SEARCHING FOR HIS CURVY GIRL

A CURVY GIRL ROMANTIC SUSPENSE

ROSE PROTECTION AGENCY
BOOK 2

MARY E THOMPSON

ROSE PROTECTION AGENCY

We hope to never meet, but if we do, we will do everything in our power to keep you safe.

Rose Protection Agency is the place to go when you have nowhere else to turn. When your life is in danger, and you don't know who to trust, they will be there. Always. No matter the time or the day, you can count on them.

Rose Protection Agency is a team of former military, special forces, and organizations you've never heard of. They are here to do what they were trained to do... Keep their country, and its citizens, safe.

No matter the cost.

Meet the protectors...

AT ROSE PROTECTION AGENCY

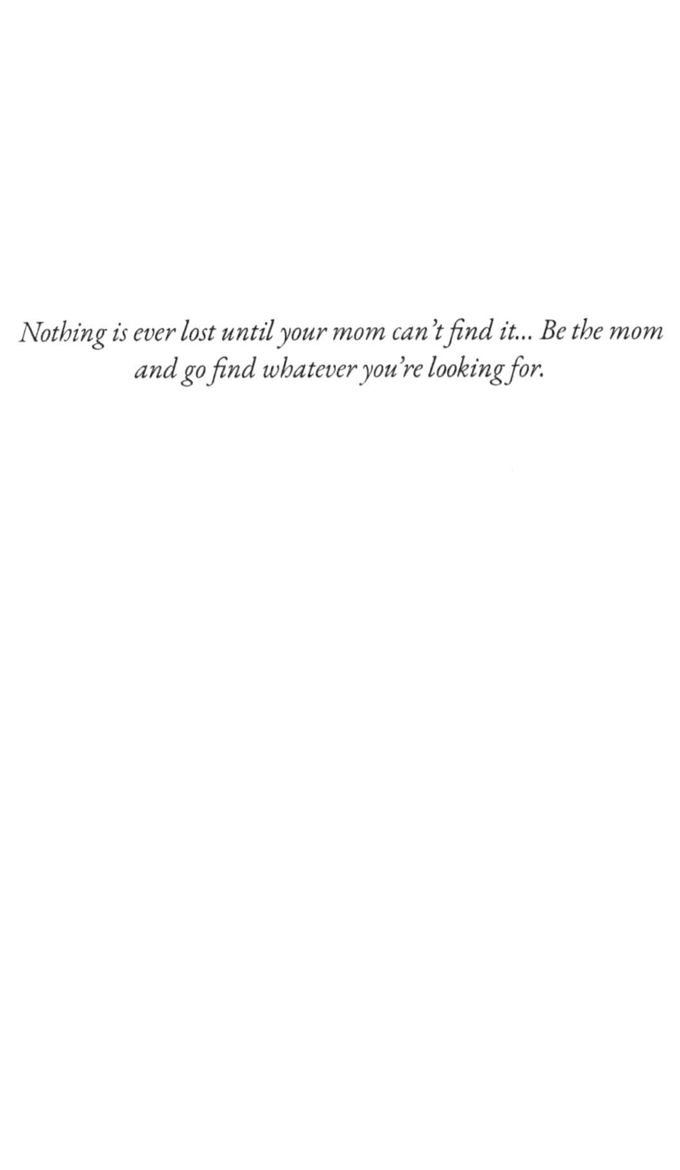

Nothing is ever lost until your mom can't find it... Be the mom and go find whatever you're looking for.

ONE

Stalking a stranger was probably a bad idea. It sounded like a bad idea to Claudia. But there was something about the dark-haired man she found herself unable to resist. A kindness she didn't expect from someone who looked like he could take down any opponent.

Sneaking into the gym for a shower was supposed to be quick. Clean up before she moved on to the next city. The next place to hide. But then she saw him.

He eyed the young woman with the black eye. As she worked the punching bag, his gaze became more intense. Claudia wondered why he was watching her, ready to defend the woman if necessary. The two of them could get enough attention from others that the guy couldn't hurt either of them.

Then he walked over, hands up and intentionally moving into her line of sight. The woman hesitated, then nodded when he asked if he could help.

Claudia couldn't tear her gaze from him. The way he moved, his subtle confidence, and the care in how he handled the injured woman all drew Claudia in. He never once touched the woman, mirroring every movement for her, patiently explaining to her how to defend herself.

Claudia had never known a man to treat a woman with that level of care. She followed the two of them around the gym, trying not to be noticed, and watched him.

When the young woman left, he stayed, finishing his workout alone before he walked out and went to an older model SUV. He was a good man. Which was why Claudia was back at the gym, watching him. Following him. Okay, fine, stalking him.

He walked out of the gym in a plain gray sweatshirt. Claudia watched from next to a sedan. She saw the sedan's owner tuck the key into a magnetic holder in the wheel well. She grabbed the key and let herself into the sedan, pulling out of the lot behind her hero.

He parked his SUV outside an apartment building not far from the gym. Claudia told herself to leave him alone. To stay away. To keep moving. Instead, she sat in the lot outside the man's apartment, watching him walk toward a building.

He unlocked the front door, then stepped back to let a young mother and her toddler walk out. She said something to him, and he smiled, replying with something that made the little boy laugh.

Claudia's throat squeezed tight. She'd never known a man like him. One who took time to be kind to strangers. One who clearly knew how to take care of himself. And who would protect her when she needed it.

Because she was definitely going to need it. She could only run for so long.

TWO WEEKS LATER, Claudia had the keys to the apartment next to her hero. Lance Kilgore was a bit of a mystery. No social media, very little online presence. Former military, but he kept his head down. He was perfect as a neighbor.

Claudia's new apartment was unfurnished, but she didn't have a choice. She needed somewhere safe. And a neighbor like Lance would ensure she was safe. Once he knew who she was.

After months of jumping from place to place, the idea of staying in one town made her anxious, but Claudia was tired of running. And her new neighbor was the kind of man she never thought existed.

It was time to introduce herself.

Claudia made every effort to pull herself together with the prettiest top she owned, enough makeup to hide the exhaustion heavy on her face, and her hair bouncy and fluffy in a way men couldn't ever seem to resist. She wasn't looking for a romance from her neighbor, but if desire led men to do things they wouldn't typically do...

Like protecting her from Michael, if and when he showed up.

Claudia checked her reflection in the mirrored front of the microwave and forced a smile until it lit up her eyes. A lifetime of faking happiness helped.

She stepped out into the hallway, checked she was alone, and locked her door. She slid the key into her pocket and flounced her hair once more, then moved in front of her new neighbor's door and knocked.

She knew he was home. She heard him arrive thirty minutes ago, and there was movement inside. But he didn't immediately open the door.

Claudia lifted her hand to knock again just as the door swung open in front of her.

He was taller up close, but everyone seemed tall compared

to her five-four. His brown hair was wet and sticking up, like he'd just gotten out of a shower and ran a towel over it. He wore a white tee and blue shorts, his feet bare.

Her gaze slid over his body, her own lighting up in a way it had never done. She'd been attracted to men before, but not like this. Not in that immediate, need you now, what will I do if I don't have you kind of way.

"Can I help you?"

Even his voice made her shiver. It also reminded her she was gawking at the poor man. She forced her smile again and met his gaze. Warm brown eyes studied her, not looking as friendly as she remembered from the day in the gym.

"Are you okay?" he asked, his tone changing as he moved toward her. He glanced into the hall.

"Hi. Sorry. I'm good. I just moved in next door and wanted to say hi to my neighbor." Claudia forced a cheerful tone and hoped he bought it.

"Okay?"

"I'm Claudia, by the way. I don't really know anyone in the area."

"Lance," he said, offering his hand.

She smiled and slipped her hand into his, suppressing the jolt that made her want to both pull away and hold on tight. "It's nice to meet you."

"You too. Is there anything else?"

"Oh, um, no, I guess not. I just wanted to say hi. If you ever need anything... well, I don't really have much, but if you want someone to watch a movie with or something, I'm right next door." Claudia pointed in the direction of her apartment so he'd know where to find her.

Lance nodded, not offering more.

"I'll let you get back to your evening," Claudia said, feeling silly for thinking she could knock on his door and he'd fall all over himself to help her out.

She turned to go back to her place, then turned back to say something else and found herself in front of a rapidly closing door. The lock clicked into place, and Claudia swallowed the disappointment racing through her.

So much for instant attraction. She would just have to wear him down.

LANCE KILGORE CLOSED the door and went back to his couch. And his beer. He was not in the mood to be social. Not this month. Not when one man he called a friend was being hunted, and another man he called a mentor was dead.

Lance still couldn't believe Samuel was dead. A part of him wanted to believe it was some sick joke, but it wasn't. Rose Protection Agency would never be the same. Lance would never be the same.

He picked up the remote and let the sound of the TV and the alcohol in his hand soothe him. If there was such a thing. Lance knew loss. He'd witnessed enough of it in his lifetime, but this loss hit differently. Harder. Because they were the protectors. They were the people called on when someone else was in danger. They weren't supposed to be the ones in danger. They weren't supposed to end up dead.

LANCE'S new neighbor came back the next day. And the one after that. And the one after that. Lance was irritated every time someone knocked on the door knowing it was going to be her. A cup of sugar, a screwdriver, a package being delivered and could he watch out for it?

Was she for real?

He was busy. He had a killer to catch. He didn't have time for another vampire woman. One who would suck the life out of him and leave him in a heap of dust. Been there, done that, had the bruised heart to remember her by.

If it wasn't for his Aunt Jackie, Lance would think all women were like that. It took him too long to spot it in Blair, but his new neighbor showed all the signs. He wouldn't get pulled in by sexy curves and a sweet smile. Not again.

No matter how determined she was to get to know him.

Lance carried himself up the stairs to his apartment, his feet dragging. He needed sleep. He'd been at it constantly since Austin and Lacey were followed leaving The Davidson Hotel and nearly killed. Almost two weeks and still no leads. It wasn't over. Lance knew that. Whoever killed Samuel was going to go after Austin again and again and again until they succeeded.

Or Rose Protection Agency took them out. Whichever came first.

They were all working around the clock to make sure Rose were the ones who came out on top of that battle. But it wasn't enough. And Lance was fucking pissed.

"Oh, hey!" Claudia said, her door opening just before Lance got to his door. "How are you?"

"Tired," Lance said, not giving her space to engage.

She didn't get the message. "You work a lot. What do you do to relax?"

The pouty look she gave him was supposed to be tempting. And fuck, it was. That brunette ponytail swung with the tilt of her head, her lips a perfect pink color. What he would do with his hand in her hair and his lips against hers. Or even better, his cock between those lips.

Lance closed his eyes to shut down the image. He was tired. That was the only reason he was fantasizing about his neighbor. She was not his type. Not anymore. He needed to ignore her, avoid her, and get the hell away from her.

"Work is relaxing," Lance lied.

Claudia tipped her head back and laughed, the column of her throat right there for his lips. Her low-cut top exposed the upper swell of her breasts. The pencil skirt she wore was a direct contrast to the laundry contained in the basket under her arm.

A quick glance showed Lance all the dirty secrets she hid beneath her polished exterior. Lacy panties, even lacier bras, tiny tanks, and too-short shorts.

He could take only so much.

She wiped an imaginary tear from her eye and smiled at him. "You're funny. No one finds work relaxing. That's why it's work."

"I like my job."

"What do you do?" She hiked the basket up, bouncing the bras inside the way he imagined her breasts would bounce if she were on top.

Son-of-a-bitch, he needed to get away from her. "I help people." He slid the key in his lock before she could ask a follow-up question. "I need to go."

Claudia tried to say something else, but Lance closed the door on her and leaned his back against it.

That was way too fucking close. She was wearing him down. It had only been three weeks since she moved in and he was having trouble not picturing her naked.

Seeing what she wore under her clothes made the task even more impossible. But he had to resist. He was not looking for a new relationship.

Too bad his sex-deprived brain didn't get the damn memo. He woke up hours later with an erection that demanded attention.

But that was second place to the phone ringing on his nightstand.

"What?"

"Walker is on his way to get you. Someone's been watching the hotel."

Lance was out of bed and tugging on clothes before his boss finished speaking. "I'll be ready."

"Thanks." Montgomery Rose hung up without another word. He didn't need to tell Lance what was at stake if they got this wrong.

Walker texted Lance as he was walking out the door. He locked up and ran down the stairs, thankful his neighbor didn't make an appearance.

CLAUDIA HADN'T SEEN Lance in a few days. She thought she heard him leaving, but since she lived in the apartment past his, she couldn't watch the peephole on her door and see when he was coming and going.

She tried to catch him a few times, but it was never him.

A week after she surprised him with her panties in the laundry basket, she swore she heard him coming up the stairs. She waited until his footsteps approached his door, then flung hers open.

But it wasn't Lance. "Um, hi." She couldn't exactly ignore the man, but he was not who she was expecting.

"Hi." He smiled at her, friendly enough, but not Lance.

"Are you moving in?" She blurted the question, hating that it came out desperate sounding.

He shook his head. "No, just staying with my buddy for a little while."

Relief filled her, and she grinned. "Oh, so Lance didn't move?"

"Nope. He'll be home later. Did you need something? I'm Austin."

She took a step forward, then stopped.

Lance was the man she saw at the gym. The one who helped that young woman with the black eye. The one who helped people. Not this Austin guy.

"Claudia. Nice to meet you. I was just going to ask Lance for a favor, but I'll catch him later. Bye." She waved and hurried back inside. She flipped the lock, hoping he wouldn't try to talk to her more.

Claudia pressed her ear to the door and waited. A door opened, then closed. She exhaled a breath and moved away from the door. Safe.

She needed to be more careful. The more people who saw her, the more exposed she was. The harder it would be to hide.

Every time she heard Lance over the next two weeks, there was another voice with him. She didn't want to be outnumbered. She thought she could trust Lance, but she didn't really know him. She couldn't take the chance that she misinterpreted his actions.

A few days after she stopped hearing Austin's voice in the hallway, Claudia decided to talk to Lance again. She waited for him to come home. She stared at the clock on the wall. When thirty-three minutes had passed, she reapplied her lipstick and walked out into the hallway.

No one was out, so she locked her door and went to his. She knocked, waiting for him to answer.

He finally did, and his gaze went right to the plate in her hand. "Hey. Are those brownies?"

She waved the plate beneath his nose, knowing the gooey chocolate would tempt even the most health-conscious man.

"They are. I was craving them today, but there's no way I can eat all of them and not hate myself for it."

"Why not?" His gaze was stuck on the brownies. She could almost see him salivating.

"I already need to lose about sixty pounds. I don't need to make that worse."

"Fuck that. You're perfect."

She couldn't hold back her smile.

He closed his eyes and shook his head. "I mean... there's nothing wrong with the way you look. You need to be happy. You're beautiful. And whoever told you otherwise is lying."

"Thank you."

He nodded, his gaze glued to her instead of the brownies.

She waited. Was he going to invite her in? Get to know her? Ask her out?

"So, the brownies?" he asked.

"Oh, um, yeah. If you're interested..."

"Hell, yes." He grabbed the plate with one hand and a brownie with the other, half of it disappearing with one bite. He groaned, and she had to clench her thighs together to stop the pulsing in her core.

"Good?"

"Damn. I guess that cup of sugar you borrowed went to good use. How in the hell did you make these?"

Claudia giggled, feeling both delighted and shy. "I enjoy baking."

"You're really damn good at it," he said, finishing the first brownie and reaching for a second. "Thanks. If you ever have other treats you want to get rid of, send them my way."

"I will," she said as he backed into his apartment.

He waved with the brownie in his hand, then closed the door with his foot, leaving her alone in the hallway.

Always alone.

But she learned something. The way to get his attention was to feed the man sugar.

That she could do.

LANCE THREADED the blue ribbon through the diamond ring. He wasn't sure if he was supposed to tie them all together or one ribbon at a time, but he figured Austin would kill him if it took forever to get the ring off the balloons and onto Lacey's finger.

Assuming she said yes to his proposal.

Lance wasn't worried about that one. He'd seen the two of them together over the last few months. Since the threat against them was taken care of and they were both safe, they'd let each other into their lives in a way Lance admired.

Austin had plenty of baggage to weigh him down, but once he accepted that he didn't have to carry it with him anymore, he was willing to be the man Lacey needed in her life.

Lance was proud to play a small part in their happy ending, being the orchestrator of their engagement. If only he could get the balloons to stay in the box. Dammit. Helium was a bitch.

A knock on the door made him swear again. In the four-and-a-half months since Claudia moved in next door, she'd forced him to spend twice as long in the gym as usual. Between her tempting treats and her tempting curves, Lance was a fucking mess.

He gave up on the box and went to the door, knowing he'd find her on the other side of it. "Can you help me?" he asked as he opened the door.

She chuckled. "That's usually my line."

"I'm pulling out my hair. I need more hands."

She was in another fancy outfit, like she was going on a date. Maybe she was.

The thought hit him square in the chest. Fuck.

"What can I do?" She followed him inside and stood next to him as he tried to remember how to breathe.

"Um, shove these balloons into the box." Lance grabbed the ribbons held together with the ring and yanked the whole thing down.

Claudia laughed as she fought with one balloon only to have another one pop back up. "Are you sure they're all going to fit in this box?"

"Yeah. We just need to get it right." Lance tried to close the lid, but three balloons escaped before he could. "Dammit."

"What is this for?"

"Gender reveal."

"Oh. Yours?"

He let go of the box and turned to face her. "I'm well aware of my gender."

Her cheeks turned red. "I meant your baby."

"No, my friend's. They're having a party at their house today, and I said I'd handle the reveal so I can sneak an engagement ring into the box for him."

"Oh, wow. That's... You're really sweet to help out."

"Yeah, well, if I can't get these balloons packed up, I'll be blowing the surprise when I walk in the door."

"We'll get it." She studied the box. "What if we cut off two of the flaps? Or tuck them in? We don't really need them, and the balloons will come out easier without them."

"We can try it," Lance said, not thinking it would matter. He shoved two sides into the box, just in case her idea didn't work, then pulled the ribbons down again.

Claudia helped him push the balloons into the box and closed one side while he held the bundle.

She laughed when some of the balloons popped out again, and the sound went right to his chest. He still wanted her. He didn't want to want her, but he did. Months of resisting her, wanting her, dreaming about her.

He couldn't think about that with her in the room. Especially if she had a date later.

She shoved the last balloon down and closed the flap on his arm, trapping it inside. "Sorry!"

Lance slowly removed his arm, not opening the box enough for a balloon to follow his escape, then pressed his hands on top of the box. "Thank you. I never could have done that."

"How are you securing it?"

"Shit. I have tape somewhere."

She looked around, then took two steps to where he'd left the tape. "Do you want to leave a loop on the end so it's easier for them to tug it off?"

"Good idea. Thanks."

"You're welcome." She spread the tape over the two edges, sealing the blue balloons and engagement ring inside the box. She pressed the edges together at the end, making a tab for Lacey to pull during the reveal.

"That's perfect."

Claudia's cheeks turned red again. "I'm happy I was here to help."

Lance lifted the box. "Did you need something?"

She shook her head and moved to the door. "Nothing urgent. It looks like you need to go." She opened the door for him and stepped into the hallway.

Lance set the box down while he locked his door, then grabbed it again. "That took longer than I expected. Thanks."

"You're welcome. Have fun." She waved and turned back toward her apartment.

He didn't repeat her words, not wanting her to enjoy a date with another man. He wanted her to be on a date with him.

Dammit.

TWO

Claudia closed the door to her apartment and swallowed the lump in her throat. She did not want to be alone, but Lance was going out. He had plans. Because he had a life.

Unlike her.

A year. For one full year, she'd been a ghost, hiding in plain sight and hoping she was safe. As the anniversary drew closer, her dreams were more insistent.

And terrifying.

Claudia pushed away from the door and went straight to her bedroom. The armor she wore when she left the apartment wasn't working the same way it had in the past. Not that day. Not when she couldn't force the memories back.

Claudia forced herself to undo each button slowly. Focus on the task. Deep breaths. Slow and calm. She was safe. She was alive. She was telling the truth. Even though no one believed her.

Therapy was a luxury she couldn't afford, but the internet was teeming with people who were willing to share advice. Some was good, some sucked, but Claudia watched all of it.

The ones who helped her the most were the ones who'd experienced their own traumas.

Claudia hated the word trauma. It felt unfair to the people who'd actually been through one. She'd only witnessed a trauma. She didn't experience the attack herself.

Tears ran down Claudia's face as the scene played out in her mind. She squeezed her eyes shut and shook her head.

"No. No more. I can't see it anymore."

She drew a breath and held it until her lungs screamed for release. She blew it out slowly, then counted again before drawing in another slow breath. One by one, the breaths calmed her racing heart. Focusing on them helped her to push the memories away.

When she was no longer shaking, she tossed her shirt in the laundry basket and unzipped her skirt, throwing it the same way. She hated the fancy clothes, but she liked the way Lance's eyes followed the silhouette of her body when she wore them.

Claudia laughed mirthlessly at herself. She'd been trying to flirt with the man for months, and he hadn't even once sought her out. She always had to go to him. He didn't want her. He might find her attractive, but men didn't wait to make a move on a woman they were interested in. Not when the woman made it perfectly clear she was available.

It was time to give up her quest to catch his attention. Maybe time to move on. Staying in the same place for so long made her complacent. She hadn't been watching her back the same as she had originally. She'd been settling in, making a life, pretending she could have the things she imagined.

But she couldn't. Michael would find her. He would come for her. He would make sure she never told anyone else what she saw.

Not that it mattered. She'd tried to tell the police, but they didn't believe her. Michael said she was lying. The police said it was a family matter, and she needed to keep them out of it.

That was the day she ran.

Until she saw Lance, and stopped running.

But Lance wouldn't protect her. He was a good man, but he had a life that didn't include her. It was time she let him live it.

Claudia dug through the plastic bins she used for her clothes to find a pair of sweatpants. One more night to plan her next move, then she'd leave Niagara Falls and find another place to go for a little while. She would clean her place, wash her laundry, and leave in the morning.

In sweats and a tank top, Claudia went to work cleaning up. She carried the laundry basket downstairs and put her first load of clothes in the wash, then went back to her apartment, turned on some music, and got to work.

The air mattress she called a bed was cheap, but it folded up into a small box so she could move with it. She stripped the sheets from it so they were clean for her next move, just in case she ended up somewhere without laundry facilities. She propped the mattress up against the wall and swept underneath, wishing she had better cleaning supplies, but they cost money.

Claudia lowered the mattress to the floor again and nibbled her lip. She dug her handbag out of the top bin and reached inside. She closed her hand around the cold metal watch and pulled it out.

Claudia sank to the floor and stared at the watch. Taking it before she left was a risk. She didn't have a lot of money, and she shared a bank account with Michael, so accessing that would have told him where she was. The watch felt like the only option.

But she hadn't been able to bring herself to pawn it. She

walked into a few stores, but when it came time to show them what she had, she always left.

Claudia didn't have a lot of fond memories of her mother. Lilian was a drunk who was always more interested in her bottle than her kids. And Claudia was not the favorite. Her brother had that honor. He and their mother would have secret conversations when she wasn't in the room. She was affectionate with him in a way she never was with Claudia.

Claudia was always jealous of their relationship. She wanted a mother. Someone to talk to about boys and makeup and life. Someone who would help her when she got her first period and had her first crush, when she lost her virginity.

Her mother was never that person. Before Claudia finished high school, her mother took her last drink. She never woke up the next morning. Her brother found Lilian and told Claudia. He promised her that he would take care of her. She would always be with him. He loved her and wouldn't let anyone take her away from him.

The watch was the only thing of value their mother ever had. A family heirloom handed down from her grandmother. Claudia often wondered why her mother held onto it, but she'd never asked. As she stared at the watch and debated using it to fund her next escape, she wondered how valuable it really was. The green stones could have been glass for all she knew, but she thought they were emeralds. The metal itself was heavy and a shiny silver color. It had to be worth something.

If she could bring herself to part with it.

Claudia stuffed it back into the handbag and shoved the bag back into the bin. She put the cover on the bin and continued cleaning.

When her bedroom and bathroom were clean and free of anything she wouldn't need in the morning, she carried her next load of laundry downstairs. She'd accumulated more things in her four months in Niagara Falls than in the eight months before that and leaving was going to be more of a challenge.

She pushed all those worries away and went back to cleaning. She put a frozen pizza in the oven, hating that she'd just been to the grocery store and would be leaving behind perfectly good food.

Maybe she could wait. Maybe she would stay until her food ran out. Then she would go.

Claudia knew she wouldn't do it. She'd gotten attached. To her fictional relationship with Lance, to the servers she worked with at the diner, even to the regular customers she had. She wanted the life she'd built.

"Too bad," she muttered to herself, sinking onto the curbside couch she'd claimed as her own two months ago. Her emotions swamped her again. All the things Michael took from her, all the opportunities he stole, felt minor compared to what she was giving up now. If it wasn't for Michael, Claudia might have been able to build a life she enjoyed. Instead, she was leaving behind the one and only thing she'd ever wanted for herself.

The timer dinged, and she went to the stove to pull out the pizza. She turned off the stove, then grabbed her keys to get her laundry.

One more load to go, one more meal in her apartment, one more night, and then she'd be gone again.

LANCE LEFT the baby shower feeling like something good had come out of Samuel's death. He would always wish their friend was still around, but Samuel would be there in spirit with his grandson when Lacey had the baby. A boy.

Austin adored his fiancée, and she felt the same about him.

Lance was happy for them. They were good together. The kind of couple that Lance believed in.

He'd never known that relationship for himself, but maybe one day.

He'd forgotten all about Claudia's date until he was getting out of his SUV. He didn't know what she drove, which he realized was weird, but he'd never seen her get into a vehicle. Their run-ins were always in the hallway.

He hoped she was still out. Or maybe home early. That would be better. But the worst would be if her date was at her place.

His gut churned as he considered that option. He took the stairs two at a time, hoping to avoid running into Claudia and her date. He turned the corner to go to his place and plowed right into her.

"Ow," she breathed, her shoulder hitting the wall.

He grabbed her waist to stop her from falling and immediately regretted the move. There was a gap between her tank top and sweatpants. His hand fit into that gap, landing on her bare skin. His dick perked up at the feel of her warm, soft flesh. "Are you okay?"

She sniffed, swallowing roughly as she avoided his gaze. "Fine. Sorry."

"I was the one who ran into you. Is your shoulder okay?"

She took a step back, removing his hand from her side. "All good."

He looked at her shoulder and saw an ugly red scrape on her perfect skin, blood seeping from the wound. "You're bleeding."

She looked at it as though she hadn't felt it. "It'll be fine."

"Claudia," he said, unable to keep the concern from his voice. He should let her go. Let her take care of herself. Ignore the desire he felt for her and move on.

But he couldn't.

"Let me help you," he whispered, reaching for her.

She tensed, but she didn't move away from him. Her eyes were red, as though she'd been crying. She was not in her usual clothes. No fancy skirt or frilly top. The sweats and tank made her softer. More approachable. Harder to resist.

"Did someone hurt you?" he growled. His fist clenched, ready to hurt whoever upset her.

"What are you talking about?"

"Your date," he snarled. "Did they hurt you? Touch you or do something you didn't want?"

"What date?"

"I thought... You didn't have a date tonight?"

She shook her head slowly.

"Why... You... I assumed when you were dressed up earlier that you had a date tonight."

"No date."

"Okay."

"Okay."

He stared at her, unable to look away. She was different tonight. She didn't flirt with him or smile. She was distant, as if she was putting space between them. He didn't like it.

"Um, can I get past you?"

"Why?"

"I'm going to get my laundry."

"No."

"No?"

"Let me take care of your shoulder first. Then I'll get your laundry for you. You shouldn't be lifting right now."

"It's just a scrape, Lance. It'll be fine."

"Please, Claudia. Let me take care of you. Of your shoulder."

She looked up at him, her eyes full of something he couldn't process. Her hazel eyes were greener tonight, almost olive with the brown mixed in. Her emotions flipped through her eyes before she nodded. "Okay."

Lance cupped her elbow and guided her back to his door. He unlocked it and pushed the door open for her to go in ahead of him. "Make yourself comfortable. I'll grab the first-aid kit."

"You have a first-aid kit?"

He nodded. "I do. I'll make sure you're okay."

"Lance?"

"Yeah?"

"Thank you."

He nodded and forced himself to walk away. He would do something stupid if he didn't. Something like kiss her.

He grabbed the first-aid kit and went back to the living room. She was standing near the door, as if debating on running when he wasn't in the room.

"You can sit," he told her.

"I didn't want to ruin your couch or anything."

"I don't fucking care about the couch. I care about you. Come sit."

She flinched at his language, and he made a mental note not to swear at her. Or around her, if he could remember. But she approached him.

He reached a hand out to her and guided her to the couch. She perched on the edge of the cushion, not settling in or getting comfortable.

He wanted her comfortable at his place. To lay back and put her feet up. To stretch out on his couch and make the place her own.

He'd never seen her apartment, but he had a feeling she made it feel like a home. She put her own touches on what would otherwise be a boring white space.

He'd tried to do the same, but it wasn't perfect. It was a place he laid his head. He spent more hours at the office than anywhere else, but having his own apartment was a necessity.

Lance opened the first-aid kit and retrieved an alcohol wipe. Her cut wasn't bad enough for stitches, but it was still bleeding. He opened the wipe and used it to chase the blood trickling down her arm. When it was red, he tossed it on his table and grabbed another one, moving closer to the cut.

He worked slowly, making sure he didn't hurt her more. She sat perfectly still, not even breathing, it seemed.

"This is going to hurt," he said before he moved to the actual cut. "I'm sorry."

"It's fine," she whispered.

He glanced at her face and found her staring straight ahead, her lip clenched between her teeth. "I'm sorry I hurt you."

"It's fine," she said again, her tone even softer.

He hated that he hurt her. That he was hurting her again by cleaning the wound. He was half-hard from touching her, and she was trying not to cry because it hurt so badly.

Lance made quick work of the alcohol wipe on her cut, then tore into a gauze pad. He applied antibiotic ointment to the pad and covered the wound with it. He taped it in place, hoping it would heal without causing her too much pain. "It should stop bleeding soon. If it doesn't, I can try some other things."

"It's fine," she said, standing immediately. "I need to go."

"Claudia, please let me help you. Sit, relax. I'll get your laundry."

"You don't have to do that."

"I know, but you'd already be back in your apartment if I hadn't slammed into you. I wasn't paying attention to where I was going, and I should have slowed down."

She laughed mirthlessly. "You were probably hoping to avoid your crazy neighbor who won't leave you alone. I get it."

"That's not exactly true."

"What is true?"

Lance drew a breath and stared at her. He liked this version of her. No fancy clothes. No makeup. No heels. Just a woman who wasn't trying to put on a show for someone else. He'd never seen her like that, and it was doing things to him.

Dangerous things.

"I didn't want to see you with another man," Lance confessed.

"What?"

Lance shook his head. "I thought you were on a date. I didn't want to see you with someone else. To run into you in the hallway with another man. So I was hurrying up the stairs just in case."

"Why would you care?"

He breathed a laugh. "I shouldn't."

She stared at him, a game of chicken to see who would break first.

Lance tore his gaze from hers and went to the door. "Stay here. I'll get your laundry. I'll be right back."

"Lance?"

He turned back to meet her gaze. "Yeah?"

She smiled at him. She didn't say anything else, just smiled.

He grinned back, laughing as he went to retrieve her laundry.

Weird night.

THREE

Claudia sat on his couch and replayed his words in her head. He didn't want to see her with someone else. All the times she thought he was indifferent to her, he was hiding a desire for her she'd never noticed.

She would be the first to admit she wasn't very experienced with men. She'd dated some, slept with a few more, but she'd never had any relationships that lasted longer than a month or two.

No one she'd loved or wanted a future with. Not that she was there with Lance, but she'd been chasing him for months. It figured he would decide he was interested when she decided it was time to go.

Could she stick around?

Did she want to?

She was still considering her answers to those questions when Lance came back into the apartment with her laundry basket under his arm.

"Do you want me to put this stuff at your place?"

"Oh, I can take it." She stood, feeling foolish for thinking he wanted her to hang out longer. He was a good man, and he was taking care of her, not flirting with her.

He twisted his body to block her from grabbing the basket. "That's not what I asked, Claudia. I said you shouldn't be carrying this. I can put it in your apartment, if you're okay with giving me your keys."

"I'll go with you," she said in a rush. She did not want him to see her apartment. Between the bare walls, the used couch, and the air mattress on the floor, she knew what he would think if he saw where she lived.

"Why don't we eat first?" Lance suggested, setting the basket on the floor and closing the door behind him.

"You don't have to—"

"I want to," he said, his hand on her arm shutting her up in a hurry.

Claudia nodded. She liked this side of him. The side he'd never shown her. It was the side she had seen all those months ago when he showed the girl in the gym how to defend herself. The protector. The man who would never let anyone get hurt.

Lance guided her back to the couch and handed her a remote. "Why don't you find something for us to watch while I figure out dinner?"

Claudia nodded. The cardboard imitation of pizza she'd eaten for dinner was barely food, and she was already hungry again. Dinner with Lance would be infinitely better than dinner alone.

Claudia figured out how to work his remote and picked a movie that sounded funny. She'd never seen it before, but they didn't have a lot of TV options when she was growing up. They barely had power most of the time, and cable was never a necessity when they couldn't afford to pay the electric bill.

"This is one of my favorite movies," Lance said as the opening credits started. "You too?"

She shook her head. "I've never seen it."

"Oh, you have to. It's so good." Lance hummed along with the opening music. It showed four kids, each doing their own thing, in a small town.

Claudia watched as the kids all came together at one house and planned out an epic adventure. About the time they got to a creepy restaurant owned by not so great people, Lance set a plate of food in front of her.

"This smells amazing," she said with a groan.

Lance grinned. "Thanks. Family recipe."

Claudia looked at the fluffy biscuits topped with a melting pad of butter, perfectly browned crispy chicken, and bright green broccoli. "Did you do a lot of cooking with your parents?"

Lance shook his head and sat next to her. "I never knew my dad. I'm not sure if he was not a great guy or if my mom wasn't sure who my father was, but I never met anyone who was my father. My mom died when I was eight."

"Oh. I'm sorry. You said family recipe..."

Lance chuckled. "My mom's best friend raised me. She took me in when my mom died. Refused to let me go into foster care. She produced a document that my mom had signed when I was born saying if anything ever happened to my mom, Aunt Jackie would be my guardian. She fought hard because the courts wanted to say it wasn't legal, but she didn't give up until they awarded her full custody of me."

"Wow. She sounds like a force to be reckoned with."

"Oh, yeah. She still is. She decides something and stops at nothing to make it happen. She's the only family I have."

"You're lucky to have her."

"I am. And I know that well. She put her entire life on hold for me. Refused to do anything for herself until I was able to stand on my own."

"You're still close?"

"We are. She got married when I was in the Army. Great man. He treats her like a queen."

Claudia smiled. "That's good."

"She deserves it. She dated some real jerks when I was young, before I moved in with her. I remember my mom telling me to be a good man when I grew up. To not be like Aunt Jackie's boyfriends. I don't remember what happened with them, but I learned young how to treat a woman."

Claudia had seen it. Not that Lance knew, but she'd witnessed the way he treated women. Not just the one at the gym, but the neighbors and anyone he interacted with. He was a good man. The best.

Which made her feel guilty for deceiving him.

"How about you? Are you close to your family?"

She laughed. "No. My mom was an alcoholic. Drank herself to death when I was in high school. My brother was my guardian until I turned eighteen."

"Are you close to him?"

Claudia shook her head, hating the tightness in her chest and throat. She had to pretend to be normal, or he'd notice something. "I haven't seen him in a year. He didn't get the same lessons you did about how to treat women."

"Did he hurt you?"

"No. Never." At least that part was the truth. He never once laid a hand on Claudia. He looked like he wanted to sometimes, but he never did. She knew he was dangerous. People feared him. But he'd never shown her his violence.

That was the hardest thing about what she saw. She'd never seen that side of him. The violent, aggressive, evil side.

But it existed.

"I'm sorry you're not closer."

"Thanks," Claudia whispered, not feeling the same at all.

One year of running, one year of memories. She wasn't sure she could keep going. Keep running. Keep hiding.

But she had to because she knew without a doubt if Michael ever caught up to her, he would kill her, too.

Or make her wish she was dead.

LANCE DIDN'T WANT to force Claudia into a conversation she didn't want to have, so he let the movie fill the silence between them. He ate his dinner and was happy to see she devoured hers as well.

When both plates were empty, he carried them to the kitchen and slid them into the dishwasher with the rest of the pots and pans he'd used to prepare dinner.

He settled on the couch again, fighting to urge to reach for Claudia. They'd never spent so much time together. She'd never been in his apartment, and he'd never seen the inside of hers. They weren't friends who hung out or called each other or did things together. They weren't even really friends.

But he wished that was different. He wanted to know her. To touch her and kiss her and hold her. To understand why she didn't like talking about her family. To know all her secrets.

Claudia chuckled at the movie, and gasped when the bad guys caught up to the kids on the pirate ship. She sighed with happiness when the kids were rescued and found the jewels to pay for their homes so their families didn't have to move.

Lance watched Claudia. He knew the movie by heart, but he didn't know her as well yet. He smiled when she smiled, he frowned when she frowned. And the whole time, he ached for her.

He couldn't remember the last time he wanted a woman the way he wanted Claudia. Months of flirting and talking and being annoyed by her made him want her in his life. It made him want to get to know her.

Admitting he'd been hoping to avoid her and a date made her smile, but she didn't say or do anything about it. Did that mean she wasn't interested, or that she didn't feel right making the first move?

"What?" she asked.

Lance realized she was staring at him, a questioning look in her eyes.

"Do I have something on my face?"

He shook his head. "No, you're perfect. I was just thinking I don't know you very well."

Her cheeks turned pink, and she pushed to stand, wincing when she moved her injured arm.

"Does it still hurt?" Lance felt like an ass for running into her and hurting her.

"It'll be fine. Thank you for taking care of me. And getting my laundry."

She went around the couch the long way so she didn't have to go past him.

He met her near the door. "Let me carry this to your apartment for you." He reached for the laundry basket before she could.

She nibbled her lower lip and nodded. "Thanks."

Lance took the victory and opened his door, stepping back to let her go first.

She moved into the hall, glancing both ways to make sure she wasn't going to get run over again, then turned to go to her apartment.

Lance pulled his door closed but didn't bother to lock it. He hitched her basket onto his hip and followed her.

Claudia pulled out her keys and unlocked her door quickly. She turned back to him, trying to reach for the basket. "I can get it from here."

"I'll set it inside for you. I don't have to come in."

"It's not that."

He shook his head. "It's okay."

"No, it's just…" She pushed the door open wider, and he saw into her apartment.

It was not what he expected. No artwork hung on the walls. There was a couch, but nothing else in the living room. No TV, no stereo, no coffee table. Her kitchen was neat and clean, but he wondered if it was because she didn't have the money for things or because she was particular.

The way she looked around his apartment made him wonder if she'd been envious of how full his place was.

Aunt Jackie insisted he make it look as if he lived in the place instead of just existing there, and it was vastly different from Claudia's apartment.

"All my money goes to rent," she said softly.

"There's nothing wrong with the way you live," Lance hurried to tell her. "Nothing at all. You're making it work. You don't need more than you have."

"Your place is so nice, though. Relaxing. My couch was on the side of the road."

"But it's yours. You should be proud of that."

"How can I be proud of this place?"

"Because you're doing it on your own. You said your mom wasn't great, and it sounds like your brother isn't much better. It's hard to overcome family disappointments like that. To start over when you're all alone. My mom's parents wanted nothing to do with her when she got pregnant. They were very religious and kicked her out since she wasn't married. We lived in plenty of places that had furniture we found on the curb with no TV and very little food. It takes a long time to claw your way out of situations like that."

"You're being nice."

Lance shook his head and took a step toward her. He set

the laundry basket on the floor inside the door. "You are strong, Claudia. I see it in your eyes. You don't give up. You are just like Aunt Jackie."

She breathed a laugh. "Hardly. I wish I was half as strong as you say she is."

"Then maybe I read things between us all wrong."

"What do you mean?"

"I mean... Oh, hell." Lance closed the distance between them. He cupped her jaw and brought her lips to his. He inhaled the scent of her, teasing her lips with his tongue.

She opened for him, sighing into the kiss and slipping her hands around his waist.

He plunged his tongue into her mouth, needing the taste of her. He yanked her flush to his body and groaned at the feel of her softness pressed against him.

She whimpered, and something in his head exploded.

He let go of her. Instantly. He took a step back. If he didn't stop, he wouldn't stop. And he had to stop.

"I... I need to go. I... Good night."

Her fingertips brushed her lips as she watched him retreat.

Fuck. He kissed her. He didn't ask her if it was okay. He didn't give her a chance to stop him. He just grabbed her and kissed her as though she was already his.

And that sound she made... that whimper... He had to go. If he didn't, he might not have been able to stop at all.

He rushed back to his apartment and closed the door, locking it to make it harder for him to get back to her.

She didn't ask for him to kiss her.

But now she knew how he felt. If she was okay with what happened, she knew where to find him.

MICHAEL REYNOLDS STALKED through his living room. He grabbed a coaster and threw it at the wall, sneering when the wall cracked.

"Dude, what is wrong with you today?" Hector asked.

Michael glared at his so-called friend. Hector would turn Michael in without a second thought if he knew anything. Hector was the lowest of the low, and a worthless piece of shit.

"Do you need to get laid? I can make some calls. Have a few girls here in ten minutes."

"I need to find my sister," Michael said.

"Why? She left. Let her go."

"I can't."

"Whatever. I'm going to get some girls here. You want a brunette?"

"Yeah," Michael said. Maybe sex would take his mind off the date. He never meant to kill that woman a year ago. But the bitch wouldn't listen. He told her he had the drugs she wanted, but instead of bringing the money she owed him, she wanted to trade.

It wasn't the first time Michael had been willing to trade for drugs. She said a friend told her he'd take her as payment, and she was his type. Brunette, shorter than him, with lots of curves. He got hard when she asked if she was acceptable.

Then she tried to call the shots. Said she didn't like it the way he wanted it. He told her she wouldn't get her drugs unless she did what he said.

She agreed, then tried to change things in the middle. His erection faltered, and she laughed at him.

He didn't mean to hit her so many times. Or for her to fall and crack her skull open on the table.

He got rid of her, but when the cops showed up the next day, Michael found out Claudia had seen something. Her disappearing wasn't a coincidence, and it wasn't innocent. She ran. She knew what he did, and she ran.

Not only that, but she told the cops. She ratted him out. She turned her back on him and tried to get him locked up.

And he'd spent a year trying to find her. A year of wondering what else she knew. What else she'd seen.

A knock on the door brought Michael back to the present.

Hector opened the door and let in the two girls.

The brunette found Michael immediately, her smile lighting up her eyes when she took him in.

He jerked his head toward the back, where his room was. Hector was already working on his belt, his other hand on the blonde's fake boob. Michael wasn't interested in watching his friend fuck her. Hector didn't care who was in the room, but Michael knew how to treat a woman. He knew what happened in the bedroom was special.

The brunette followed him. Michael closed the bedroom door and locked it so they weren't interrupted.

She smiled, then dropped to her knees.

Sex was definitely a good idea. He'd already forgotten about Claudia.

FOUR

Everything changed for Claudia with Lance's kiss. Not only could she not stop smiling, she didn't want to keep running. Maybe she could have something with Lance. Maybe not, but she had hope for the first time in more than a year.

It was a funny feeling, hope. Like bubbles rising up in a pool, tickling her the entire way up, but they never reached the surface. They just made her tingle every time she thought about Lance and his kiss.

Not about the way he ran right afterward. She wasn't going to worry about that. It was nerves. Or something. But it didn't mean he didn't want her. He wouldn't have kissed her the way he did if he didn't want her.

But she had some sense of pride, and she wasn't going to chase him down.

"Busy today, isn't it?" Mallory asked.

Claudia chuckled. "Hard to keep up." The diner where they worked was dead quiet. Claudia kept busy by filling salt and pepper shakers and wiping down tables that hadn't been used. It was better than sitting around.

Which was what Mallory was doing since she was almost eight months pregnant. She was rolling up silverware in napkins, resting her feet, and rubbing her belly.

"Is he kicking today?" Claudia asked with a nod to Mallory's belly.

"So much. When I'm on my feet, it rocks him, I guess. That's what the doctors say. It's soothing for him. When I sit, he's bored, so he's busier."

"Are you excited to meet him?"

Mallory's smile was dreamy and joyful. "So ready. We had a baby shower over the weekend with our families. Andrew is setting up the crib today when I get home."

"Aw, that's so fun!"

"It is. He can't wait to be a dad."

"My friend did a gender reveal for friends of his over the weekend. It seems a lot of people are having babies right now."

"Your friend?" Mallory asked, pursing her lips and raising her brows. "Is this the same friend who's put that smile on your face all day?"

"What smile?" Claudia asked, unable to stop her laughter.

Mallory gave her a look that called bullshit on her attempt to hide her smile.

"He's my neighbor."

"Andrew was my neighbor, too. That's how we met."

"You never told me that."

Mallory shrugged. "It was before you and I met, obviously." She rubbed her belly. "But yeah. He would come over to talk to me sometimes. When he asked me out, it was almost a shock because it felt like we'd already been dating. His lease was up before mine, and he moved in with me a few months after we started dating."

"That's so sweet."

"What about your guy?"

"We don't know each other that well. I guess I'm the one who initiates all our conversations."

"That smile says there's more to the story than that."

Claudia chuckled, her cheeks warming.

"Definitely more to the story."

"He kissed me on Saturday night."

Mallory squealed. "That's awesome!"

"I think so. But then he ran. I don't really know why."

"Ask him."

"I haven't seen him since. And I... I don't know. What if he was wrapped up in the moment and regrets it?"

"Do you really think that's what happened?"

Claudia slowly shook her head. "No, but I don't know what happened."

"Well, then I think you need to talk to him. Today. Don't wait any longer to find out what's going on."

"What if he says it was a mistake?"

"Then you know and can move on."

Claudia sucked in a breath and nodded. Mallory was right. Wondering what Lance was thinking wasn't getting her anywhere, but asking him would tell her what she needed to know.

"I expect details next time we work together."

"I hope I have details for you."

"You will. I have a good feeling about this." She winced and grabbed her side. "That was a good one. He's going to be a soccer player."

Claudia chuckled as the door opened. She smiled at the new customer, then glanced back at Mallory. "I'll take this one?"

Mallory nodded. "Thanks. I'll get the next one."

Claudia smiled, calculating how much of her tips she could give to Mallory. She was the closest Claudia had to a friend in years, and she wanted to give back to the woman who'd been kind to her since she started working at the diner. Claudia would miss Mallory when she went on maternity leave, but if Claudia stuck around, she would see Mallory again.

THE REST of the shift went by quickly. Lunch hit, and they were busier until it was time for Claudia to head home. She stuck half her tips in Mallory's envelope, hoping it would help.

Mallory promised to share pictures of the crib and completed nursery when they worked together a few days later, and Claudia promised to share what happened with Lance.

First, she had to work up the nerve to talk to him.

The weather was turning colder, and Claudia wondered how she'd make the half-mile walk to the diner from her apartment when winter fully arrived. She needed to find a winter coat if she was staying in Niagara Falls much longer.

When she got home, she stripped out of her grease-scented clothes and jumped in the shower. The warm water helped ease the chill that soaked in on her walk home.

Claudia debated what to wear and finally decided not to go overboard. The first time Lance kissed her was when she looked like herself instead of like the woman she pretended to be, so she went for comfortable and casual. Cotton panties and her most comfortable cotton bra, both purple with lace trim, then sweatpants and a tee that proudly displayed Claudia's new city. She looked like a tourist, but she didn't really care.

Lance worked during the day, but Claudia decided she would stick her head out when she heard him come home that evening. See if he wanted to have dinner together, or watch another one of his favorite movies. She didn't really care as long as she got to see him.

One of the perks of her job was taking home extra food, so Claudia heated up her burger and fries and settled on her couch to enjoy her lunch. She'd just finished when someone knocked on her door.

She didn't get visitors, and she hadn't ordered anything. She ignored the knock, knowing whoever it was had the wrong apartment.

They knocked again, and she sighed and set her plate on the couch. She went to the door and looked through the peephole.

A man faced away from her, looking back at the stairs.

"Can I help you?" Claudia called through the door.

"I have a delivery for your neighbor. Can you sign for it?" he asked, pointing toward Lance's apartment.

"Um..."

"I'm in kind of a hurry, and I was hoping you knew him. Could take this for him."

Claudia sighed and shook her head. She was being para-noid. She'd been on the run for a year, and in that time, she'd never once felt like she was in danger. Someone delivering something to Lance? Why was she worried about that?

"It's okay if you can't," the guy said, starting to move away from the door.

"No, it's fine." Claudia unlocked the door and swung it open.

And came face-to-face with Michael. "So nice of you to help out."

Before she could react, he pushed her backward into her apartment, following her inside and locking the door. "Michael."

"Nice to see you, sis." He blocked her one and only exit as

he swept his gaze around her apartment. "I see you've been doing well for yourself."

"What are you doing here?"

"I'm here to get what's mine."

"What are you talking about?"

"Did you think you could steal from me, and I wouldn't notice? Or maybe you were too busy telling the cops you saw me with that whore a year ago."

"I don't know what you're talking about," Claudia whispered, her voice faltering at the anger in his gaze.

"Don't fucking lie to me!" Michael shouted.

Claudia flinched. She's almost forgotten what it was like when he yelled. How scared she was. But it rushed back in a second.

"Well, I'm going to get Mom's watch. And then I'm going to take you home. Make sure you clear my name. The fucking cops haven't left me alone since you told them I killed that bitch. They're always hanging around."

"You did kill her," Claudia breathed.

"No one would have missed her."

"She was a person. Her niece was in my class. She would come pick her niece up sometimes. I knew her, Michael."

"Fuck," Michael breathed.

Claudia watched the emotions flicker across his face. None of them were regret. Anger, resentment, fury. That last one was directed at Claudia.

"Where's Mom's watch?" he growled.

"I don't have it," Claudia lied.

Michael pulled a knife out of his back pocket. "Yeah? Let's see if that's true." He stabbed the knife into the couch, dragging the blade across the back of the couch.

"No!" Claudia cried.

Michael was on her so fast, she didn't even process his movement until he punched her.

The crack of her nose breaking was immediately accompanied by the worst pain Claudia had ever felt in her life. Tears rushed to her eyes and poured down her face with the blood that erupted from her nose.

"You have no right to tell me no," Michael snapped.

Claudia dropped to her knees, blood pouring down her front and soaking into the carpet. She tried to stop the blood, but she didn't know what to do.

Michael moved around her, back to the couch. He slid his knife effortlessly through the cushions on the couch, then the pillows, tossing them when he didn't find what he was looking for.

Claudia wanted to cry out, to stop him, to get help, but she knew her brother. If she let him have his tantrum, he would leave her alone. His threat of taking her home was empty. He just wanted the watch.

The watch Claudia couldn't give him because it was the only thing she had that could help her escape again.

A crash in the kitchen drew her gaze to where Michael yanked drawers from the cabinets and rummaged through them, sometimes snapping them off, and dumped them. He pulled doors open, not bothering to be careful and pulling two of them from the hinges.

Then he was back in front of her. "Where's Mom's watch?"

"I don't have it," Claudia lied again.

Michael grabbed her hair and tilted her head back. He pressed the knife to her throat so tight she couldn't swallow without feeling the bite of the steel against her skin.

"Please," Claudia whispered.

"Tell me where the watch is and I'll leave," Michael demanded.

Claudia pointed to her bedroom, and Michael released her.

He stomped into her room, and she squeezed her eyes shut. She didn't want to think about him in her bedroom.

The hiss of her air mattress deflating told her he cut it. Bins were toppled, tossed around, then he was back at the door. "Where?"

"In my handbag," she said.

He went back into the room, and she debated running. She could get to the door before he found the watch. She could run.

Lids were pried off bins, and more items were tossed.

Claudia pushed to her feet, her head spinning when she did. She swallowed the urge to vomit and took a step toward the door. Then another. And another. She tried to be quiet but fast, and she had her hand on the doorknob when she heard his steps behind her.

"Oh, no. No no no. You're not going anywhere!" Michael was on her before she could pull the door open.

He wrapped an arm around her waist and hauled her back to the center of the living room. He threw her onto the floor, face down in the bloodstain.

"How could you do this to me, Claudia? I've given you everything. I've always taken care of you. And you repay me by stealing from me, ratting me out to the cops, and trying to run? Where did you think you were going to go?"

Claudia cried, wishing she'd left before Lance kissed her.

Michael upended the handbag where Claudia stashed the watch, all her things pouring out into the pool of blood. Except the watch.

"Where is it?" Michael growled.

"It's in the zipper," Claudia admitted.

Michael tore the zipper open and reached inside. He dropped the handbag on top of the pile of things, his hand wrapped around the watch. He brought it to his face, looking closely at it.

Then turned his angry gaze to Claudia.

"You're never going to steal from me again."

Claudia shook her head, the move making her nauseous. "I won't. I promise."

"Your promise doesn't mean anything to me anymore."

"What... What does that mean?"

"It means I don't trust you, Claudia. How can I? After all this..." He paused and shook his head. "Let's go."

"Go? What do you mean?"

"We're going home, little sister. Where you belong."

"No! I don't want to go back."

Michael pulled out his knife again and put it to her throat. "You don't get a say in this."

"Michael, please."

"Shut up," he snapped. "Get up. We're leaving. And if you say anything to anyone on our way out, I'll bury them next to that bitch I killed a year ago. And you'll get to watch."

Tears ran down her face, but she stopped arguing. He wasn't lying. He would do it. Michael was cruel, but he wasn't someone who made empty threats.

Claudia let him haul her to her feet and lead her out of the apartment building, past the worried-looking neighbor who asked if she was okay.

"Tripped over the dog," Michael said. "Caught the edge of the couch. We're going to the emergency room right now."

"Take care," the woman said, smiling at Michael's fake concern.

He pressed the knife against Claudia's side, keeping her silent as he led her to his truck.

And drove away for good.

LANCE CLIMBED the stairs to his apartment and felt his lips lift in a smile. He hit his keys against the wall. He stomped his feet down the hall. There was no way Claudia would ignore him. A week of nothing? She would definitely stick her head out when she heard all the noise he was making.

He was almost to his door and still nothing. What the hell? She got on him constantly about letting people rest and not interrupting their neighbors. It wasn't his fault the building was from the last century and not the recent half. The sound barrier between the units was nonexistent, and she had no trouble reminding him.

Or she didn't. Until a week ago.

Lance glanced at the door just past his. His next-door neighbor was on his doorstep the day she moved in, introducing herself and trying to be friends. Friends. Lance didn't have friends. He had coworkers and family, although the latter was nowhere near Niagara Falls.

Lance jangled his keys, making sure they hit the doorknob before he turned the key and let himself into his apartment.

Nothing. It wasn't like Claudia at all to ignore him. Something wasn't right. Was she still mad at him?

The last time he saw her, he kissed her. Without her permission. He hated that he did, but fuck, he was tempted by her too much. He'd finally reached his breaking point and kissed her.

He regretted it. Not the kiss, that was hot as fuck, but not asking her. Not making sure she was on board before he put his hands on her.

He'd been working crazy hours and hadn't been able to check in with her since, but he thought she would say something. Unless she was really upset.

And dammit, he missed her. He missed the cheery smile she gave him when he was being an asshole. And he missed the daily spank bank material when she touched his arm and laughed, tilting her chest forward just far enough to give him a peek at her ample cleavage. And the weekly laundry routine that gave him a hard-on he had to take care of immediately when he spotted her lacy panties and even lacier bras. Bras that could not possibly contain those full breasts he got a peek at.

"Fuck," he breathed to himself, debating on taking care of the erection already growing at just the thought of his neighbor. She was not supposed to be tempting him the way she did. Lance knew better than to think he could be a forever kind of guy. He'd tried and failed miserably at the task, and he was not looking to repeat past mistakes.

Or get fucked over by another woman who wanted nothing to do with a man who didn't know how to wine and dine her but could only fuck her into oblivion. Apparently there were plenty of other men with that same skill. And his last girlfriend was happy to leave him for one of them. One who also knew how to wine and dine her.

The fucker.

Well, if that didn't take care of his dick, nothing would. Lance took his anger and carried it to Claudia's door, ready to give her a piece of his mind for ignoring him for a damn week. He raised his hand and pounded on the door, stepping back when it swung open on the first hit.

"Fuck me," Lance breathed.

Her apartment was trashed. Cushions sliced, freezer wide open, cabinet doors and drawers smashed. Lacy things were ripped and tossed all over the apartment.

Lance had his phone in his hand before he could process what he was doing.

"Yeah." Montgomery would know what to do.

"My neighbor is gone."

"Hey, good news. You've been bitching since she moved in."

"No. No, she's gone. She's been taken."

"What?" Montgomery's tone changed in an instant. "How do you know?"

"Because I'm standing in her apartment. There's blood. Her handbag was dumped in the middle of it. She's gone. I have to find her."

"I'm on my way."

Lance hung up the phone and made his way through the rest of the apartment. There was no sign of Claudia, as he expected. The place stunk of rotten food from the freezer thawing and stale from being closed up for days.

A week. He hadn't seen her in a week, and instead of noticing something wasn't right, Lance sat in his apartment and got pissed that he didn't hear anything from her. She was in danger, and he did nothing.

But he knew now. And he would find her.

FIVE

Montgomery burst into the apartment with Walker right behind him. Both men scanned the room, seeing all the same things Lance had already gone over in his mind.

Furniture sliced apart like someone was looking for something. Cabinets and air mattress treated with the same care. And blood that said so was Claudia.

Lance wanted to hit something, but he couldn't touch anything. Everything was exactly as he had found it twenty minutes ago.

"When's the last time you saw her?" Montgomery asked.

"Saturday. After the baby shower," Lance said.

Walker's brows shot up, but he didn't comment.

"What can you tell us about her? Or about this building. Cameras? Any security?" Montgomery asked, moving through the apartment without touching anything.

Lance shook his head. "Nothing. I don't really know much about her. She moved in right after Samuel died. Saturday was the first time I'd been in her place. It looks like she never really settled in."

"She was running," Walker said.

Lance swallowed roughly and nodded. "Clothes in bins and an air mattress made me think the same."

"Do you know if the building has cameras?" Montgomery asked.

"Not that I know of."

Montgomery pulled out his phone and read something, then put it away. "Marcus is on his way up."

Lance nodded. He let Claudia down. She'd been trying to get his attention for months. He thought she was just an annoying woman who wanted him, not a woman who needed him. He could have helped her. Protected her. Made sure whoever was after her never got to her.

But he didn't know.

"Did anyone touch anything?" Captain Marcus Patrick asked as he walked in the door. His police badge and gun demanded respect, but the man himself was why Lance respected him. Marcus had been through hell with dirty cops in his department and threats against himself and his wife, and he never let any of it steal his integrity.

"No, sir," Lance answered. "I was the first one here."

"Did you break in?"

Lance shook his head. "I live next door. Claudia and I talked. I don't think I'd be so bold as to say we were friends, but we talked."

"You last saw her when?"

"A week ago. In the evening."

"What happened that night?"

"After the baby shower, I came home. I was rushing up the stairs and ran into her, literally. She slammed her shoulder against the wall in the hallway. I took her to my apartment to patch her up. We watched a movie and had dinner. She was doing laundry, and I helped her with it since I'd hurt her. I brought it back over here for her, and... Um, and then I left."

"After?" Marcus prodded.

Lance sighed. "I kissed her, sir. I... She was always dressed up in these fancy-ass clothes, but that night, she looked like... I don't know. She was in sweats, and she was real somehow. Like she wasn't pretending to be someone else. When I saw her in the hallway, it looked like she'd been crying. I asked her if someone hurt her."

"What did she say?"

Lance thought back and realized she had never answered. "I thought she had a date. I asked if her date hurt her, and she said she didn't have a date, but she never answered me about someone hurting her."

"Meaning whoever was after her could have hurt her before you saw her, then came back and did this?" Marcus asked, gesturing to the bloodstain on the floor.

Lance closed his eyes. How did he miss all of that? How did he get so distracted that he never noticed what was right in front of him for months?

"What else can you tell me about her? Name? Work? Anything?"

"Claudia Smith. I've never seen her outside the building, so I'm not sure if she drives or works or anything," Lance said.

"And you think Claudia Smith is her real name?" Marcus asked.

Lance took a step back. He'd never considered it wasn't. Did she lie to him about who she was? Was anything she said to him the truth? "I don't know."

"I'll check in with the office and see what they know. Chances are she was working somewhere that would pay her under the table. A restaurant or something like that where she could bring home cash. Want me to keep you informed?" Marcus asked Montgomery.

"Yeah. We want to help," Montgomery said without hesitation.

"I'll get a team here to collect what we can. Can you hang around and wait for them?" Marcus asked.

"We're not going anywhere," Montgomery said.

Marcus nodded, then let himself out of the apartment.

Montgomery and Walker shared a look that Lance ignored. He didn't care what they thought, what anyone thought. He needed to know what happened to her.

Who was after her? He wished he'd asked her more questions, gotten to know her. He wracked his brain to find anything she might have said over the last four months that would clue him in on where she could be.

But he had no answers.

Marcus's team showed up and asked them to leave. Montgomery said something to the cops and got them permission to stick around, as long as they didn't get in the way.

The team had barely gotten started when Marcus was back. "Claudia Smith is the name she gave the office when she moved in. Specifically asked to be in the apartment next to you, Lance. Said she had to be in this building and had to be next door to you. The office had a diner around the corner on file as her place of employment. I'm heading over there next."

Montgomery met Lance's gaze. "Do you want to stay here or go with Marcus?"

"I'll go."

Marcus nodded and led the way to his SUV. Lance didn't say anything as they drove the three blocks to the small diner Lance had passed by hundreds of times but never been in.

Marcus commanded the attention of the entire room when he walked in. A very pregnant woman smiled and asked if they were there to eat.

"We're looking for an employee. Is there a manager on duty?" Marcus asked.

"I knew Claudia didn't just walk," the pregnant woman said. "What happened to her?"

"Are you a friend?" Marcus asked.

She nodded. "I am. Mallory. We've been working together for months. She's not overly talkative, but she's so kind. She always lets me sit and rest when I'm having a bad day. Covers my tables and still gives me the tips. Most people would be resentful of me not pulling my weight, but Claudia never once complained. She sneaks her own tips into my envelope and thinks I don't notice. I keep trying to give it back to her, but she refuses to accept anything."

"Sounds like her," Lance said.

"Are you her neighbor? The one who kissed her and ran?"

Lance's cheeks heated with her direct question. "How do you know that?"

Mallory shrugged. "She told me."

"She told you?" Marcus asked. "When did you see her last?"

"She was here on Monday. We worked the lunch shift together, and she couldn't stop smiling. She told me you helped with a gender reveal for a friend, and you guys kissed. I told her to talk to you. Ask you why you ran after you kissed her."

Marcus looked at Lance, either waiting for an answer or for more details.

Either way, Claudia never talked to him. "I haven't seen her since that night. Saturday. She never asked me... I didn't see her after that."

"She was pretty determined to talk to you that night. I told her it didn't make sense to wait. She was going to tell me what you said. She was supposed to be here on Wednesday, but she didn't show up."

"No one cared to report it?" Marcus asked.

Mallory glared at him. "Captain, we are servers in a tiny diner that most people pass by without noticing. People stop showing up for work all the time. Eventually, they come get their last check, but if someone finds somewhere better than here to work, they don't always pause to let the bosses know."

"But she didn't do that. You haven't heard from her?"

Mallory shook her head. "Nope. But I never saw her outside work."

"Seems to be the trend," Marcus said, sliding a glance to Lance.

Mallory picked up on it and asked, "What does that mean?"

"We haven't been able to figure out what she drives or where she could be."

"She doesn't drive. She walks. I don't know if she has a license, but she definitely does not have a car," Mallory said.

"That answers one question," Marcus said. "Do you know if there are employee files anywhere?"

Mallory nodded and waved him toward the kitchen. "There's an office back here. The owner is here today. I don't think he's spoken to Claudia since he hired her, but he can give you any of the official stuff. His name is Evan."

"Thank you," Marcus told Mallory.

"You're welcome. I hope she's okay. Claudia is good people." Mallory winked at Lance. "And she deserves an explanation."

Lance's cheeks warmed as Mallory turned and went back to work.

"Something I should know?" Marcus asked.

"Just felt too close. I held her away for months, and in one night, I crossed a line."

Marcus turned to face Lance fully, crossing his arms over his chest. "What line?"

"Kissing her. Nothing beyond that. But I didn't ask her before I did it. I acted on instinct, and I felt like an asshole, so I took off. I had to clear my head before I could face her again. I wanted to apologize."

"And that's it?"

"Yes, sir. I had nothing to do with her disappearance. I want to find her."

"Okay." Marcus knocked on the door marked *OFFICE*.

"Yeah?" a voice inside asked.

Marcus opened the door and flashed his badge. "Captain Marcus Patrick. I'd like to ask you a few questions about one of your employees. We have reason to believe she's been kidnapped."

"Shit," the man said. "Come in. I'm Evan Wilson. I own this place. You're talking about Claudia, aren't you?"

"Yes, sir. We need to see her employment application and any records you have on her."

Evan opened a file cabinet and flipped through files until he found the right one. He handed it to Marcus. "I don't get a lot of details about people. Identification and application is pretty much it."

Marcus opened the file and flipped through the two pages before he handed the folder to Lance. A photocopy of a license and a single-page application were the only things in the file.

"This is fake," Lance said, looking at the license. "It's not even a really good fake."

Evan shrugged. "I get people in here who need a place to work. Who don't have anywhere else to turn. She didn't seem dangerous or like she was a criminal. She said she needed a way to make some money."

"So you knew her license wasn't valid?" Marcus asked.

Evan hesitated, then nodded. "She told me someone was after her. She couldn't have her real ID hitting anything."

"Did she show it to you?"

Evan nodded again.

"Where is she from?"

"Kansas."

CLAUDIA SAT on the bed in her room and tried not to cry. A week ago, Lance kissed her, and she fooled herself into thinking she could have a life. A real life. With someone who cared about her.

But she wasn't destined for that.

Her room was dark, but it was still daylight outside. Michael boarded up her window and removed all the lamps from her room except one that was near the door. Where she couldn't reach.

Because he chained her to the bed.

Twice a day, he let her use the bathroom, but other than that, he kept her in her room. He brought her food, sat and talked to her, and mostly left her alone.

She thought he would kill her, but he didn't. The entire drive from Niagara Falls back to Kansas, he told her he was going to make her regret running. That he was protecting her. But he didn't lay a hand on her.

Yet.

The locks on the outside of her door clicked and unlocked, then Michael was there. He held a bag she hoped was full of food.

Michael walked in and closed the door. He grabbed the chair from next to the door and carried it to where she sat on the bed. "I brought you dinner."

Claudia didn't say anything. She couldn't. If she spoke, he might hurt her again.

"Are you not grateful?" Michael barked.

"Thank you," she whispered.

"That's better." He smoothed the hair back from her face and pressed his lips to her hairline. He stayed there, holding her close. He inhaled deeply and caressed her head, like a lover would do.

Claudia didn't move. Her shoulder had healed from the tiny cut when she ran into Lance, but her nose still throbbed. She knew it was broken, but Michael refused to take her somewhere to have it looked at. He offered to straighten it himself, but she said it was fine and didn't mention it again. But it still hurt like a son-of-a-bitch.

Michael finally released her and sat on the chair he brought over. "I thought we could have dinner together. We haven't done that much lately. I miss spending time with you." He opened the bag and handed her a sandwich. "When you were gone, I realized how little time we'd spent together lately. You started working and thought you were better than me."

"I never…" Claudia wanted to argue, but he glared at her, and she stopped talking.

"It's okay. You are better than me. Mom always said I needed to make sure you were taken care of. I love you, Claudia. I want only the best for you."

Claudia nodded and unwrapped her sandwich. It was ham, which she hated, but when she hadn't eaten a normal meal in five days, she wasn't going to be picky. She took a bite and found mustard and pepper-jack cheese. All things she hated.

"How's your sandwich?" Michael asked as though they were having a nice, normal meal together.

"It's good," she forced out.

"Good. I want to take care of you again. You don't need to worry about anything when you're with me. I'll never let anyone hurt you. Just like I always promised when we were younger."

Claudia nodded, feeling the tears welling up in her eyes. She couldn't cry. If she did, he'd get mad at her. He said she was being ungrateful when she cried. Or weak. It didn't matter to Michael. Neither were okay.

"We need to go to the police station sometime. They questioned me when you disappeared. I swore I didn't have anything to do with you running off, but they didn't believe me. I can't keep working if they're going to watch me like they have been, so I need you to tell them I didn't do anything to you."

Hope blossomed in her chest. If she could talk to the police, maybe she could get away from Michael. She could run. She could call Lance. Even if it was just to tell him she appreciated him giving her hope. Letting her believe there was still good in the world.

"Of course, we can't have you going there looking like you do." Michael reached over and grabbed her nose before Claudia knew what he was doing. He shoved it, the snap bringing tears to her eyes and making her stomach revolt the food she'd just eaten.

Claudia gagged and turned her head to the side, vomiting onto the floor next to her bed.

Michael jumped up. "What the fuck is wrong with you?"

"That hurt," Claudia breathed, the pain radiating across her face.

"I was trying to help you. All I ever do is take care of you, and you repay me by throwing up all over me?" Michael punched her side, sending her rolling to the other side of the bed.

Claudia fought against the pain and the nausea. She laid there, struggling not to pass out as Michael threw the chair he was in against the wall and let himself out, locking the door again.

Claudia let the tears fall and mingle with the blood once more pouring from her nose and stopped fighting the pain, letting it claim her and drag her to sleep.

SIX

Lance felt like a caged animal. He paced the office, wanting to rush to Kansas and turn the entire fucking state on its head until he found Claudia. But he couldn't. Not until he knew what the hell he was looking for.

It had been two days since he discovered Claudia lied to him about who she was. A full week since she disappeared. Since someone hurt her and took her right out from under his fucking nose.

Lance thought back over every interaction they had to remember something, but he had zero ideas of where she could be.

"Hey," someone said, clapping him on the back before Lance could brace himself for the contact.

Lance flinched, fists coming up to defend himself against someone he didn't need to fight.

Damien Joseph had his hands up in defense, palms out to show Lance he wasn't there to fight.

"Sorry," Lance mumbled.

"All good. I take it you haven't heard anything." Damien leaned against Walker's desk, crossing his ankles and his arms.

Lance shook his head. "It's a big fucking state. Almost three million people. And without a name, finding her is pretty fucking hard."

"The ID didn't help?" Damien asked.

"Marcus ran it through the database he has, but it didn't narrow it down enough. She must have had it made somewhere with a different picture than she used on her real license."

"Damn. What's next?"

"Fuck if I know. Montgomery looks like he's gearing up for something, so I don't even know if I'm going to be able to keep going."

"You're giving up?"

Lance closed his eyes and pictured Claudia in his mind. The fancy clothes, the perfect hair, the makeup that hid so much from him. He didn't know her. Did she want to be found? He believed anyone who was injured like she had to have been wanted to be found, but what if she wasn't the one hurt? What if she ran because she hurt someone else?

Damien was watching Lance when he opened his eyes.

"What if she wasn't the one hurt?"

Damien straightened at the question. "Did anyone test the blood?"

"I don't know. I need to call Marcus."

Damien didn't move as Lance found Marcus's phone number and called.

"Patrick."

"It's Lance. Did you test the blood? Do we know if it was Claudia's? Or whatever her name is?"

Marcus tapped a keyboard, the sound audible through the phone. He was silent for a minute. "Blood is female, but there's no match in our system to anyone."

"Which means it could be hers, or it could be another female who was there."

"Yeah, but without a match to anything, we have no way of knowing."

"Is there a system for that?"

"The FBI will have to do that."

"What do you mean?"

"It's kidnapping. They're taking it over. Now that we know she's gone, she didn't show up for work, we have reason to believe it's foul play, the FBI is taking over."

"Who has the case?"

"Adam and Lorelei. They'll find her."

"I still want to know what's going on."

"They are aware. They should be coming to see you soon."

"Thanks, Marcus."

"Sorry we didn't find answers yet."

"Me, too." Lance hung up and told Damien what Marcus said.

"They just walked in," Damien replied.

"They did?"

"While you were talking, they went to Montgomery's office." Damien pointed.

Lance stood and saw agents Adam Johnson and Lorelei Sloane talking to Montgomery. Lance didn't wait for an invitation to join them.

Montgomery saw Lance coming and waved him in before Lance got to the door. "I guess you know they're taking the case."

"I just called Marcus to make sure it's Claudia's blood. He told me he'd turned it over."

"We understand she's your neighbor?" Adam asked.

Lance nodded. "We don't know each other well, but yeah. She lives next door to me."

"And she requested that. Do you remember meeting her before she moved in?"

Lance shook his head. "I never did. She knocked on my door the day she moved in, but we'd never met before then."

Lorelei flipped a tablet to face Lance. She tapped the screen.

Lance saw the front of his gym. It was sunny, bright like spring or summer, not dreary like the last few days had been as fall grabbed hold of the area.

The video played, and he watched himself walk out the front door. He stared at the screen, trying to remember when it occurred. A few seconds after he walked out, Claudia walked out behind him. She stayed a little away from him, but it was definitely her. And she was definitely following him.

She watched him until he drove out of the parking lot, then she walked the other way.

The video jumped to another day. Lance walked out of the gym, but this time, Claudia was next to a car. She followed him out of the parking lot.

"When was this?"

"Early May. Two days apart. We figured if she requested living near you, she saw you somewhere."

"So you were stalking me?"

"You were easier to follow than she was since we knew some of your routine. It looks like she saw you one day and decided to follow you. You never saw her?"

Lance thought back to early May. "Samuel."

"What?" Montgomery asked.

"It was right around the time Samuel died. He was killed on May second, so this had to be right after. There was a girl at the gym..."

"Claudia?" Adam asked.

"No. Younger. She was alone, probably around twenty. She had a black eye. She was working out, but it was obvious she was scared. I talked to her, showed her a few moves. How to defend herself, how to throw a punch, pressure points to go after if someone attacked her."

"She was in danger?"

Lance shook his head. "She wouldn't say. I asked if she was okay, and she blew me off. I persisted and asked if I could spot her on the bag. She tried to ignore me, but I gave her tips, anyway. It wasn't long before she was listening to me."

"You think Claudia saw you with this young woman?" Montgomery asked.

"I think it's possible."

"What happened to the woman?" Lorelei asked.

Lance smiled. "I saw her again a month later. She thanked me and said she was leaving town alone and that she was safe."

Lorelei grinned and closed her eyes. She nodded.

"If that's how Claudia saw you, it sounds like she must have decided you would protect her, too. I assume that's why she asked to have an apartment near you," Adam said.

"It makes sense. If I was in danger, I'd want a neighbor who would help me," Lorelei said.

"But she never mentioned anything. She never told me she was in danger," Lance argued. "I thought she didn't have a car. She was driving?"

"We looked into the car. The owner goes to the gym. Never reported it stolen or anything. She returned the car not long after she followed you, so she must have just used it to follow you. She pulled the key from the wheel well."

"She went to all this trouble to get close to me. Why not say anything?" Lance asked.

"She must have thought you'd figure it out. Or she thought she was safe." Montgomery shrugged.

"And now she's gone, and I have no idea where to find her," Lance growled.

"Her boss at the diner said she's from Kansas?" Adam asked.

"Yes," Lance replied.

"We're focusing our search there, but anything you can tell us about her would be helpful," Lorelei said.

"I don't know anything. She didn't tell me much about herself."

"But you talked a lot, right? She came to you?" Adam asked.

Lance nodded and scrubbed a hand over his face. He wanted to remember everything, but it felt like there was a black hole where all his knowledge about Claudia should be. "She would ask for sugar or a screwdriver or be walking out the door when I was coming home and say hi."

"Did she flirt with you? Say things she shouldn't have known? Have an accent?" Lorelei asked.

"What... Yes, she flirted. At least, I thought she was. She smiled a lot and flipped her hair like women do. She would laugh at everything, even though I don't think I'm that funny."

"You're not," Montgomery interjected.

Lance flipped his boss off, and Montgomery chuckled.

"Anyway, what else?" Lorelei prompted.

"I don't remember her knowing anything weird, or wondering how she knew something. Like I said, it was always basic. She never invited me to her place or asked me out."

"But she was dressed like she worked somewhere a lot fancier than a diner?" Adam asked.

Lance nodded. "Definitely. She was always in a skirt or a dress."

"Her apartment was definitely searched, but we didn't get the idea anything was taken besides her wallet. Certainly not a wardrobe. She had only two skirts and three dresses that match what you're saying. She had a lot of casual clothes," Lorelei said.

"That's not..." Lance tried to picture her in her nice

clothes. They were always a bit of a turnoff for him, reminding him of his ex and the way things ended.

He wasn't interested in a woman who cared about her appearance, so he ignored Claudia. As much as he could ignore a woman who was always trying to get him to pay attention to her. As much as he could ignore a woman he wanted to strip out of her fancy clothes and find out what secrets she hid beneath the layers of class.

Lance was drawn to Claudia way more than he wanted to admit. After the first month she lived next door, he admitted to himself she was attractive. He still resisted her because of her appearance, but he couldn't stop himself from dreaming about her.

In his dreams, she was the woman he wanted her to be. Wild, passionate, casual. Someone who suited him.

He told himself the dreams were harmless since no one would ever know, but the fantasies he had of her became more frequent until Lance was looking forward to seeing her every day.

"Her skirts were black. Always black. If you say there were only two, I guess I believe it. Her tops changed, though. Red, pink, purple, blue, green."

"We found those," Adam said. "She must have thought you would pay more attention to her in her nicer clothes if that's what you always saw her wearing."

Lance shook his head. She was wrong. If she'd dressed the way she did the last day he saw her, he would have known more about who she was. He would have known the moment she disappeared. He would have been chasing her down by now.

But instead, he believed the picture she showed him. He believed she was an uptight bitch like his ex. A woman who would only stick around as long as he was taking care of her, then find another man who could do a better job of it.

Lance didn't know Claudia because she didn't want him to know her. She hid the truth from him. She chose him because she saw him at the gym, but then she hid everything. She pretended to be someone else. She didn't tell him she was in danger.

What the hell was he supposed to do with that? Was he supposed to race to her side and save her when she didn't ask him to? Or did he let the FBI handle it and move on?

"We have the picture from her fake license out there, but it's not very good, so we haven't gotten any traction. We have the video footage from the gym, but again, it's not great. She was careful, which makes us wonder if whoever she's been running from had law enforcement connections," Lorelei said.

"Then why would you have her picture everywhere? Doesn't that help whoever is after her find her?" Lance demanded.

"We're hoping it makes whoever she was running from tip their hand. If we get a call, it's likely either someone who wants to help or someone who wants to know what we know. Either way, it gives us somewhere to look," Adam explained.

"I hope you know what you're doing," Lance growled.

"We do. And we will keep you informed so you know what we're doing. Even if you aren't willing to admit how much she means to you." Lorelei raised an eyebrow and dared Lance to argue.

Lance just nodded.

"Thank you both," Montgomery said, more diplomatic than Lance. "We appreciate the help, and the information."

"We just hope we have good news next time we talk," Adam said.

"So do we." Montgomery walked Lorelei and Adam out, leaving Lance alone in the office.

Lance sank onto the couch and dropped his head into his hands. He didn't know what to do. Claudia, or whatever her name was, was in danger. He felt an obligation to protect people. It was his job, and it was in his DNA. He'd been doing it forever.

But he didn't know if she wanted his protection, or needed it. What if he was wrong, and instead of finding a woman in danger, he showed whoever was after her where she was? Or maybe she was the dangerous one?

CLAUDIA WAS LOSING track of the days. She wanted to have faith and trust that she would be saved from the hell she was in, but no one cared enough about her to notice she was missing. No one knew who she was. No one was going to come looking for her.

She cried herself to sleep at night when she thought about the life she could have had. The life she fantasized about with Lance. She was a fool to keep him the dark. If she'd told him everything, he would be there.

Or not.

He never seemed open to her advances, no matter what she did. Even when he kissed her, he ran. Men didn't do that. Not unless they regretted their actions.

All her dreams about Lance were just that. Dreams. Silly ideas by a silly girl, just like her mother used to tell her when Claudia would talk about the future she wanted. Her mother would laugh. She said they didn't have money for Claudia to go to college, and she'd be lucky if she finished high school.

Michael made sure Claudia finished high school after their mother died. He pushed her to take classes at the community college when they had money. He was always proud of her and her accomplishments. Until she started earning her own money.

Things changed when Claudia talked about moving out. She wanted independence, but Michael told her she didn't need to leave. They fought about it, and eventually, he convinced her to stay. Over the years, she worked and saved her money, contributing to the household expenses.

But then he wanted more. Things needed to be repaired, and she had the job, so she paid. He found out how much money she was making and asked where it was all going. She confessed she had a savings account, and he got angry. Forced her to put all her money into an account they both had access to. Said she owed him for raising her. For loving her enough to give up his future to take care of her.

That was three years ago. Claudia's meager savings account became their joint checking account, something that hovered around empty all the time. Claudia knew she had to do something, find a way to hold on to money for her future, but then Michael killed that woman.

A fist pounding on her door made her jump. Claudia scrambled to sit as the locks clicked open. The door slammed against the wall and revealed Michael's friend, Hector.

Claudia curled her feet under her. Hector scared her. Not just because of his size, but the look in his eyes when he looked at her. Predatory. Possessive.

"Sup, Claudia," Hector said, stepping into the room.

"What do you want?"

"Is that how you talk to a friend?"

"We're not friends. Where's Michael?"

"He had to run an errand. Said he'd be back soon."

Claudia swallowed roughly. Michael was the one who chained her up, but Hector was the one who scared her. "What are you doing in here?"

Hector took a step toward her, his gaze sliding down her body. "I just wanted to see how you're doing. Anything you need?" He licked his lips, his gaze locked on her crotch.

Claudia fought against her tears. She was trapped. The man in front of her had made no secret that he wanted her, and he finally had her alone.

She'd evaded him before, running out the door when he'd tried to touch her. She snuck out the window once, but Michael put bars on it. Not to mention, she was still chained to the bed.

"I'm fine," Claudia said, hoping he was more talk than action.

"Well, there's something I need." He was across the room fast, much faster than she expected. He grabbed her breast and squeezed it hard, bringing tears to her eyes.

"Ow!"

"Shut up, you bitch. You've been teasing me for years. Now it's time for me to take what I want from you."

SEVEN

Claudia screamed. She tried to hit Hector, but she couldn't do anything with her hands chained. He tore at her shirt and exposed her bra. She tried to cover herself.

He was stronger. He shoved her onto the bed and climbed on top of her. She felt his hard length against her stomach. His breath billowed over her face as he brought his mouth to hers.

She jerked her head forward, catching him off-guard, and head-butted his cheek.

"Ow! You bitch!" He leaned back enough to cup his cheek, but he didn't get off of her. "You're going to pay for that."

He grabbed her shirt and tore it through. He shoved the cup of her bra down and pinched her nipple hard enough that she cried out in pain. His other hand went to her waist.

She bucked her hips, trying everything she could to get him off her. She screamed and cried and kicked and fought.

He was still stronger.

Her sweats started to move, exposing her panties to his gaze. He moved back so he could slide them lower.

She crossed her legs, fighting with every inch of herself to fend him off. Her throat was sore from screaming so loud, so much, but she couldn't stop fighting him.

He released her breast, and she quickly covered it back up with her bra. Her skin was sore, raw, from his aggressive touch. He wrapped both hands around her ankles and squeezed hard. Hard enough that she was sure he would snap a bone or two.

"Stop! Please! Don't do this!"

He pried her legs apart and laughed. "I'll do whatever the fuck I want."

"The hell you will!" Michael growled from the open bedroom door.

Claudia hadn't heard him return, and from the look on Hector's face, neither had he.

"You want a turn? I'll let you go first. I'll hold her down for you," Hector said, eyeing Michael.

"Get your hands off her," Michael threatened.

Hector released Claudia's ankles, but the red imprints from his fingers remained.

Michael noticed the marks, his gaze traveling up Claudia to her exposed panties and torn shirt. Anguish and anger battled in his eyes.

"You know she's a tease. I was just—"

Hector didn't get to finish his statement before Michael throat-punched him.

Claudia gasped as Hector dropped to his knees, clutching his throat.

Michael came to her and sat on the side of the bed.

Claudia shied away from him, scooting over so he wouldn't touch her. Hector's offer rang in her ears. She knew the words weren't empty. Michael had looked at her with desire. More than once. He usually wiped the look off his face when he realized someone else noticed, but clearly Hector saw the same thing she'd convinced herself she wasn't actually seeing.

"I'm sorry he touched you," Michael said, his voice soft and compassionate. "I never should have left him here with you. It's my fault." He closed his eyes and drew a heavy breath. "He will never touch you again. I promise you that."

"Thank you," Claudia whispered. Even those two words hurt to push past her sore throat.

"When I heard you screaming..." Michael swung his gaze to Hector, still crumpled on the floor. "I only want to protect you. That's all I've ever wanted. I love you, Claudia."

"Thank you," she said.

"Do you love me?" he asked.

Claudia swallowed the thick feeling in her bruised throat. She couldn't tell him the truth. But he would know if she was lying. "Of course."

He reached for her, slowly, and she let him pull her into his arms. His touch was gentle and caring, unlike the way he'd been treating her since he dragged her from her apartment ten days ago.

Claudia's eyes filled with tears. She felt safe. It made no sense when she was chained up, but Michael protected her from Hector. She didn't know how he knew she was in danger, but he did, and he was there for her. He saved her.

But if he hadn't dragged her back there, he wouldn't have had to. How could she feel safe with him and threatened by him?

Hector inhaled a full breath and pushed to his feet. The look in his eyes was one of pure hatred. He moved to the bedroom door, and as soon as he stepped out, he started to close it.

Michael was fast, and he stopped Hector from locking them in the bedroom together. Hector tried to slam the door on Michael's foot, but Michael was stronger and overpowered Hector.

"You will regret ever coming in here," Michael growled. He yanked the door open as Hector retreated.

The door slammed closed again, leaving Claudia alone. She heard a crash and jumped. Another crash. Grunting and yelling, then a single gunshot.

And silence.

Her heart pounded, a rapid beat of fear and unknown. Her ears strained for any sound.

Then she heard footsteps.

She sucked in a terrified breath. If it was Hector, he would finish what he started.

If it was Michael…

Claudia stared at the door, waiting for someone to appear. Waiting for the door to open. Waiting for…

The knob turned. Michael pushed the door open. Blood was spattered on his left side. His eye was showing signs of a bruise. There was a tear in his shirt.

"Hector won't touch you again. But you're going to be alone tonight. Just for a few hours. I promise I'll be back."

Claudia nodded.

Michael stared at her for a long moment, then closed the door and locked it. All three locks engaged slowly, like Michael wasn't sure about what he was doing. Then his footsteps retreated.

Claudia was alone again. In a house with a murderer. And his latest victim.

She had to get out, or Hector would not be Michael's last victim.

LANCE'S HEAD hit his desk and woke him up. He forced himself upright, then out of his seat.

He'd been staring at the computer for hours. Days, really. Claudia had been missing for almost two full weeks. The FBI had no leads, Rose Protection Agency had other cases, and no one seemed to care that Claudia was gone.

Except for Lance.

And he didn't even know if he should keep looking.

He'd chased random leads about missing women and women who appeared to be in danger from half the country, but none of them had much information. He didn't know how the FBI agents who chased down missing people handled it. He was losing his mind, and it had only been two weeks. To have case after case with little to no information about the person who disappeared would make Lance crazy.

He walked through the office, the silence around him deafening. He checked his phone and saw it was two-fifty-six in the morning. Everyone had left hours ago, but Lance couldn't do it. Claudia was out there. She was in danger. And she was alone.

Lance used the bathroom, then went to the break room. He started a new pot of coffee and grabbed a stale muffin from the meeting two days ago. His stomach rumbled. He hadn't had a decent meal in days, and he'd barely left the building.

When the coffee was done and his muffin was gone, Lance carried a fresh cup back to his desk and dove in again. If Claudia was from Kansas, he had to assume whoever took her was back in Kansas. He could be wrong, but his scattershot search hadn't resulted in anything valuable yet, so he focused on Kansas.

She moved in next door to him in May, which meant she had to have left home in April or earlier. Lance searched through missing persons reports from April in Kansas, but found nothing. A few kids, two women who were both later found, and a man whose body was discovered a week after he went missing.

Lance went farther back, month-by-month. Person after missing person filled his screen. Many of them were still missing. A few had been found and returned home. More bodies were found. And even more had never been found.

The thought of never finding Claudia sent Lance to his feet. What would be worse? Never finding her or finding her body? He didn't know. What he did know was he couldn't sit there with only his thoughts to keep him company.

He checked the time again, but he knew Aunt Jackie would be awake. She'd been a night owl her entire life. An artist who worked from home in her studio and frequently spent her nights dreaming up a new piece and bringing it to life as the rest of her town slept.

"I hope you're not calling for bail money because it's a pretty long trip for me and you'll be stuck there for a while," Aunt Jackie said when she picked up.

Lance chuckled, needing the laugh more than he cared to admit. "No bail money. Just wanted to hear your voice."

"Uh oh. I know that tone. What's wrong? Case getting to you?"

Lance leaned back in his chair and rubbed his eyes. "Yeah."

"You are the most dependable man I've ever known in my life. You will always prevail."

"Don't let Rico hear you say that." Aunt Jackie married a tolerant and kind man when she moved to Oregon. After raising Lance and putting her dreams on hold to make sure he had a good life, she picked up and moved across the country while he was in the Army. She met Rico a few years after she moved, and the man took his time convincing Jackie they were perfect for each other, including waiting until he met Lance to ask his permission to marry her.

Aunt Jackie guffawed. "Oh, please. That man would agree

with me. He knows if anyone ever needs anything, you're the one to call."

"I'm not sure if I can do it this time."

"Tell me what's going on."

Lance pictured Jackie in his mind. Her dark brown skin was always warm and soothing to him. She held him when he cried more times than he could count, crying with him when his mother died and taking over the role without hesitation. He heard the swish of her hair as she no doubt tossed her waist-length braids behind her back. Fabric rustled before a creak told him she was on her feet and pacing her studio.

"I interrupted your night, didn't I?"

"You are never an interruption. Now, quit stalling. What's going on?"

Lance sighed and started at the beginning. He told Jackie about Claudia showing up around the time Samuel died, then her worming her way into his life without him even realizing it.

"She sounds like Rico."

Lance chuckled at the thought. "I guess we both need to be hit over the head with someone right in front of us before we know we want them in our lives."

"Yes, well, I finally listened. It sounds like you still need the reminder."

"She lied to me, though."

"And you don't do well with that. Not after that witch broke your heart."

"Can you blame me?"

Jackie's sigh sank into Lance. "You are such a good man, Lance. Your mama would have been so proud of you. She loved you. Oh, she loved you. But she missed out on teaching you valuable lessons about women. I did, too. I should have done better telling you how hard relationships are, but I always worried you would resent me for not being your mama.”

“I love you, Aunt Jackie. You did everything for me.”

“I tried. But I knew there was a big hole missing where she would have been. Your mama didn’t date after you were born because you were her priority. I thought I had to do the same, but instead of helping you, it didn’t allow you to learn how relationships work.”

“I know how they work,” Lance grumbled.

“Okay, tough man. You can say that, but you never saw the inside of one. Not from the outside. That witch did you dirty. She wasn’t worthy of you.”

“That’s not what she says.”

“She’s wrong. She was looking for things that don’t matter. She wants wealth and power. You were offering love and security.”

“It wasn’t enough.”

“Maybe not for her, but one day she’ll realize what she threw away. But this isn’t about her. This is about you and Claudia. It sounds like she’s a woman who knows what a catch you are.”

“Then why did she lie to me?”

“I didn’t tell you when I was attacked,” Aunt Jackie whispered.

Lance’s gut clenched. He still remembered the day he found out Aunt Jackie’s boss assaulted her. She’d already quit her job and filed a restraining order against her former boss, but Lance still wanted to go after the asshole for thinking he had a right to put his hands on a woman who said no.

“I was ashamed,” Aunt Jackie continued. “I had a hard time accepting I did nothing wrong. Women are told we are here to serve men. It wasn’t very long ago that we were first recognized as independent and not property. In some countries, women are still property, and that history is ingrained in all of us, even as we fight against it. I thought I did something wrong. That I invited it somehow."

"You didn't," Lance growled.

"I know that now, love, but at the time... I struggled a lot. If your Claudia is running from someone or something, she might be feeling similar guilt."

"If she thought she could trust me to help her, why wouldn't she have told me?"

"My guess would be she saw you with that young woman at the gym and believed you would never hurt a woman. But that didn't mean she thought she could trust you with the darkest of her secrets."

"I guess," Lance said.

"You're feeling twitchy, aren't you? Dying to get out there."

"Yeah."

"What if you just go? Take some time off and go to... Where? Kansas?"

"Yeah. That's what her boss said."

"What if you go there?"

"It's a big fucking state."

"So? New York is even bigger."

Lance let out a laugh. "True, but what if she's not in Kansas?"

"What if she is?"

Lance drew a sharp breath. He trusted Aunt Jackie. Could he do it? "It's an FBI case. I'm not sure they'd be okay with me going and looking for her."

"You won't know until you ask, my love. Or you could say your uncle is Catholic and you were taught to ask for forgiveness," Aunt Jackie teased.

Lance laughed. "I'm sure Rico would be happy to take some of the blame for me going rogue."

Aunt Jackie laughed. "Oh, he'd be the same calm man he always is. And he'd do anything for you, just like I would."

"Do you think I'll find her?"

"I think you'll find her. But I think you need to figure out what you're going to do when you do. These cases don't always turn out the way you hope."

The thought of finding her body flashed in his mind. "My boss's sister was missing for twelve years. She escaped her captor and called his best friend, who's now her husband."

"A happy ending."

"It was." Lance was quiet for a minute. "Do you think I might get one, too?"

"Oh, my love, I know you will. If there was ever a man who deserved happiness, it is you. I'd like to think your mama is watching you right now, maybe watching Claudia, and guiding you back together."

"I don't know. Maybe."

"You know what the next right step is. You always do."

Lance exhaled a laugh. "I wish I had your confidence."

"The fourteen-year-old boy who wanted to beat up my old boss knew the next steps. The eighteen-year-old man who joined the Army knew the next steps. The thirty-six-year-old warrior on the other end of this phone knows the next steps, too. I know it."

"Thanks, Aunt Jackie. I miss you."

"I miss you, too, my love. Come out and visit us sometime. Maybe bring your Claudia with you."

"I'll see about Claudia, but I will come soon, or you can come here."

"Be careful what you wish for. We just might."

"I would love that. I love you. Love to Uncle Rico."

"We love you, Lance. Talk soon. Keep me posted."

"I will."

Lance hung up the phone and smiled. Aunt Jackie always made him feel like he could do anything.

Going to Kansas? He dismissed the idea before, but the longer he looked at reports online, the less he felt like he could do anything from Niagara Falls.

If he did find something on Claudia, and he was still in New York, it would be way too long before he could get to her.

Lance knew it was the right move. He just had to convince the powers that be to allow it.

EIGHT

"No," Montgomery said. "No. Just... what the hell are you thinking?"

"I'm thinking she could be in danger."

"And you're what? Just going to drive around the fucking state and ask if anyone knows a woman whose name might be Claudia but might not be who might be from somewhere in Kansas but might not be? It makes no sense."

"I can't just sit here. I can't."

"Mont," Zeke said from the chair next to Lance.

Montgomery glared at his friend and second in command. Something unspoken passed between them. Something that had Montgomery sighing. "Son of a bitch."

"Give us a day," Zeke said, holding up a hand before Lance spoke. "One day to figure a few things out. See if we can send someone with you. Can you do that?"

Lance nodded. "Yeah. Thank you."

Zeke nodded and gave a slight jerk of his head toward the door.

Lance got the hint and left the office, knowing there was more between the two men than he knew. Zeke and Montgomery were not just coworkers but best friends and brothers-in-law after Zeke married Montgomery's sister.

Who also went missing years ago. Lance knew the two of them understood more than he did what hell Claudia could be facing.

Sitting around for one more day was the last thing Lance wanted to do, but he would follow orders. He hadn't slept much, and he could use some more time to research the state and figure out where to start his search.

He dug up everything he could about the state of Kansas. He learned about the big cities in the state and the smaller towns. When he looked at the missing persons reports, he noticed a very loose pattern. It could be nothing, or it could lead him to Claudia.

By lunchtime, Lance was dragging. He decided to go home and get some sleep before he took off for Kansas. Flying would be faster, but if he drove, he was more inconspicuous. It would take two full days of driving to get there, which made him debate the options, but all that mattered was getting to Claudia.

Lance stopped by Berkeley's desk on his way out and filled her in on what was going on. As the office manager, he knew she was aware of everything and wondered if she could give him some hope.

"You look exhausted," Berkeley said when Lance walked out from the back.

Lance breathed a laugh. "Yeah. I feel it. I'm going to try to get some sleep."

"You're not going to sneak off to Kansas, are you?"

Lance shook his head. "Zeke said to give them a day. I'll honor that."

"And if they say no?"

"I plead the Fifth."

Berkeley chuckled. "I didn't know them when Nina disappeared, but I imagine they felt the same way you do now. It can't be easy knowing someone you care about is missing and hurt. I'm really sorry, Lance."

"Thanks, Berk. I hope I find her."

"I have no doubt you will."

"Do you think they're going to give me approval to go?"

Berkeley nodded. "It might not be a blank check and a get out of jail free thing, but I think they'll tell you to go."

"I hope so." Lance leaned on the counter, resting his head on his hands.

"Go home. Get some sleep. You'll feel better tomorrow."

Lance stood upright and nodded. "I hope so. Thanks, Berk. Call me if something changes."

"I will." Her phone rang and drew her attention.

Lance walked out into the bright midday sunshine and squinted. He didn't bring a jacket and realized the weather had changed while he was inside and searching for Claudia. October brought cold and hinted at an early winter.

Lance hurried to his SUV and cranked it up, pulling out of the lot and heading home. The police had left the building a week ago, but Claudia's apartment was still taped off. Lance stared at her door as he hesitated in front of his own. Was there a clue in there?

Before he could talk himself out of it, Lance was entering Claudia's apartment. It hadn't changed since the day he walked in and found the bloodstain in the middle of the living room. The stench of the rotten food still hung in the air even though the fridge and freezer were closed.

Lance went to the sliding glass door on the far side of the unit. He unlocked it and pushed it open, then he went to the fridge. He spent the next hour cleaning out all the food in her fridge and freezer, dumping everything and taking the trash down to the dumpster. The police had processed the scene, and the FBI had given clearance to clean the place, so Lance set about doing that.

He wiped down the kitchen counters and removed the cabinet doors that hung on broken hinges. Once the kitchen was as good as he could make it, he moved to the bathroom. A part of him felt odd being in Claudia's space, but he wanted to help. When he brought her home, and he would, he didn't want her to have to deal with the mess left behind.

Once the bathroom was clean, Lance focused on her bedroom. He rolled up the deflated air mattress and carried it to the dumpster. The bins where she kept her clothes were cracked and tipped over, but they still worked. Lance went about setting her things back to where he assumed they would have been.

He debated moving her possessions into his apartment, but he didn't do it. If she wanted to move in with him when she got back, he would happily have her there, but he couldn't make more assumptions about the woman.

The last space Lance tackled was the living room. The couch needed to be thrown out. It was sliced apart and not salvageable. He checked that there wasn't anything buried in the cushions, then muscled the couch to the dumpster and left it on the curb where large items were dropped for collection.

He stopped at his apartment to get cleaning supplies, then got to work on the carpet. He had to close his eyes a few times, wishing he'd been home when she was taken. He would have heard her. He would have protected her.

But he was avoiding her. He was beating himself up for forcing himself on her with that kiss, and she was taken right out from under him.

He would find her.

It took him an hour to clean the carpet, and he knew it still wasn't clean. The blood had soaked in and replacing the carpet was the best option, but without the approval of the complex, he'd done his best.

And he felt it.

Lance let himself out of her apartment and closed the door behind him. He was about to turn when he heard someone coming up the stairs.

"Good afternoon," Mrs. Mitchell said.

"Hi, Mrs. Mitchell. How are you?"

"I'm good, honey. How are you? How's your friend?"

"The woman who lives there?"

Mrs. Mitchell nodded. "I assumed you were checking on her."

"What do you mean? She's missing."

"Oh. I didn't realize. The day she broke her nose, that man—"

"Man? You saw her with a man?"

Mrs. Mitchell balked at Lance's aggression.

"I apologize, Mrs. Mitchell. She's been missing for two weeks. No one has seen her or heard from her. We assume she was injured and taken, but no one saw anything. Will you tell me what you saw?"

Mrs. Mitchell shrugged. "She was with a man. He was a few inches taller than her. She had blood all over face and down her shirt."

"Where did you see them?"

"Outside. They'd just come out of the building. He was holding her elbow. Said she tripped over the dog and hit the edge of the couch. He said they were going to the emergency room."

Lance exhaled a long breath.

"They didn't go to the emergency room, did they?"

"No, they didn't. And I believe he's the one who hurt her. Would you be able to sit for a sketch artist? Describe the man?"

Mrs. Mitchell shrugged. "I didn't get a good look at him."

"Anything you can tell the FBI would help."

"I can try."

"Thank you, Mrs. Mitchell." Lance pulled out his phone and called Lorelei Sloane. He told her what Mrs. Mitchell said, and Lorelei said they'd be over shortly. He invited Mrs. Mitchell into his apartment and got her a glass of water.

"She was always very sweet to me," Mrs. Mitchell said. "Held the door and helped me carry my groceries upstairs a few times when she saw me coming into the building. Never set foot in my apartment. Was particular about that. She brought me pie a few times from that diner where she worked. I wish I'd realized she was in danger."

"I've been feeling the same. I had no idea."

"She liked you. I asked her once about it, and she blushed furiously and changed the subject. Then I saw her with that other man and thought I must have misread the situation."

"We're not together."

"But you'd like to be."

A knock on his door saved Lance from answering.

Lorelei and Adam thanked Mrs. Mitchell for her help, then sat with her and recorded everything she said. Another knock on the door sent Adam to answer it. He hugged a woman Lance didn't recognize.

"Kyra works with my cousin, and she's a talented artist. On such short notice, she agreed to help out with the sketch." Adam introduced Kyra to Mrs. Mitchell, then he and Lorelei joined Lance in his kitchen.

"How did we not know there was someone who saw them?" Lorelei asked.

Lance shook his head. "I don't know. She saw me coming out of Claudia's apartment and asked how she was."

"You were in her apartment?" Adam asked.

"I wanted to clean the place up for her."

"That was kind of you," Lorelei said.

"I'm going to Kansas. Hopefully tomorrow. I can't sit around here and do nothing."

"Montgomery called us. We're going to put you in touch with a few people in the state. Mostly in the cities, but they'll be closer than we are." Lorelei watched Kyra and Mrs. Mitchell as she spoke.

"Thank you. I... Hopefully this helps, but I need to find her."

Adam and Lorelei shared a look. "We understand. When Lorelei was missing, I went out of my mind. We all did."

"I remember," Lance said.

Lorelei was kidnapped by someone she was looking into and left for dead when they realized she knew enough to take them down. She was lucky she was found when she was, but her injuries left her with temporary amnesia.

They were quiet for a few minutes as Kyra and Mrs. Mitchell finished the sketch. Mrs. Mitchell nodded before Kyra turned the sketch to the rest of them.

"This is the man who was with your missing woman." Kyra tore off the page and handed it to Adam. "Hopefully it helps find her."

Adam hugged her. "Thank you for doing this. Again."

Kyra grinned. "Always happy to help. We all are." Kyra hugged Lorelei, then offered her hand to Lance. "You work for Rose Protection Agency?"

"I do. Lance Kilgore. It's nice to meet you."

"You, too. Kyra O'Keefe."

"Slade's wife?"

Kyra chuckled. "That's me. Also the admin for F-BOMB."

"Thank you for your help."

"Any time. I hope you find your friend."

"Me, too."

Adam walked with Kyra to the door, and Lorelei sat next to Mrs. Mitchell.

Lance felt like a stranger in his own apartment. But it was all in the name of finding Claudia. One step closer.

Kyra left, and Adam turned to Lance. "We're going to run this through our databases and see if we get a hit on it. We'll start with Kansas and go from there. If we get something, we'll all be going to Kansas."

"Thank you both for getting here so quickly. I really appreciate it."

"We're going to bring her home," Lorelei said. "I know we will."

Lance nodded, feeling better for the first time since Claudia disappeared. The agents left his apartment with Mrs. Mitchell, walking her to her apartment, and Lance's body demanded rest.

He took a quick shower, then collapsed onto his bed, ready for Claudia to be home.

"I'M HOME," Michael said through the door. He knocked on it twice, then continued on by like he'd been doing since the night he disposed of Hector's body.

Claudia jumped at his words. He'd been spending more and more time with her since he killed his friend. Letting himself into her room and talking to her. He shared stories about their mother, telling Claudia that Lillian taught him the most important thing was to protect those you love.

She wasn't up for another night of talking about their mother, but she knew she didn't have a choice. If Michael wanted to talk to her, she couldn't do anything about it.

He hadn't hurt her since he killed Hector. He'd been...

different. Almost kind. Not that he was letting her go, but he acted like he cared. If it was possible.

The locks clicked as he turned them. Claudia sat up on the bed, pulling her feet under her as Michael opened the door. He carried a large bag of food into the room, her stomach rumbling as the scent hit her.

"Is that Joe's?" she asked before she could stop herself.

Michael grinned, his face transforming with her question. "It is. I knew you'd remember."

Claudia nodded, the nostalgia wrapping around her as Michael carried the food closer. He set the bag on her bed, then unlocked the chains holding her. With the chains released, he grabbed his chair from next to the door and sat down.

"I thought it would be nice to have this. It's been a long time since we did."

Claudia nodded, her mouth watering as Michael retrieved grilled mac and cheese sandwiches and fries. "Mom loved taking us there."

Michael's hand stalled halfway between them. He nodded after a second and handed Claudia her sandwich. "It was the only place she could afford to take us. She slept with Joe so he would give us food."

"What?" Claudia asked, the happy memories suddenly feeling wrong. "No."

Michael nodded. "You never noticed that she would disappear with him when we got there? He'd hand us a roll of quarters to play the games, and she would go with him. When they came back, he would bring us food."

"I..." Claudia tried to come up with a better explanation, but she failed. Their mother always wore low-cut tops and tight skirts when they went there. Claudia thought it was odd since the place was casual, but she never considered her mother was screwing the owner to get them food. "But she worked. She had money. Didn't she?"

Michael laughed mirthlessly. "She was a whore, Claudia. She screwed whoever would take her and traded sex for whatever she needed."

"No. No, she was..." Claudia tried to remember a time when her mother had a regular job. She would go out at night and sleep most of the day. Michael was the one who took care of Claudia. He was the one who made sure she had food and got to school. He was the one who raised her. "That's why she never told me who my father was."

Michael shrugged. "She never knew."

Claudia put her sandwich down, unable to bring herself to eat it. The one good memory she had of her childhood was tainted, stained by the truth. "I always thought she hated me. That she resented me for existing. She would tell me I nearly bankrupted her. That I ruined her for men."

"She was a beautiful woman," Michael whispered.

"She was an alcoholic, Michael. She didn't take care of herself. And now you're telling me she was a prostitute."

"She did the best she could. Her life was hard. She worked her ass off, and I did what I could to help her."

"You were a child, too."

"I was the man of the house. I still am. She told me it was my responsibility to take care of both of you."

"Who was taking care of you? You were only nine when I was born, Michael. You were still a kid, and you raised me."

"I was man enough," Michael said in a tone that made all the hair on Claudia's body stand up.

"What do you mean by that?"

"I mean I took care of both of you. I protected you. I made sure she was safe and came home. I calmed her down."

"Michael, what are you telling me?" Claudia whispered, his words hitting her. She remembered when their mother would freak out. When she would come home drunk and strip in the living room. Claudia spent most of her time in her bedroom, and when her mother came home in one of her moods, she stayed there.

Michael jumped up and glared at her. "I'm the man of the house, Claudia. I'm the man. I made sure Lilian was taken care of. I did whatever it took to calm her down."

"Did she assault you?"

Michael shook his head. "You're making what we had sound wrong. I was the man. I was responsible for making sure she was taken care of. Just like I'm responsible for you."

Claudia's throat tightened as the truth of what happened between her mother and brother hit her. "Michael."

"Don't look at me like that! Don't pity me. I learned how to take care of a woman when the rest of my friends were barely figuring out how their dicks worked. Lilian was good to me. She loved me. And I loved her. Just like I love you."

Claudia shook her head, fear building inside her.

"I need to go," Michael growled. "I'll be back later." He started for the door, then stopped and went back to her.

Claudia flinched as he got closer.

He stopped, then glared at her and reached for the chains. He locked them around her wrists again, then slammed his way out of the room, locking her inside once more.

Claudia stared after her brother. Tears rolled down her cheeks for the little boy and what he went through.

And maybe a little for herself and the future she saw if she didn't get away from Michael. She had to find a way out.

Now.

NINE

Lance stifled his groan and shifted away from the man snoring next to him. The man on his other side was staring at his newspaper, opening it with a flick of his wrist and spreading the pages into Lance's personal space before folding the pages to read each story.

Lance closed his eyes and drew a breath. Only thirty more minutes until he landed. If he was lucky, maybe longer than that before Montgomery and the FBI figured out Lance jumped on a plane first thing that morning to head to Kansas.

He had planned to drive, to have his own vehicle, but waiting two days to be in the same state as Claudia, he hoped, was too long. Especially after Mrs. Mitchell confirmed she left with a man who'd obviously hurt her.

Lance wanted to punch everything.

Sleep hadn't come easily to him, but once he was out, he slept for hours. When he woke up, all he knew was sitting around and waiting for more information to come through was going to drive him insane. So he left. He packed a bag, locked up his weapons, and booked a flight to Kansas on his personal credit card.

If he was lucky, he'd get a call from Adam and Lorelei and he'd be boots on the ground to get Claudia once he landed.

Fifteen minutes.

The plane dinged before the announcement came on that all electronic devices needed to be stowed for landing, and Lance sat up straight in his seat. He didn't check a bag and didn't have a plan, but he was going to make one fast.

With the time change, it was almost ten in the morning in Kansas, but was an hour later in Niagara Falls. His one-hour layover had been uneventful, but Lance had a feeling as soon as he turned on his phone, he was going to get an earful about skipping town.

Lance waited until he followed his fellow passengers off the plane before he stopped and turned his phone on. As he expected, there were calls and texts from Montgomery and Griffin Knapp, Lance's current partner. He liked Griffin, but they were still figuring each other out, and Lance hadn't filled him in on everything going on.

The one message Lance was most interested in came from neither of them but from Adam Johnson.

Lance hit play on the voicemail and listened to Adam's message.

"Hey, Lance. A partial match came up on the sketch Kyra did. It's only seventy-five match, but when we looked into the guy, we have a reason to believe he could be who we're looking for. We're looking at getting a team together to check out the location in northeastern Kansas. Guy's name is Michael Reynolds, but he has a sister who's been missing for a year. His sister's name is Claudia. I'll send you an update as soon as I have more information about a team heading there. Talk soon."

Lance listened to the message again, relief flooding him. They found her. Or at least, they found her brother, who matched the drawing from Mrs. Mitchell. It was the best, and only, lead they'd had in weeks. And Lance was not going to sit around and wait for more information.

Lance made his way through the airport to the rental car booths. He stopped at the quietest one and asked if they had anything available. He paid for the car and followed the directions the bored attendant gave him for finding a vehicle, then pulled out of the lot and away from the airport.

Once Lance was heading north, he listened to the messages from Montgomery and Griffin. Montgomery's messages went from when will you be in to where the hell are you to what the fuck are you doing. Lance was sure his boss had already tracked his location and his credit cards and knew exactly where Lance was.

He'd deal with that in a little while.

Lance played Griffin's message next. Griffin was less forceful and more diplomatic than Montgomery, but no less pissed off.

"Montgomery said you've skipped town. What the fuck, partner? I know we've only been working together a little while, but I thought we were good. I'd have been there with you if you called. Call me."

Lance felt like a dick for cutting his partner out of his decisions and knew that warranted a reply. He tapped the screen to return Griffin's call first.

"Where are you?" Griffin hissed into the phone. The noises in the background said Griffin was at work, and likely getting shit for Lance's behavior.

"I'm in Kansas," Lance said.

"Fuck. I figured. Why didn't you let me know?"

"Were you going to rat me out?"

"I was going to be your backup, asshole. But maybe this partnership isn't going to work out."

"I couldn't sit around any longer. I was going fucking nuts."

"And you think the rest of us like when someone is missing? I know we don't really know each other, but I thought being on this team meant working together."

"It does," Lance said, knowing he was causing an issue that didn't need to be there. Griffin was new, and Lance wasn't helping. He told Montgomery the guy should have been paired with someone else, but Montgomery said they were the match and to get the hell over it.

"Yeah, it seems like it."

"Listen, I know I'm too close to this. I know I'm emotionally involved. But that's why I couldn't drag you into it. If I fuck it up, I don't want you taking the fall for me."

"That's what partners fucking do. What's your plan? Do you even know where you're going?"

"Northeast Kansas. Michael Reynolds."

"And then what are you going to do?"

"I don't know yet."

"The FBI is getting a team together. Instead of sending a team from here, they're looking to send local agents. But it's going to be tomorrow at the earliest before they can do anything."

"She might not have that long."

"Shut up and listen to me, asshole."

Lance stopped talking, recognizing the tone of his partner's voice as one that demanded respect.

"I'm going to send you the address. I might get fired for it, so you better fucking make it work. Montgomery was debating on sending a team until you skipped town. Now he's pissed, but he knows why you went. I'm guessing you're going to be there long before anyone else can be. Find a place to lie low. Do some recon, and don't draw attention to yourself."

"I can't—"

"I said shut up. No one can know you're there. This guy... He has connections. He's not just a random guy. He's the local dealer. The cops haven't been able to pin anything on him, but they've had him as a person of interest in a bunch of cases. He is not going to take it lightly if you charge in against him."

"Understood."

"I hope you do." Griffin was quiet for a few seconds. "I gotta go. You better fucking fix this when you get back, partner."

"I will," Lance assured him, knowing Griffin put his career on the line to help find Claudia.

Even more so when a text came through a minute later.

Lance waited until he saw a rest stop, then pulled over and read the text. It included an address two hours from where he was. He put the address into his phone and got back on the road, ready to find Claudia and bring her home.

LANCE DROVE into the small town where Michael Reynolds lived. It was early afternoon, which meant kids were in school, families were at work, and, in general, the town was quiet.

Lance found a small cafe to grab a sandwich and a cup of coffee. The server was less interested in conversation than Lance was and dropped off his food, then left him alone.

As he ate, Lance looked around the place. Wallpaper from decades ago peeled at the edges. Chips in the checkerboard tiles made him wonder if the place was safe to be in, let alone serving food. The booths were more duct tape than vinyl.

The food was decent and cheap, and Lance took his time, not wanting to appear too much in a rush. When he finished eating, he left enough cash for a decent tip but not so big it would make him memorable. He hoped.

He was already a visitor in the small town that clearly knew he didn't belong, and any additional attention wasn't a good idea. Lance returned to his rental and made his way around the town, past the local schools and the factory at the edge of town that seemed to employ half the residents if the vehicles in the lot were any indication.

Lance turned onto Michael Reynolds' street and checked the addresses of the houses as he drove past. He couldn't risk slowing down to check out the house, but he didn't race either. The numbers climbed as Lance's heart pounded. He didn't know what he hoped for, but a quiet street with no sign of anything wrong wasn't it.

As he approached the Reynolds' house, Lance debated knocking on the door or pulling over or just breaking in and finding her, but he couldn't do any of the above. He had to figure out what was going on and wait for backup.

A truck was in the driveway, parked nearly sideways, taking up all the space in front of the house. It blocked the front door and the windows, making it impossible to see if there was anyone inside the house. And making it impossible to see if anyone left the house.

Lance's gut twisted. The house was as rundown as the cafe where he had lunch with peeling paint on the wood siding, cracks splitting the driveway and steps to the door. The yard was more weeds than grass and high enough to hide any small animals that dared get close to the house.

Lance had no doubt the house was one kids would avoid on Halloween in a few weeks. One he would have avoided as a kid himself.

He continued down the road, hating that Claudia could be inside that house right now and all he did was drive by.

Lance spent the rest of the day learning his way around the town. He booked a hotel room close to the interstate and paid in cash, using an alias the team knew and could track.

When he was settled in his hotel room, Lance finally gave in and called Montgomery.

"I should fire your ass right fucking now," Montgomery said as he answered the phone.

"I couldn't sit around any longer. And it sounds like coming here was a good idea."

"Not that you knew that when you left. What the hell are you thinking?"

"I'm thinking she's in danger, boss. If I'd been paying better attention—"

"Or she didn't want you to know," Montgomery barked. "But you're there now, so I guess we have to make the best of it. What did you find? I'm assuming you have the address and went to the house."

"Uh, yeah. But nothing stood out. There was a truck in the driveway when I went by. The house looks like a shithole. It's falling apart."

"Did you get a plate on the truck?"

Lance shared the number and the make and model. "It matched."

"Yeah. The agency is working toward a plan. But you know how this goes."

"They don't have any confirmation, so they're going to tip him off, and he's going to do something stupid."

"You would know that well," Montgomery growled.

"I can't let anything else happen to her, boss. I'm going to go back there tonight and see if I can find any evidence of her being in the house."

"And what if you do? Are you going to be able to walk away?"

Lance blew out a breath and chose not to lie to his boss.

"This guy is dangerous. Even if he's not guilty of all the things they think he might be guilty of, he's too close to too much to be innocent."

"All the more reason to get her out of there ASAP."

"I know. But if you get caught…"

"I won't."

"Be safe, Lance. Fuck, I hate that you're there alone."

"I'll be fine. I'll check in as soon as I can."

"You fucking better. No more solo missions, you got me?"

"Yes, sir."

"Fuck." Montgomery hung up without another word.

Lance knew he crossed a line. If it wasn't Claudia, he never would have taken the chance, but he couldn't let her disappear.

As dusk fell, Lance went back into the town, driving around again and finding a street a few blocks from the house with vehicles parked along the curb. He added his rental to the cars parked and climbed out.

The chill in the air stole his breath. He tugged his jacket tighter around himself and pulled a hat low over his head to hide as many of his features as possible.

The walk to Michael Reynolds' house was easy enough. Lance knew the way and didn't take time debating where to come from. He tried to find data on the house, a floor plan or something, but there was no information about it online.

As Lance walked down the street toward the house, he noticed the truck he saw there earlier was gone. He hadn't noticed it driving away, which meant Michael could come back any second, but Lance couldn't just walk by. He had to go into the house.

The street was quiet, and the house was dark. Shadows were plentiful, giving Lance cover as he moved from the heaving sidewalk up to the front door of the house.

Lance checked that his hair was covered as he moved to the door. He tested the doorknob, but it was locked.

He looked around, hidden on the dark porch, and dug out a lock pick from his wallet. Before he touched anything else, he slid his gloves on, then made quick work of the front door, wiping off his prints from testing the door.

He opened the door slowly, hoping he was right and Michael Reynolds was out.

The living room was empty, the house quiet. Lance closed the front door silently and moved into the space, wishing he had a gun, and listened for anything to tell him he wasn't alone.

A slight sound down the hallway had Lance moving in that direction. He stuck to the wall, knowing that if someone was there, his only advantage was the element of surprise.

A dark stain in the middle of the living room floor made Lance pause. Without a team, he couldn't be sure, but he was fairly certain it was blood. A lot of it. He closed his eyes and prayed it wasn't Claudia's, then kept moving toward the hallway until he came to a door.

With a padlock on the outside.

CLAUDIA HEARD the front door open and close, but Michael's footsteps didn't sound through the house. She tried to slow her breathing, wondering what was going on. She hated being trapped in her room, unable to defend herself if...

Someone was outside her door.

Claudia's heart slammed against her chest. Was it Michael? He had no reason to sneak around the house. What if she was wrong and Hector wasn't dead? What if he came back to finish what he started while Michael was out on a run?

Claudia sat up on the bed and curled her feet under her. She searched for something, anything, she could use to defend herself, but there was nothing. Michael made sure of it.

She barely breathed as the person outside moved past her

room, then returned. They were quiet for a minute, then the lock on her door moved.

Claudia didn't know what a heart attack felt like, but she was positive she was having one as she sat there and waited for whoever was outside the door to get in. She couldn't do anything besides wait as they messed with the locks, one after another.

When the last one snicked open, Claudia braced herself on the bed. Maybe she could shock whoever it was. Catch them off guard and hurt them before they hurt her.

The door opened slowly, a head peeking through the opening for a flash. Then the door opened all the way, and Claudia nearly collapsed.

"Lance?"

TEN

Claudia had to be dreaming. Why would Lance be there? She screwed her eyes closed, then opened them again.

He was closer.

"Are you okay?" He brushed her hair back from her face, his gaze scanning her. "We have to go."

"I can't."

"Claudia, he hurt you. I know he did. I'm getting you out of here before he comes back."

She shook her head. "No, I... I don't want to stay, but I can't leave." She held up her arm to show him the chain holding her in place.

"Fuck me. He—" Lance swallowed and slammed his eyes closed. He shook his head once, then focused on the chains, not her. "I... Let me see what I can do."

Claudia held her arms out for him to look closer. The lighting in the room was dim and probably made it harder for him to see, but he didn't make a comment about it. He also didn't make a comment about her general state, the way she and the room smelled, or anything besides getting her to safety.

She wanted to cry with relief. Even if he couldn't get her out of there, he knew where she was. Michael might kill her, but Lance would know. Michael would not get away with another murder.

Lance ran his hand down the chains to where they were attached to the heavy wooden bed. He tugged, but nothing budged. Claudia had already tried that. Many times.

"Do you know where the key is?"

"He keeps it with him."

"Dammit. All right." Lance looked around the room. He ran a hand down his face. He exhaled roughly, then checked his watch. "We can't take long to figure this out. He could come back any minute. I'll try to pick the lock. Can you hold your hand up for a few minutes so I can see?"

Claudia nodded.

Lance took her right hand and held it up where he wanted it.

Almost instantly, her muscles started to shake. Being chained up for weeks hadn't helped her physical strength. She used her other hand to support the one in the air, then shoved her knee under both hands to be still.

Lance worked on the lock on her wrist. He was patient and focused.

Claudia watched him and prayed he would get her free. That he would be able to save her. That she was—

The lock opened. A sob fell from her lips. She drew a breath and tried to stifle her hope.

"Halfway there." Lance moved her free hand to the bottom and helped her position the other wrist on top for him to work on.

Claudia stared again, foolishly allowing hope to blossom inside her. Lance's concentration never faltered as he worked to free her other hand. When that lock opened, she swallowed the relief that washed through her. She was far from free.

"Let's go."

A vehicle rumbled outside, and they looked at each other. The noise faded as the vehicle passed the house, and Lance grabbed her hand.

"We need to go right now. Are you okay to walk?"

Claudia nodded, deciding she'd do whatever Lance told her to do if it meant getting away from Michael.

Lance led her to the bedroom door. He looked out, then moved into the hallway. He held her hand, tugging her behind him.

Claudia stayed close to Lance, not more than a step behind him. He opened the front door and stopped, backing her up inside the house.

Lance looked back at her. "Do you need to get anything? Your wallet wasn't in your apartment. Is it here? ID? Anything? Fuck, shoes?"

Claudia glanced around the room, spotting the bloodstain in the middle of the floor. For half a second, she felt bad for Hector. He was an asshole who was happy to hurt her, but that didn't mean he deserved to die.

"Claudia?"

She drew a breath and continued her search. She spotted her hot-pink wallet sticking out from under the coffee table. "There."

Lance checked out the front door, then released her hand to grab her wallet.

He was back in less than five seconds, but that was all it took for the overwhelming fear to sink back in and bring Claudia to her knees.

"Shit," Lance breathed. "Claudia. I need you up. I need you to stand. Can you do that for me, sweetheart?"

Her breath trembled through her, stealing all her strength. Tears flowed down her cheeks.

Lance scooped her up, holding her in his arms as he

stepped out of the house and into the cold evening air. It was a slap in the face, a reminder of what she'd missed.

"I can walk," she whispered.

"Are you sure?"

Claudia nodded.

Lance paused on the porch and slowly lowered her bare feet to the ground. He held her steady until she nodded, then grabbed her hand again.

Then he led her into the darkness.

Lance went to the sidewalk, head down as he walked.

Claudia followed suit, ducking her shoulders and hiding herself as they walked quickly down the street where Claudia grew up toward town.

Lance took a right, then a left, then stopped in front of an SUV. He unlocked it with a key instead of letting it beep and opened the passenger door for her.

Claudia didn't want to let go of his hand, but she did, letting him close her inside the vehicle. She watched as he ran around the front and climbed in next to her. He reached for her hand as soon as he was in the vehicle, then locked the door and started the engine, pulling away from the curb without another word.

A few minutes later, Lance parked behind a cheap motel at the edge of town. He turned off the SUV and squeezed her hand. "We're in room two-seventeen. The stairs are right there. We're going to get out of the car, go up the stairs, and I'm going to make sure it's safe. Then you're going to take a shower while I update my team. Are you okay with that?"

Claudia nodded, starting to feel the shock of everything that had just happened. She realized she was clenching Lance's hand tight when he rubbed his thumb over her hand. "Sorry."

"It's okay, Claudia. I'm going to get out. I'll be right there, or you can get out, too. It's up to you."

She nodded, debating what to do as he opened his door

and rushed around to hers. She jumped when he opened her door. She took his offered hand, then let him guide her up the stairs and to the room.

Once they were inside, curtains drawn tight and locks engaged, Lance guided her toward the bathroom but stopped halfway there. "You don't have to take a shower right now, but I want you to feel like yourself. I... I have to ask if he... Did he... Do we need to go to the hospital for a rape kit?"

The last words rushed out of his mouth so fast Claudia wasn't sure she heard them correctly. When they finally processed, she shook her head. "No. No, he never..."

Lance swallowed roughly, his gaze sticking to her face instead of straying to her torn shirt like it had earlier, and nodded. "I don't have any of your things, or anything that would fit you, but you can wear my clothes for now. We'll get you whatever you need tomorrow."

"Tomorrow?" she squeaked.

Lance hesitated before he spoke. "We can leave right now if you'd rather. What do you want to do?"

"I... I don't know. I don't want him to find me again."

"He will never touch you again, Claudia. I promise you that."

Michael made the same promise about Hector before he killed him. Was Lance...? No, she couldn't even think it. She inhaled a shaky breath and nodded. Everything felt shaky.

"Take a shower. You'll feel better after that. I'll get some clothes you can wear. We'll make a plan when you're out."

She nodded again.

"You're safe now."

She swallowed back the sob that threatened to come out and went to the bathroom. She paused before she closed the door all the way and met Lance's gaze. "Thank you for finding me."

"You're so welcome, sweetheart."

She smiled at him, then closed the door between them, knowing she made the right decision when she moved in next door to him.

LANCE WAITED until the shower turned on to move. He dug through his suitcase for clothes as the shower curtain slid along the metal rod. The sound of the water changed, telling him she was finally in the shower.

He didn't know what he expected to find when he went to the house, but Claudia chained to a bed was not it. He wanted to strangle the fucker with his bare hands for leaving her like that, but he had to get her out of there.

Lance punched the wall, his knuckles protesting the move and splitting open with the contact. Lance needed the pain to focus on. It was better than replaying the look on Claudia's face when he peeked in that door. The fear. The pain. The resolution.

Fuck.

Lance pushed the thought away and grabbed clothes that would have to do. A dark tee, gray sweatpants, and a pair of his clean boxer briefs. It was the best he had.

Lance took the clothes to the bathroom area and knocked on the door. "Claudia? I have clothes. Can I put them in there for you?"

"Yeah," she said softly, her voice shaky.

Lance opened the door. "I'm coming in now. Can I take the clothes you were wearing?"

"Burn them."

"I'll get rid of them, sweetheart."

Claudia's breath hitched, but she didn't say anything else.

Lance took her clothes out of the room and closed the

door again. He took the bag from the trashcan under the sink and stuffed her clothes inside, tying the bag tight. He stuffed that bag in the one from the trashcan next to the TV and tied it again, then shoved the bag into the bottom of his suitcase.

The water still ran, so Lance sat on the edge of the bed and unlocked his phone. He debated who to call first, but he knew Montgomery was the right one.

"Rose."

"I found her," Lance said.

"Jesus, are you serious?"

"Yeah. She was chained to a fucking bed. That son-of-a-bitch..." Lance couldn't finish his thought.

"Is she with you now?"

"Yeah. She's in the shower. She's freaked the hell out. She thinks he's going to find her again."

"You're still at the same hotel?"

"Yeah."

"Hang tight. Griffin will be to you in less than an hour."

"What? How?"

"He wanted to back you up. Told me he was going whether I approved it or not. He took a flight a few hours ago. He's on the ground and on his way to you already."

"Seriously?"

"Yeah. I'll update the FBI on what's going on. Assuming she can identify Michael Reynolds as the man who was holding her, they will bring him in. As it is, she was chained up in his house, that's enough to haul his ass in." Montgomery sounded as revolted by the situation as Lance was.

"I have her clothes."

"Fuck me. Did he...?"

"She said no," Lance said. The shower turned off, and Lance looked at the door. "She's out of the shower. I'm going to get packed up so we can hit the road. I don't think she wants to stay here. Can you have the FBI get rid of the rental?"

"They'll want to check it out anyway, but yeah. Griffin can get you guys out of there. Be safe."

"Thanks, boss. And thank you... For all of this."

"I've been there. If I could have... I know how you're feeling. Just be careful."

"We will. Talk soon." Lance hung up and exhaled a long breath. He wasn't fired, and he wasn't alone. His team came through for him, like they always did. Even when he didn't think they would.

The bathroom door opened slowly, revealing Claudia in Lance's clothes. Her wet curls hung past her shoulders. In the harsh light of the bathroom vanity, the bruises on her face were more prominent and ugly.

But Lance thought she was beautiful. The urge to pull her into his arms and hold her until Michael was either in jail or the ground was strong.

"Thank you for the clothes," Claudia whispered.

Lance stood and approached her. He saw the way she shrunk as he drew closer, but she didn't move away from him. He tucked her hair behind her ear and slid his fingers down her arm. "Do you feel any better?"

She shrugged.

"I'm so sorry I didn't keep you safe." Lance could barely push the words out.

Her gaze snapped to his. "How could you have kept me safe?"

"I... I wish I hadn't pushed you away for so long. That you'd felt like you could trust me enough to tell me what was really going on. That you hadn't needed to lie to me about who you are and why you were living next door to me."

Claudia swallowed roughly and nodded, not saying another word.

"My partner is on his way here. He will be here soon. When he gets here, it's up to you what we do."

"What do you mean?"

"We can stay here for the night and try to sleep, or we can get on the road and leave. I'm not sure we'll be able to get flights without raising too much suspicion. We can try, but—"

"No. I don't think I can… I would rather know we can stop and I can get out whenever I want."

Lance nodded, hating that she was locked up for weeks, chained up, and suffered God knew what at the hands of a man who was supposed to protect her. "Okay. We can drive. We will follow your lead, Claudia. I promise you."

"Can I ask you something?"

"Anything."

"Why are you here? I mean, the last time I saw you, you were running out of my apartment like you regretted—"

"No. I never regretted kissing you. Not for a second." Lance exhaled a breath and weighed his next words. She deserved the truth, but how much of the truth? "I regretted kissing you without asking you first. Without making sure you were okay with it. I never should have forced myself on you. I was… That night, I… God, it feels like forever ago."

"It was," Claudia said.

Lance sat on one bed and gestured to Claudia to sit on the other, letting her have the bed farther from the door.

She moved over and sat on the edge, nibbling her lip.

"Right before you moved in, one of my coworkers was killed. He was on a routine job, but it wasn't so routine, and he was killed. Another one of our teammates almost died, and he was in danger for a long time. He's safe now… Austin. He met you one day coming into my apartment?"

Claudia nodded.

"He's safe, and he's happy, and it all… Aside from losing Samuel, everything worked out. But I was not in a great place when you moved in. And you were bright and light and talkative, and I wasn't looking for that. I wasn't looking for anything. You reminded me of my ex, who always dressed in those skirts you wore and cheated on me with a man who has more money and cares more about appearances than I do."

"I..." She exhaled a laugh. "The clothes were supposed to entice you, and instead they pushed you away."

Lance smiled and shrugged. "But you... I didn't want to like you. I wanted to dismiss you, but you kept showing up. I was drawn to you, even though I didn't want to be, and that night... I've regretted kissing you because I should have given you the choice. I should have asked you before I did anything. I ran because I was ashamed of my behavior, and I stayed away, I stayed at the office, for days. I couldn't face you. I thought you hated me when you weren't in the hall and didn't bump into me constantly. And the longer I avoided you, the harder it was to believe I was wrong."

"But I was gone."

Lance nodded. "And when I realized that... When I realized you were gone, I spent every minute looking for you."

"You did?"

"Yes. Your boss at the diner knew you were from Kansas. The property manager told us you insisted on the apartment next to mine. The gym had footage of you following me. And Mrs. Mitchell asked how you were doing. That's what finally led me here. She was able to describe Michael well enough that we got a sketch of him. As soon as we had that, I got on a plane. By the time I landed, we had an address. That was this morning."

"This morning?"

Lance nodded. "I'm sorry it took me so long. That you had to sit there for weeks... That you..." Lance closed his eyes tight and fought against the regret racing through him. "I will never forgive myself for letting you get taken right out from under my nose."

Claudia moved to sit next to him, her warmth pressing against his side. "But you came for me. You found me."

"I'm never letting him near you again."

A knock on the door made them both jump.

"He found me," Claudia whispered. "He's going to kill us both."

"It's Griffin," Griffin said from the other side of the door.

"It's my partner," Lance said.

Claudia hovered behind him, her fingers digging into his sides. "He could be working with Michael."

"He's not. His name is Griffin Knapp. My boss told me he was on his way. He's here to help. I told you he was coming, remember?"

Claudia's breath shook. She held it, and Lance held his with her, then she exhaled. "I'm sorry. I forgot. I'm sorry." Claudia collapsed behind him.

Lance turned and picked her up, setting her on the bed. "Let me let him in, then I'll be right back."

Claudia nodded, tears streaming down her face.

Lance kissed her forehead, then moved across the room to unlock the door. "She's terrified of you. Go slow," he told his partner when he opened the door.

"She's here?"

Lance nodded and stepped back to let Griffin into the room. Griffin closed the door, then faced Claudia. "Claudia, this is Griffin Knapp. He's going to get us home."

Claudia stared at the two men, her tears not slowing or stopping.

Lance moved to her slowly, watching as her gaze tracked him. She would be okay. Eventually.

"Are you ready to leave? To get the hell out of Kansas?" Lance asked.

Claudia nodded. "Far away from Michael."

"Sounds good to me. Let's go, sweetheart."

ELEVEN

Claudia curled up in the backseat of the SUV Griffin drove to town. She didn't ask Lance about the vehicle he'd driven to get her from Michael's house. She didn't ask much.

The men talked in soft tones as they headed east. Claudia knew they could have chosen to jump on a plane and ignore her protests, but Lance had been nothing but amazing. She felt a sense of pride that she'd chosen him as her protector all those months ago and was right about the man. She had to find a way to alleviate his guilt that she hadn't opened up to him and Michael found her. That wasn't on Lance. It was on her. And Michael.

A few hours into their drive, they stopped at a rest area, and the men switched drivers. Both stayed up front, giving Claudia the entire backseat to herself. She didn't think she could have handled someone else so close to her after everything, and it meant a lot that they understood that without her having to explain herself.

At some point, Claudia must have fallen asleep because she woke to her name being called softly and a hand on her shoulder. She startled awake, jumping away from whoever was talking to her and knocked her head on the window.

"Shit. Are you okay? I didn't mean to scare you." Lance. It was just Lance. She was safe. With Lance.

"I'm good." Claudia rubbed the sore part of her head and closed her eyes against the bright light of the... Gas station.

"We're getting gas, but we can run into the store and see if you can find some clothes." Lance nodded toward the hood of the SUV.

Claudia followed his gaze to the big-box store next to the gas station. She'd gotten rid of all her clothes, including her bra, when Lance rescued her. She didn't know what was waiting for her back in her apartment in Niagara Falls, but since Michael knew where that was, she couldn't go back. All she had was literally on her back, and it wasn't hers.

But walking into a store like that, one with cameras and people and a chance at being caught was terrifying.

"You can wear my hat, and we will be by your side every step. One of us can also go in and the other can stay in the SUV with you. If you want." Lance's tone was comforting, not impatient or frustrated.

Claudia looked up at the only person who'd come for her and nodded. She trusted him. He'd proven more than once that she could, and she would again. "You'll stay with me?"

"Every step, sweetheart."

"Okay. I'll go in. With the hat."

Lance grinned at her, and Claudia felt like she made the right decision. Not because of his joy, but because it made her feel good to take a step toward normal.

Griffin finished pumping gas and climbed back into the passenger seat. Lance told him they were going to go to the store, and Griffin nodded, turning in his seat to meet Claudia's gaze. "We're not going to let anyone get close to you."

"Thank you," Claudia whispered.

Griffin turned to face out the windshield, and Claudia wondered how she'd managed to get not one but two attractive men as her personal protectors. There was something unspoken between the two men, something she didn't understand, but there was a trust between them that was inherent and reached beyond verbal communication. Claudia had never known that kind of connection. Not personally.

Lance parked the SUV under a light in the lot and looked back at her before the two men got out. He waited until Griffin made it to his side before opening the door for Claudia to get out.

Griffin offered her his hand and nodded when she took it. As soon as she was out, he handed her over to Lance and closed the door.

Lance wrapped an arm around Claudia's shoulders and held her close to him. She tentatively slid her hand around his waist. His grip on her tightened when she did, and she assumed that meant he was okay with her touching him.

Griffin followed behind them, never more than a few steps away, as the three of them moved through the store. They went to the shoes first, finding something for Claudia to wear since she was still barefoot. With a pair of slip-on shoes in place, they head for the women's section. The two men stood guard as Claudia found a handful of outfits that would fit her. Lance steered her toward outerwear and suggested a coat. She picked out something soft and cozy, then nibbled her lip.

"What about… personal items?" Lance asked, reading her mind.

Claudia nodded. "I… um, yeah."

"Do you want us to hang back?" Lance asked.

Claudia shook her head, a sliver of fear winding around her neck at the idea.

Lance hugged her to his side again and led the way to the undergarments. He didn't say a word as Claudia searched for sizes of panties, grabbed packs of socks, then moved to the bra section. She'd never been shopping for a bra with a man before, let alone two. She glanced at Griffin, who appeared as uninterested as possible, then at Lance.

Lance's gaze bounced from her to the store and back to her. He didn't appear to judge her choices, or the size she was looking at.

Thinking of what happened to her last bra, Claudia's eyes filled with tears and blurred the cotton and lace in front of her. She drew a shaky breath and tried to let it out without either man noticing the tenuous hold on her emotions.

"You're safe," Lance whispered, his heat sinking into her as he moved closer. "We're not going to let anything happen to you. But we can go if you need to. Walk out right now and leave everything here."

Claudia shook her head. "No. I... I can do this."

"Do you want help?" Lance sounded like the last thing he wanted to do was pick out her bra, but it was sweet he offered.

"I'm almost done." Claudia forced the emotions back and grabbed three options in her size, then hesitated and picked up a bralette. "Let's go."

Griffin led the way to the checkouts and paid for everything before Claudia could think about how she was going to afford it all. Lance held her close on the walk back to the SUV.

They were almost to the vehicle when a large truck pulled into the lot. Tires screeched, and Claudia jumped, terror gripping her.

Lance pulled her into his arms and hurried her toward their SUV, leaving Griffin to follow.

Doors slammed on the truck, and the driver and passenger went into the store, but Claudia's panic did not subside.

"You're safe," Lance said. He crouched in front of her, meeting her gaze as she sat on the edge of the seat inside the SUV. He made a show of breathing, and after a minute,

Claudia matched his breath. "Good. Breathe with me, sweetheart. You're safe. We got you."

Claudia breathed again, her heart slowing as she accepted his words.

"Do you feel better?"

Claudia nodded.

"Are you ready to go?" Lance stood and rested his hand on the door.

Her heart raced again. She closed her eyes and chastised herself. She could not insist a man she barely knew hold her in the backseat of an SUV as he whisked her away into the night. It wasn't fair. She could handle it.

"What do you need, Claudia?"

"I..."

"Anything, sweetheart. You tell us, and we will make it happen."

"Can you hold me?"

Lance didn't hesitate. He moved toward her and pulled her into his arms, shielding her from the outside world with his large body.

Claudia trembled with relief, or fear, or some combination of both. Tears welled up once more and overflowed onto his shirt as he held her.

After a minute, Lance pulled back and bent to meet her gaze again. "Do you want me to ride back here with you?"

Claudia nodded, hating her weakness but needing him close.

Lance nudged her over and sat with her, again, not needing words to tell Griffin to take over driving. Griffin slid behind the wheel without another word, and they were off again.

Lance pulled Claudia to his side and held her close. She hugged him around his middle and rested her head on his shoulder, his warmth and presence sinking into her and making her feel safe for the first time in... maybe her entire life.

LANCE'S back was killing him. He was sore and stiff, but there was no way in hell he was going to risk moving.

"Is she out?" Griffin whispered.

"Yeah," Lance said.

Griffin nodded.

"Thanks," Lance told his partner.

Griffin met Lance's gaze in the rearview mirror and nodded once.

Lance leaned his head back against the headrest and closed his eyes. If Griffin hadn't shown up, they would have been stuck in Kansas longer. Lance wasn't ready to drive all the way back to Niagara Falls immediately, but with someone to swap the driving with, they would make it.

The feel of Claudia against him and the gentle sway of the road put Lance to sleep before long. He knew Griffin would keep them safe and on track and sleeping would mean he could take another shift soon and didn't fight it.

When Lance woke, the clock on the dashboard read six-oh-eight. Claudia still slept, and Griffin stared out the windshield, his gaze drifting to the mirrors every few seconds.

Lance put his hand on Griffin's shoulder to let him know he was awake, and Griffin nodded, not breaking his concentration.

"Columbia, Missouri."

Lance nodded. It had been about two hours since they stopped, and he'd slept for about an hour. It wasn't much, so he closed his eyes and went back to sleep.

The next time Lance woke, another two hours had passed,

and Griffin was slowing the SUV down and getting ready to exit the interstate.

"Need gas," Griffin said.

Lance nodded and shifted, hoping his movements would wake Claudia up so he wouldn't scare her again.

He hated the fear in her eyes when he woke her up at their last stop. It was the same look he saw when he opened the bedroom door. He wanted to ask what she'd been through, but he hadn't been able to bring himself to voice the questions.

Claudia stirred, freezing for a second before she settled against him once more. She woke up slowly, not jerking awake this time, and blinked up at Lance.

"Good morning," he said with a smile.

"Hey." She sat up, extracting herself from his body.

He missed the feel of her already. "We're stopping for gas."

"Where are we?"

"Just outside Saint Louis," Griffin answered. He pulled into a gas station and parked, getting out without waiting for them.

"Do you want to get something to eat?" Lance asked, nodding toward the large convenience store attached to the gas station.

Claudia nodded and stretched. He tried hard not to notice the way her breasts moved under his shirt. He was half-hard and all-creep. She still hadn't told him it was okay he'd kissed her, and he had to remember that. "Do you think I can put on some of the clothes I bought?"

"I don't see why not," Lance said. "Do you want to take the bag in or just one or two things?"

"Probably just one or two things." Claudia's cheeks turned pink.

Lance reached for the bags in the trunk of the SUV and handed them to Claudia. He tried not to watch as she searched through and found one of the bras she bought. She pulled out her new coat and bit the tag off it, then stuffed the rest of the items back into the bags. She bit the tag off the bra, then shoved it into the pocket of her new coat and pulled the coat on.

"I'm ready," she said without meeting his gaze.

Lance nodded and slid out of the SUV. He waited for her, then met Griffin's gaze.

Griffin nodded back.

Lance guided Claudia into the store, searching for restroom signs and steering her toward them. Both restrooms had multiple stalls and no way for him to go in with her without drawing lots of attention.

Claudia looked up at him with fear in her eyes.

"I'll be right here. I'm not moving until you come out."

"Okay," she whispered.

Lance watched her walk into the restroom until the door swung closed behind her and cut her off from his view. He counted the seconds until she appeared again, still wrapped up in her coat but looking a little more sure of herself. "Good?"

Claudia nodded, then surprised him when she took his hand.

Lance smiled and squeezed her hand.

They walked through the store and ordered breakfast from the self-serve screen near the takeout counter. When Griffin approached, Lance excused himself to use the bathroom while they waited for their food to be prepared.

They carried breakfast to the SUV and ate before Lance took over driving. Claudia asked if she could sit up front with him, and Griffin took the backseat, stretching out and resting his head on the headrest to sleep.

Claudia took Lance's hand again and held it tight as he drove. He was silent, letting her decide if she wanted to talk. The hours passed without a word spoken. Lance didn't mind the quiet. He drove across Illinois and halfway through Indiana to Indianapolis before they stopped for lunch.

All of them were ready to keep going, so they grabbed a quick lunch and Lance kept driving. Another four hours passed before they stopped for gas, then Griffin took the last shift of driving, getting them back to Niagara Falls.

Claudia sat in the backseat alone for the last stretch and sighed when they crossed the North Grand Island Bridge and arrived in Niagara Falls. "I didn't think I'd ever be back here."

"You're safe here," Lance said. "We are going to protect you, Claudia."

"Thank you," Claudia whispered.

Lance turned to look at her and smiled. Twenty-four hours ago, she'd been chained to a bed. A prisoner in her own childhood home. If it weren't for a chance encounter with the one neighbor who knew something, she'd still be there.

He was not going to let her get hurt ever again. No matter what it took.

MICHAEL SCREAMED at the walls of the tiny cabin where he'd been for a day. He was furious. Claudia was gone, and the cops were on him. That bitch got away and found someone who believed her.

Fucking bitch.

When Michael made it home after his date, he could tell something wasn't right. It wasn't until he got to Claudia's door and saw the lock hanging off the hinge that he realized she was gone. Her cuffs had been unlocked, the same as the front door, and she was gone.

She didn't do it herself, though. She had help. Help that brought hell to his doorstep.

Michael was lucky to get the fuck out of there when he did, the sirens echoing in the night as he drove away.

They'd never find him at the cabin. It belonged to Hector's father, a man who'd been dead and gone for a decade. Hector brought Michael out there to hunt more than once, and a few times to meet up with women. Hector's truck was there, used to deliver Hector's body a week ago.

No one knew Michael was there, just like no one knew about the place at all. But Michael wasn't a fucking pussy. He wasn't going to hide out forever and wait for the cops to stop looking for him. He was going to find Claudia. It was his job to take care of her, to protect her. He was the man of the house, and she belonged to him.

The trip back to Niagara Falls was long, but Michael would make it one more time. One more trip to claim Claudia, to remind her she belonged to him, to take her back. No matter what.

He just had to figure out who had her. Who had the nerve to steal her from her home and act like she needed help. Michael would find whoever took Claudia from him. And he would make sure they understood the error they made.

And that it would be their last.

TWELVE

Lance drove straight to the office. He knew Griffin would alert Montgomery, and anyone who needed to be there would be when they arrived. He was happy to see he was right when he pulled into the parking lot and found a crowd waiting for them.

"What's going on?" Claudia asked nervously.

"This is our team. They're here to make sure you get inside safely," Lance told her.

"Oh. Are you not going inside?"

"I am, we both are, but they are here to make sure we're all safe."

Claudia nodded, and Lance met Montgomery's gaze. Montgomery moved toward Claudia's door.

"That's our boss. Montgomery Rose. He's going to open your door. We're right behind you," Lance told her.

Claudia released Lance's hand and turned to the door. When Montgomery locked eyes with her, she nodded, and he opened the door.

"Nice to finally meet you, Claudia. Let's get you inside." Montgomery offered Claudia his hand, and she slid out of the

SUV. Montgomery blocked her from behind as she headed for the front door.

Lance and Griffin got out and followed the small crowd of protectors into the building. Once they were through the security door, Lance pulled Griffin to the side.

Griffin raised his brows at Lance for him to talk.

"Thank you. I… I should have reached out to you, and I apologize for not filling you in on everything. Your showing up meant a lot."

Griffin didn't say anything for a minute, then sighed. "I know I haven't been a part of this team for long, but I came here because of Samuel. When I got out, I was a little lost, as we all are. Samuel did volunteer work at the VA. I was in a session with him once, and he said the thing that helped him the most was finding a new purpose. For him, that was helping others. But he mentioned Rose one day. That he found his second calling here. Helping people in a different way. He was still taking orders, but he was taking orders that he was allowed to weigh in on. I liked that idea."

"It's part of why—"

"I wasn't done," Griffin snapped.

Lance held up his hands and rolled his lips in.

"The hardest thing for me was having to shut up and take an order I didn't believe in. It's why I didn't stay in longer. I knew no matter how high my rank was, there would always be someone who could tell me what to do and when and how. I didn't like that. Hearing Samuel talk about this place showed me there was somewhere for me to go that gave me the chance to do things differently. When you left without a word, I almost quit. That's not what I signed up for. I need a partner I can count on. If that's not you, and if that's not how this team operates, then I'll go."

Lance waited a beat. He didn't want to interrupt again. He raised his brows, and Griffin nodded.

"Go ahead."

"It is how we operate. And I shouldn't have gone solo on this one. Being a part of this team has given me something I didn't always have. I hope you stick around because I do think it's the right place for you."

"And you're the right partner?" Griffin narrowed his eyes at Lance.

"I hope so. Your showing up in Kansas… that told me all I need to know about you." Lance offered his hand.

Griffin stared at it for a minute, then clasped hands with Lance and shook. "Keep me in the loop. You obviously have a connection with her, and she seems to be a good person. Let's stop this asshole."

"Agreed."

Griffin clapped Lance on the back and shoved him toward the bullpen. They circled around the desks in the center of the room and went to Montgomery's office, where Claudia sat on the couch with Lorelei Sloane.

Lance didn't wait for an invitation to walk into the office, meeting his boss's gaze and seeing the punishment that was coming his way as soon as things with Claudia were resolved.

"…anywhere he would go? Where he would hide?" Lorelei was asking Claudia.

Lance fought against his anger. Michael Reynolds slipped away. Fuck.

Claudia shook her head. "I don't know."

"Did he say anything to you? Tell you where he was going to be when Mr. Kilgore rescued you?"

"He didn't tell me anything. I don't know anything. He abducted me. He forced himself into my apartment and broke my nose. He dragged me back to Kansas. He chained me up and would have killed me if he didn't have a sick and twisted view of our relationship. He…"

"I think she needs a few minutes," Lance said, stepping forward.

"Kilgore," Montgomery warned.

Lance returned his boss's glare and stood his ground.

Lorelei Sloane stood and faced Lance. "He's right. Let's take a beat and give her a chance to get settled." Lorelei stopped in front of Lance. "Can we have a word with you?"

Lance nodded and followed Lorelei and Adam out of the office. Montgomery followed behind them, but Griffin stayed with Claudia, something Lance appreciated. She knew him. Sort of. And she would feel better with Griffin in the room with her.

Montgomery led them to the small conference room to talk in private. He stood inside the door, arms crossed, and raised his brows at Adam when he looked at Montgomery.

Adam nodded and faced Lance, accepting the permission Montgomery was handing over to rip Lance a new one. "What the hell were you thinking?"

"I was thinking there was a woman chained to a bed and I couldn't leave her there," Lance growled.

"What about when you left Niagara Falls?" Lorelei asked.

"Are you seriously going to stand there and tell me I shouldn't have done it? As far as I know, your husband ignored orders and saved your life. I would assume you of all people would agree with my actions," Lance told her.

Lorelei sighed heavily and shook her head. "My history is not a blanket approval for everyone in this city to do whatever the fuck they want. Yes, your actions likely saved her life. But Reynolds wasn't there. We've had agents on the house, and he hasn't come back. He doesn't own any other property, and as far as we can tell, not a lot of people in town actually liked him."

"What's to like about a man who abducts and murders people?" Lance asked.

"We're all on the same side here," Adam said. "But until we bring Michael Reynolds in, Claudia's not safe."

"She's been through hell. You didn't see her when I got there. She hadn't showered in days, maybe weeks. She was wearing a torn and bloody shirt, there was vomit in the room, and the whole place stunk."

"Has she told you what he did to her?"

"She said she didn't need a rape kit, but I haven't asked about anything else," Lance admitted. "I saved her clothes. I don't know if you can get anything from them, but just in case, I kept them."

"That was smart," Lorelei said. "We can test them for semen and—"

Lance growled at the word.

Lorelei, Adam, and Montgomery looked at him.

Lance shook his head. "He's her brother."

"He also had her chained to a bed. We have no idea who else had access to the house, or if he was selling her while she was there. She might not have wanted to admit anything to you, or wanted to face what happened to her. We need to find out." Adam's words did nothing to quiet the rage in Lance's head.

"Do you think she'll talk to you?" Lorelei asked.

Lance shrugged. "I... I don't know. I can try."

"Can you do it without getting..." She waved her hand at his face. "All like this?"

Lance drew a breath and let it out slowly. "I'll try."

Lorelei and Adam exchanged a glance, then looked at Lance.

"I'll go in with you. You ask her questions, and I'll just listen," Lorelei said. "We need to know what information she's telling you. The sooner we know, the better."

"I'll get her clothes to the lab, if that's okay with you," Adam said.

Lance nodded.

"Are we all good then?" Montgomery asked.

Lance looked at the others and nodded. It was the best he could hope for. He just prayed he could handle the answers Claudia shared.

CLAUDIA SAT on the couch with her hands clasped together and detailed everything that happened since she opened her door and found Michael on the other side of it. She told Lance about her brother hitting her and threatening to kill her and anyone else she said anything to when he dragged her out, and the entire drive back to Kansas.

"You believed he would follow through if you didn't listen," Lance said, not asked.

Claudia looked up at him and nodded. She swallowed back the fear in her throat. The last time she told someone what she saw, they didn't believe her. "A year ago…" She drew a breath. "A year ago, I left because I saw him kill someone."

"What?" Agent Sloane barked.

Lance silenced her with a sharp look, and the agent fell silent again, resuming her seat behind the desk.

"Can you tell me what you saw?" Lance asked.

Claudia debated, but it was Lance. If there was anyone she could tell, it would be him. "I grew up in the house where you found me. We both did. When our mother died, we stayed. Michael is older than me, and he was my guardian. I was seventeen, so it wasn't long, but even after, I stayed. I didn't have other options. I wanted to be a teacher, but I didn't have money for college, so I started working at the local daycare and taking classes when I could afford to. Michael always seemed to have money, but he doesn't work much. There were rumors about him selling drugs, but I never saw it. A year ago, I came home and heard noises in his room. I thought someone broke in, but he was in there with a woman. He hit her. More than once. She fell and hit her head. I could tell she was dead by the amount of blood."

"Did you tell anyone?" Lance asked.

Claudia nodded. "I left. I don't think Michael knew I was there, and I went to the police. Her niece was one of the kids in my class, so I knew her name and told the police what I saw. They brought Michael in for questioning, but whatever he told them, they believed because they let him go. Never charged him. That's when I ran."

"Fucking hell," Lance breathed.

"I know what he's capable of. He had a friend... Hector was mean. He came in one day when I was there. He said I was done teasing him. He grabbed me... Hector didn't care that I said no, he was going to force himself on me. Michael came home. He heard me screaming and pulled Hector off me. He dragged him out of my room. A minute later, I heard a gunshot." Claudia felt numb retelling them what happened.

"How old were you when that happened?"

She looked up at Lance and shook her head. "That was last week."

Lance jerked back. His gaze flipped to Agent Sloane, then back to Claudia. "This happened last week?"

Claudia nodded. "I was chained up. There was no way for me to fight back. Michael left Hector there to make sure I didn't get away, I guess. I don't know. But it proves he'll kill people."

"Do you feel you owe Michael for protecting you? Would you keep information from us—"

"No," Claudia snapped. She shook her head, insulted the agent would suggest such a thing. "He kidnapped me. He broke my nose. He told me he's in love with me. He's sick. Do

I want him to get help? Yes. But am I going to hide things from you to protect him? No." She fought her tears, hating that anyone would think that of her. "He told me our mother... She forced him into a sexual relationship. I was always jealous of how close they were. I thought... He was her favorite, and I wished she cared about me the way she cared about him. And now... I didn't know anything about it. He said she told him he was the man of the house, and he had to take care of the women. It's been fifteen years since she died, and I never knew. How did I not know?" Claudia looked at Lance like he could help her understand.

He leaned forward and took her hands. "People hide the parts of themselves they don't want others to see. And we don't typically look for something like that happening right in front of us."

"But it happened for years. It had to have. He was nine when I was born. He said he took care of her, calmed her down. He told me she would sleep with the man who owned our favorite restaurant so he would give us free food. She slept with anyone who would give her things. I never noticed any of it. She was sleeping with my brother, warping him, and I never noticed it."

"Neither of them wanted you to notice it. They probably knew what was happening was wrong," Lance said.

"He said he took care of her, and he wanted to take care of me," Claudia said, holding Lance's gaze as Michael's words settled between them.

Lance stiffened, understanding the same thing Claudia believed Michael meant. He closed his eyes. "Did he do anything to you? Did he touch you? Rape you? Anything?"

Claudia shook her head. "No. Nothing. I never... He's my brother. Half-brother, but he's still my brother. I never thought of him like that. He was there for me my whole life. My mother was never really much of a mother, so Michael made sure I got to school and had something to eat and studied. He was the one who encouraged me to take classes at the community college. It wasn't until I started talking about moving out and getting my own place that things changed between us."

"Changed how?" Lance asked.

"Little things," Claudia said with a shrug. "He needed money for repairs on the house, for groceries, for utilities. It added up in a hurry. When I asked him about it, he said he always took care of everything, but if I was going to move out, I needed to understand what that really meant."

"Do you think he was making that up?"

Claudia laughed mirthlessly. "Now I do. Before I thought he was helping me out, like he always did. I feel like the biggest idiot ever. So many things I missed."

"Don't beat yourself up over it. We all miss things." Lance ducked his head.

"I didn't know if I could tell you what was going on," Claudia whispered.

"I wish you had. If I'd known... I never would have let him anywhere near you."

"It's not your fault," Claudia said.

"It's not yours either," Lance declared.

Claudia swallowed the emotions filling her throat. She wasn't sure she would ever stop blaming herself, but she could try. With Lance's help, she could try.

Agent Sloane made a noise and moved toward the door.

Claudia shifted in her seat, realizing how close she and Lance had gotten while they talked.

Lance cleared his throat and stood, walking toward the agent.

"I'm going to update Adam and see what we can find out about the woman he killed and his friend, Hector. For what it's worth, I think Lance is right. You shouldn't blame yourself for what happened to your brother or for what he did to you and others. We will find him, and we will get justice for all the people he hurt." Agent Sloane nodded to Claudia, then Lance, then let herself out of the office.

Claudia watched the other woman go and felt marginally better.

"I'm sorry for everything you've been through. And for taking so long to find you."

Claudia looked up at him and smiled. "You found me. I didn't even have hope that would happen."

Lance nodded. "I'm happy to hear you... that nothing worse happened to you."

She chuckled. "Yeah. Me, too."

"And I'm sorry for kissing you. I... I got carried away. I had no right, and I never should have—"

Claudia shook her head and stood. "Stop apologizing for that. You... I wanted you to kiss me for months. I never for one second felt like you overstepped. I assumed you regretted it."

"No. Not for a second," Lance said.

Claudia moved closer to him. "That's good to know."

Lance took a step toward her. "Did you?"

Claudia shook her head. "Not for a second."

Lance's lips quirked up at the edges. "That's good to know."

Claudia grinned. "It's been a while, though. I might need a refresher on what it was like."

"Oh yeah?" Lance cupped her cheek, his thumb dancing over her skin.

Goosebumps rose all over her body. She nodded.

Lance leaned closer, his head tilting to the side. He gave her plenty of time to pull back before his lips brushed hers.

Claudia sighed into his mouth and gripped his shirt at the waist. She tugged him closer and licked his lips.

He groaned and opened for her, slicking his tongue against hers. His other hand slid across her back and pulled her closer.

She felt him harden against her belly and smiled.

He pulled back, his smile echoing hers. "What are you smiling about?"

"You. This. I never expected..." She looked over his shoulder at the people approaching the door. "We're about to have company."

Lance looked over his shoulder and sighed. "Duty calls. But we're going to finish that conversation later."

Claudia grinned. It felt weird to be so happy when she'd been in captivity a day ago, but she was happy. She was safe. And she was with Lance. His hands gripping hers tight proved that.

THIRTEEN

Lance listened as the people who outranked him talked in circles. No one had any real information. They didn't know anything about Michael Reynolds or the woman Claudia mentioned or his friend Hector. They only knew he'd matched the sketch of the man who'd walked out of the apartment building with Claudia more than two weeks ago.

Yes, he was linked to a lot of drug use in his town, but there was no proof of anything. And sharing the same tiny pieces of information over and over and over again was not helping find him.

"Do we have to keep doing this?" Lance finally asked when he saw Claudia's eyes closing. "We're exhausted, and we're not getting anywhere."

Montgomery looked at Lance, then slid his gaze to Claudia. His face softened, and he closed his eyes. "Her brother has been to her apartment. It's not safe for her to go back there."

"She can stay with me," Lance said.

Montgomery shook his head even as Lance spoke. "I don't think that's far enough away. We need her safe. We can put her at The Davidson Hotel."

Everyone started talking at once, either agreeing or disagreeing with Montgomery. Lance ignored them all and focused on Claudia. "Are you okay with staying in a hotel?"

She shook her head. "I really don't have the money for that. I can just go back to my apartment. I don't want to put anyone out."

"First, you're not going back there. Second, Rose or the FBI, or hell, I will pay for a hotel to make sure you're safe. And third, I'm staying with you. If you're okay with that."

A smile peeked out from behind the exhaustion and misery. "Yeah?"

Lance nodded.

"Okay."

"Okay. You're okay with The Davidson?"

She nodded, sitting up straighter on the couch.

"We're going to The Davidson Hotel," Lance announced to the room.

Everyone stopped talking as Lance stood and offered Claudia his hand. He didn't let go of her hand when she stood next to him, not caring as everyone in the room studied them.

"You can't go alone," Adam said.

"I have a few people I can send," Montgomery said.

Adam and Montgomery had a silent conversation, which ended with a nod from Adam. Montgomery ushered everyone out of his office, catching Griffin and Damien's attention and nodding to both of them.

Griffin slid a look to Lance. Lance nodded to his partner, hoping it conveyed that he wanted the other man in the loop.

"Lance and Claudia are going to The Davidson Hotel. I'd like you both to go with them. Three of you protecting her is better than one. If you're all willing?"

Griffin nodded without hesitation.

Damien tilted his head. "As long as Jude's on leave, I'm wherever you want me to be, boss."

"Thank you. That's what I was thinking, too. And since you and Griffin worked together before, the three of you should work well. How you handle things is up to you, but grab your bags and head out."

The three of them nodded.

Montgomery left them to talk through the specifics, catching up with the FBI agents as they walked out.

"Ready when you are," Griffin said.

"Same," Damien agreed. He offered his hand to Claudia. "I'm Damien Joseph. Nice to meet you."

"You, too," Claudia said, smiling at Damien.

Damien released her hand quickly, lucky for him, then followed Griffin to the locker room. They all kept go-bags in the office for urgent situations that prevented them from going home. The practice had come in handy more than a few times.

Lance squeezed Claudia's hand and smiled when she looked up at him. "You okay with this?"

She drew a deep breath and let it out slowly. "I don't really have a choice, do I?"

Lance tucked her hair behind her ear and pulled her into his arms, holding her close for a minute. "They will find him and end all of this."

She nodded against his chest.

Damien and Griffin walked back out and nodded to Lance. Griffin held up a second bag, Lance's bag, and they headed for the door.

"They're ready if you are," Lance told Claudia.

She lifted her head from his chest and wiped her eyes. She nodded and let him lead her to the door.

THE HOTEL they were staying in was the nicest one Claudia had ever been in. By far. She guessed one night in the place was likely a week's worth of rent, but she wasn't paying for it. She didn't like that someone else was going to be, but she had to admit she felt safer in a hotel with the level of security they had over her apartment, where Michael had already been.

She tried not to think about her apartment and what it would take to get it back to decent after what she went through. She wasn't looking forward to going back there. Ever. But if Michael was caught, and if he was arrested for all the things he did, she knew she would have to figure something out.

Maybe something that involved Lance.

He hadn't let go of her hand the entire drive, and as they walked around the suite, he stayed with her. "You have a room to yourself. The three of us will use the second bedroom."

"Oh," Claudia said, more than a little disappointed. "I thought... Never mind."

"What did you think?"

She shook her head, her cheeks heating. She was being ridiculous. Of course, Lance didn't want to share a room with her. He said they were going to finish their conversation from earlier, but he clearly didn't mean when two of his teammates were in the suite with them.

"Please tell me, Claudia," Lance implored softly.

"I was hoping you'd stay with me. I... On the drive back here, I only felt safe when you..."

"I'll stay with you," he said without making her spell it all out for him.

"I feel like I'm forcing you."

"To share a bed with a beautiful woman that I can't stop thinking about? Yeah, it's a real struggle for me."

She breathed a laugh.

"Do you want to get some sleep? Or are you hungry? What do you need right now?"

"Sleep. I'm... I haven't slept well since..."

"Let's go to sleep." Lance turned to Griffin and Damien. "We're going to get some sleep."

"Together?" Damien asked.

Lance nodded. Griffin cleared his throat.

Damien glanced at them, then nodded and said goodnight. Griffin repeated the word, then Lance guided Claudia to the bedroom.

All she wanted to do was crash. She couldn't remember ever being as tired as she felt. Every noise in the house made her jump, and sleep was hard to come by when she worried about what Michael would do when she was sleeping.

But she was safe with Lance.

"We'll get you more clothes tomorrow if you need anything else," Lance said. "I know none of this is ideal."

"It's better than where I was thirty-six hours ago," Claudia whispered.

Lance smiled and reached for her, pulling her against his body. His cock twitched.

"Are we going to finish that conversation from earlier?"

His dick surged against her belly. "We don't have to right now. I don't want you to feel like I'm pressuring you into anything."

"I know you're not. I also know I spent two weeks in a prison my brother created for me. I was in danger every second, and I still am. Michael is not going to give up. He didn't come after me because a year ago I saw him kill a woman. He didn't even come after me because of our mother's watch. He came after me because he thinks we're supposed to be together. He thinks he loves me and that we should be together."

Lance squeezed her tight. "I hate that you have to be

afraid. That your voice shakes when you talk about him. That you witnessed something so awful and no one believed you."

"You believe me."

"I might not know you well, but I know you're a good person, Claudia. I know you wouldn't lie. You're helping your pregnant coworker even though you don't have much. You give food to people who can't afford it and pay for it out of your own pocket. You are kind to our neighbors, and you are always helping others. You're not the kind of person who's going to lie about something like that."

"Thank you," Claudia whispered. Until he said it, she didn't realize how much she needed to hear those words. How much they would mean to her. A year of doubts made her wonder if she should have just kept her mouth shut, but one reassurance that she was doing the right thing and she knew it was.

Lance pulled back from her just enough to meet her gaze. He lifted her chin with one finger, then leaned down to bring his lips to hers.

Claudia sighed into the kiss, meeting him in the middle and swiping her tongue along his lips.

He opened his mouth for her and teased the tip of her tongue with his. Then he tilted his head and swept his tongue through her mouth, groaning as they tasted each other.

She clutched him tighter, pressing her body to his. Her need for him, for something good, for a reminder that she was alive and okay, raced through her veins, urging her on as she whimpered and pried his shirt up, giving her access to his warm skin.

"Claudia," he groaned, breaking the kiss with sharp reality and a gust of cold air. "I... I'm not trying to force you."

"Please, Lance. Please. Maybe it's not fair of me, but I want you. I've wanted you for months. I thought I'd never see you again. See anyone again. I thought I was dead. I need this."

He stared at her for a long moment, long enough that her cheeks heated and doubts about his sincerity sank in. Then he moved, all at once, and disintegrated all her anxiety. He sealed his mouth tight over hers, swallowing the squeak that fell from her lips. He grabbed at the new clothes she wore, tugging them free of her body as he did the same with his. He squeezed and molded and caressed and loved her flesh with his fingers, jumping from one spot to another and making her head spin as she tried to anticipate where he would touch her next.

Claudia moaned, and Lance pulled back. A glance at the door was enough to tell her he didn't want his friends to hear them. "Sorry."

He shook his head. "I don't want to share you."

His words, whispered and harsh, were enough to make her knees weak. To make her feel cherished and worshipped and loved.

She knew it wasn't all that. It couldn't be. He was a man who could have had his pick of women. He didn't need to settle for her, for his neighbor who needed protection and sought it out through lies and deceit. He could have chosen a woman from anywhere. But he made her feel special. He made her feel like she wasn't lucky to be with him, she was chosen.

Lance slowed his movements when their clothes were tossed freely around the room. He stepped back and looked at her, just looked. She'd never had a man who stared at her body the way Lance did. Nor had she had one who seemed to grow harder as he did it. He licked his lips, then moved back into her personal space. "On the bed, Claudia."

She didn't waste time following his request, sitting on the bed before she moved to lie down.

He hooked her ankle in one hand and stilled her movement before caressing the faded bruise. "Can I taste you?"

"What? You...?"

"Next time if you're unsure," he said, releasing her ankle

and making her head spin with the promise he possibly didn't intend to make.

Claudia wasn't a virgin, and she hadn't been for many years, but she also wasn't used to a man who was vocal about his intentions. Most of the men she'd slept with climbed into bed, crawled on top of her, pumped until they were done, then left. A few had stuck around for more than one occasion and had made an effort to ensure she enjoyed herself. One in particular was good to her. He made her feel special. He waited until they'd been together for a few weeks before they slept together. He made her feel special. Until he disappeared one day, and she never heard from him again.

The memory of him threatened to drag Claudia out of her current state, so she shoved it to the side and focused on Lance. He kissed her skin, laving at her flesh with his tongue. She trembled at the feel of it, leaning into his affections. He smiled against her stomach and nipped lightly at her hip. "You taste good."

"I taste like motel soap and road trip," she countered.

"I guess I like those things," he whispered against the underside of her boob. He looked over the swollen skin at her, waiting for approval.

"We're naked and in bed. You don't need to ask for permission."

He closed his eyes and rolled his lower lip between his teeth. "I don't want to make any assumptions. Any more assumptions. I want you, Claudia. But what you went through—"

She shut him up with a hard kiss, yanking him on top of her and wrapping her legs around his hips. She didn't want to think about what she'd been through, and she definitely didn't want to stop what she was about to go through because of it.

Lance resisted for a second or two, then sank into the kiss and gave it back to her just as fiercely as she kissed him. His tongue thrust into her mouth as his erection nestled at the apex of her thighs.

The feel of him against her made her want to tighten her legs and bring him inside her, but thankfully, he had more braincells than she did and pulled back.

He jumped off the bed and searched his pockets for a condom, producing one before he climbed over her again. He held himself off her and kissed her just as urgently, as though the pause hadn't happened.

Claudia arched against him, the friction she needed holding her orgasm just barely out of reach. She groaned with frustration, and Lance rolled to the side, leaving a hand between her thighs as he took his weight off her.

His fingers teased her sensitive flesh, pulling the orgasm from the depths of her to the surface in record time. His lips never left hers, swallowing the moans and whimpers she emitted with ease as he toyed with her clit.

She trembled in his arms, and he slid his fingers through her folds to her soaked core. He dragged the wetness back to her clit and exposed her clit to his ministrations, dragging an orgasm from her in near-record time.

Claudia threw her head back, biting her lip as her orgasm poured over her, everything splintering with the intensity of it. She expected to be done, but was surprised to find he hadn't withdrawn his fingers and was kissing his way down her throat. He brought her nipple into his mouth and tugged on it with his teeth. The jolt connected all her pleasure centers and resulted in an orgasm that nearly had her screaming.

"No more," she begged. "No more, or I'll scream."

Lance reluctantly lifted his head, his regret clear in the debate in his eyes. He kissed her chest, paying special attention to her breasts, and brought his lips back to hers. His fingers didn't retreat from her core, but he gave her a break and casually caressed her body.

When their kissing included teeth and tongues and pants and moans, Lance rolled the condom on and lined up between her thighs. His gaze strayed to her entrance, then back to her face. "One day, I'm not going to stop until you do scream, Claudia. I want to hear you beg me for more, screaming my name, and coming until you can't breathe."

"I... I think I might like that," she whispered.

"Good. For right now, I'm going to sink into your perfect body and feel how good we are together."

"What if we're not?" she asked, the words a whisper.

He chuckled, his face disbelieving. "Not possible. There hasn't been one moment since we met that I thought we wouldn't be."

"Since we met?"

He nodded. "I thought you were different, Claudia. I wish I'd known the real you from the start. I wanted to. I wanted you from day one. And there's no doubt this is going to make me regret not giving you a chance before. But all we have is right now, and I'm not looking to waste another second."

She trembled at his words, nodding as he leaned over her to kiss her. With his lips on hers, he pushed inside her body. She exhaled a moan and wrapped her legs around him, not letting him retreat when he tried.

"Fuck, you feel good," he gasped against her lips.

"Don't stop," she begged.

"Not a chance." He withdrew enough to plunge back in, his strokes short with her legs tight around him.

His body rubbed against her, inside and out, and made her dizzy with pleasure. She didn't know she could come again, especially the way they were, but as he thrust into her, she knew there was no way to stop it.

"Lance," she whispered.

"Fuck. Again? I'm close, Claudia. Are you going to come with me?"

"I might."

Lance pushed himself up, changing the angle inside and out.

Claudia sighed at the loss of his body rubbing hers until he reached between them and slid a slick thumb over her clit.

"Oh, God."

"Damn. Fuck. Come on, Claudia. Come with me." His thumb pressed harder and rubbed faster, sending her from right there to past the point of no return in seconds.

"Yes. Oh, shit. Fuck. Yes." Claudia did her best not to shout the words as her orgasm burst from her and dragged Lance over the edge with her, his grunt of pleasure echoing in her ear as he collapsed on top of her, his hand pinned between them.

"Holy shit," Lance whispered, rolling to the side as soon as he landed on her and dragging her with him. "I told you we would be good."

"I didn't know it would be that good," Claudia said before she could measure her words. Her cheeks burned with the casual admission.

Lance propped himself up and looked at her, a cocky smile leading the way as he leaned over to kiss her. "I did," he whispered against her lips. He kissed her until she writhed against him and he had to find a new condom.

FOURTEEN

Claudia had never spent the night with a man. It was a new experience, and one she was pretty sure she was a fan of. A big fan. Lance had only two condoms on him, but he was a very creative lover. So creative Claudia was sore long before morning but not at all willing to tell him to stop.

Lance kissed her shoulder, his erection rising against her ass. His teeth sank into the column of her neck.

Claudia moaned softly and turned to face him. "Did you get any sleep?"

Lance nodded. "I got enough. I was a lot more interested in you, though."

"You are very distracting."

"I didn't hear you complaining last night."

She chuckled. "I was not going to complain about any of the things you did."

"Neither was I," Lance said, crawling over her and kissing her soundly. His tongue tasted like her, just like hers tasted like him. His erection pulsed against her thigh, and way too quickly, Lance rolled off the bed. "I think we need a shower."

"We?" Claudia asked.

Lance offered her his hand and grinned. "We."

Claudia followed him into the attached bathroom and waited as he adjusted the water temperature. He stepped into the shower first, then blocked the water for her to stand with him.

"Is it too hot for you? Too cold?"

She reached her hand behind him to feel the water. "It's good."

Lance pulled her against him and held her tight for a minute, the water running over their bodies and soothing Claudia the same way it did when she showered in the motel room.

As they stood there, she felt herself relaxing. Feeling the safety he offered her without asking for anything in return. She never expected to end up in a fancy hotel room with him, but she couldn't lie and say she didn't hope she would end up naked with him at some point.

"What are you thinking?" he whispered against her soaked hair.

"I'm thinking this isn't how I hoped things would go, but I'm not disappointed to be here with you."

"I'm not either."

"Thank you for finding me. For looking for me and not giving up on me. I..." Her throat tightened. "I never expected you to come for me."

Lance drew a breath. He opened his mouth to say something, but a loud banging came from the bedroom. "Shit."

"What is that?" Claudia asked.

"It's Damien and Griffin. They're trying to get into the room for some reason. Don't move."

Claudia nodded, pressing her body against the wall of the shower. Lance stepped out and wrapped a towel around his waist, using another one to dry his hair as he hurried out of the bathroom.

She didn't move when he was gone, staring at the doorway where he disappeared. She sucked in one after another breath and tried not to throw up.

"Claudia. Fuck, Claudia. You're safe, sweetheart. I'm right here with you." Lance sounded far away. Like he was in another room. Or being kept from her.

Cold rushed over her, then she felt something that made her jerk. She slipped, but before she fell, she was caught. She fought him, hitting back and trying to get free of Michael as he held her tight to his body.

"Listen to my voice, Claudia. You're safe with me, sweetheart. It's Lance. I'm not going to hurt you. I'm so sorry, Claudia. Listen to my voice. Hear what I'm saying. Please breathe, sweetheart. Breathe. There you go. Breathe with me. In and out, Claudia. I've got you, honey. I'm not going to let anyone hurt you."

Claudia realized she was in Lance's arms, not Michael's. She stopped fighting him, reality crashing around her. They were on the floor of the shower. The water was off. His towel was still on, but it was soaked like he'd gotten into the shower with it around his waist.

"I'm sorry," she said, her voice shaking with the words.

"Do not apologize to me, honey. You're okay. You're safe. I'm sorry I didn't know you would be triggered by something."

She shook her head. "I didn't... I thought they were trying to break in. That it was Michael."

"I'm sorry, Claudia. Shit. I'll kick their asses."

"It's okay. I... It's okay."

"Do you want me to turn the water back on?"

She shook her head and tried to extract herself from his arms.

"You don't have to get up right now if you don't want to. We can sit here as long as you want."

She drew a shaky breath and knew she had to stop relying on him. She had to find a way to be normal. "I'm fine."

The look on his face said he didn't believe her for a second, but he let her have the lie and helped her to stand. He grabbed a clean towel and wrapped it around her shoulders, then rubbed her arms. "Are you okay?"

She nodded, not meeting his gaze, and went to the bedroom to find something to wear, ignoring the fact that they never actually washed themselves.

After a minute, Lance walked out of the bathroom with a dry towel around his waist.

"What did they need?" Claudia asked, proud that most of the shakiness was out of her voice.

"There's an update. Montgomery is on his way."

Claudia inhaled sharply. She didn't know what she expected. A year of no one believing her about what Michael did made her question if he would ever be punished, but a day with Lance and his team and there was a lot of power behind stopping Michael.

If they could find him.

"Okay," Claudia finally said. She kept her back to Lance as she dug through the bag of clothes he bought her the day before. She pulled on panties beneath the towel she held around her body, then added sweatpants. She positioned her towel around her shoulders to hide her upper body and put her bra on. With it secure, she added a tee and rubbed her hair with the towel.

She spent the night in Lance's arms, then had a panic attack in the shower. She wasn't okay. She wasn't going to be for a long time. And the last thing she needed to do was drag him any farther into her orbit and end up destroying him the same way Michael destroyed her.

"I'm ready," Claudia said after a minute.

"Claudia," Lance said, his voice sounding strained. "I don't want you pulling back from me."

"I'm not. I'm ready to talk to your boss. Hear what he found out."

Lance didn't move.

Claudia wanted to run, but she wasn't strong enough to do it alone. Not again. She wouldn't make it if Michael found her again. He would kill her. Without a doubt. But she couldn't hide in a hotel paid for by Lance's boss forever either. She had to find a middle ground. And whatever Montgomery had to say would go a long way toward figuring out what that was.

Lance sighed after a minute, then moved to the door. Claudia noticed he'd gotten dressed in the time she had, and he wore his own pair of sweats and a tee. He looked way too good for a man dressed so casually, but he always did in her opinion.

Griffin smiled at Claudia when she walked out of the room and offered her a cup of coffee. He asked how she slept and if she wanted something to eat.

Before Claudia answered, there was a knock on the door, and she crouched behind the counter.

"FUCK," Lance breathed, going to Claudia as Damien went for the door. Lance crouched in front of her and spoke softly to her. "Hey, look at me. You're here with me. No one is here to hurt you, Claudia. Please breathe with me, sweetheart."

She finally met his gaze and sucked in a breath.

Relief swamped him as she slowly came back to him, her panic receding as her tears dried up.

"Panic attack?" Montgomery asked.

"Whenever someone knocks. So maybe we don't pound on the doors for a bit," Lance snapped.

"I didn't know," Griffin said.

"Neither did I," Montgomery said. He looked past Lance to Claudia. "I apologize. Are you okay?"

Claudia nodded, obviously trying to pull herself together. Lance ached to pull her back into his arms and make her forget her brother showing up at her door.

"Do you want us to bring someone in for you to speak to?" Montgomery offered.

"A therapist?" Claudia asked.

"Yes."

Claudia shook her head vehemently. "I don't need a therapist."

"With all due respect, we all need help sometimes."

"Are you in therapy?" she spat.

To Lance's surprise, Montgomery nodded. "I am."

Lance caught the mirrored looks of shock on Griffin and Damien's faces, but none of them commented.

"Does it help?" Claudia asked.

Montgomery shrugged. "My struggles differ from yours, but it helps. Sometimes it's good to take a step back and have someone who isn't emotionally involved in your issues give you perspective."

Claudia considered his words, then nodded. "I'll think about it. If that's okay."

Montgomery nodded and offered her his hand. "Of course."

Claudia let Montgomery help her to stand.

Lance moved to the side, feeling like a third wheel between his boss and the woman he'd spent the night buried inside of. It was a shitty fucking feeling.

"Lance said you have news?" Claudia said, looking up at Montgomery.

"I do. Should we sit?" Montgomery gestured to the couch.

Lance hung back, letting Claudia and Montgomery sit together on the couch. It hurt, but she was terrified, and he understood that.

"We found reports on the woman you mentioned and Michael's friend, Hector. There's been no one who's seen either of them since the dates you mentioned. The FBI had the blood tested from the floor in your house, and it didn't come back as a match for anyone, but that just means it's someone who isn't in their system."

"Hector was never arrested as far as I know. He and Michael were always getting away with stuff," Claudia said.

"Do you think there was a cop they were working with? Someone who would hide what they did?" Montgomery asked.

Claudia shook her head. "I don't know. I wish I did, but I tried not to pay attention to what they were doing."

"It's okay. We also found a property in Hector's name, but it was obvious no one had been there for a while. We didn't find any family."

"His father died a while ago, I think. Maybe ten years. Michael mentioned it," Claudia said.

Montgomery nodded, looking at notes on his phone. "We also didn't find his vehicle. There's one registered to Hector, but it seems to be missing with him. Do you know where he might go? If he was alive? Maybe Michael is using Hector's vehicle and knows of a place to hide where Hector would have gone."

Claudia shook her head slowly. "I never liked Hector. He always looked at me like he... well, like he was going to do exactly what he said he was going to do to me. I stayed away from him. If Michael said Hector was coming over, I made sure I wasn't there. I'm sorry."

"You have nothing to apologize for. We're just trying to

find out what we can. If you're okay with it, I have some pictures of other people who've gone missing in the last few years. People who are believed to have had ties to your brother and Hector. I wanted to show you these pictures and see if you remember seeing any of them at your house. Are you okay with that?" Montgomery asked.

Lance stood and watched Claudia. He could tell she was worn out. The panic attacks were taking a toll, and she was crashing after the adrenaline rushes.

But she nodded and let Montgomery show her the pictures.

Lance stayed close, the need to protect her weighing on him heavily. The first few pictures didn't get a reaction from Claudia, but after a few, she stopped Montgomery.

"All these people are missing?" she asked.

"Yes."

"And you think my brother had something to do with it?"

"It's possible."

"This one," Claudia pointed to the picture Montgomery had just shown her. "She's sixteen. She's young. Why do you think my brother had something to do with her disappearance?"

Montgomery was not one for weighing his words, and to see him do just that had Lance taking a step forward.

"The local police are severely overworked. They have more cases than they can handle. Yours was one of the many. Your coworkers reported you missing, but your brother repeatedly told them you were fine and you'd gone on vacation or you were visiting family or something else over the last year. Your disappearance was one sheet in a folder somewhere, and it was with dozens of others that were similar. Someone completely changed their routine, and the people who would know something made it seem as if the police were overreacting. With no evidence of foul play and no leads on where you would have gone, they didn't put much effort into finding you. This girl was the same. Her mother is known as an addict who barely noticed when her daughter was around."

"And my brother is her dealer," Claudia said with very little emotion.

"That's the working assumption."

Claudia exhaled roughly, but Montgomery wasn't done.

"After what you told us yesterday about your mother, it's possible your brother was involved with this girl."

"What? No. Why would he do that?" Claudia asked, her voice trembling.

"He could have taken her as payment."

"Payment?"

Montgomery nodded and let his declaration sink in.

Claudia closed her eyes, tears leaking around the lids. She shook her head but didn't argue with Montgomery's suggestion. "How did I not see any of this? I've lived with him my entire life, and I had no idea what he was doing."

"He didn't want you to," Montgomery said. "He knew you were a good person and would turn him in. You turned him in, but the police didn't believe you. That woman has never been found, and now that a year has passed and Michael confessed to you, they have a good reason to take your accusations more seriously."

"She's still dead," Claudia said.

"Yes, but finding her body would give her family closure. And finding your brother could stop him from hurting others. He's still out there, and we have no idea where he is or who he could be with. He has to have help to avoid everyone who's looking for him, and if we find out which of these people he's actually been involved with, we can narrow down where he could be."

"He's going to come back here," Claudia whispered, almost threatening. "He's going to come here and kill me."

"If he was going to kill you, he would have done it before," Montgomery said with very little emotion.

"Fucking hell," Lance gasped.

Montgomery looked at him, and Lance glared at his boss. "Sorry, Claudia," Montgomery said.

"He wanted me to go to the police station with him. He said the cops were starting to ask too many questions about where I was, and he needed me to go with him to prove I was alive," Claudia said.

Lance drew back at that news. She hadn't mentioned it before. But it made sense why Michael tried to straighten her nose. He wanted her presentable.

"So he knew they were closing in on him. He knew he was under investigation. And he knew you were a key to all of it," Montgomery said.

"I didn't hang around with my brother. I don't know…" She stared at the folder Montgomery tossed on the table. She pushed a few pictures to the side, exposing the one that only showed a name. Amber Courtney. "She's missing?"

Montgomery nodded when Claudia looked up at him. "She is. Six months. Do you know her?"

Claudia nodded, fresh tears building in her eyes. "Amber was a friend of mine. We took classes together at the community college. She met Michael once. We were studying for a final, and we ran into him. She asked me if I was being abused by him. I told her he was my brother and had never hit me. She said if I ever needed help to call her."

"When was the last time you spoke to her?"

Claudia shook her head. "It's been two years maybe? We didn't have a lot of classes together because she was in school full time and I wasn't. Why… what happened to her?"

"No one knows. She disappeared from her college. Her car was left in the parking lot for weeks. The college didn't report her absent because student attendance isn't recorded. She wasn't working, and no one noticed she was gone until almost three weeks had passed when one of her classmates asked a professor. They both said it was strange and called the police." Montgomery met Claudia's gaze.

"He thought she was helping me, didn't he? That's what you think?"

Montgomery shook his head. "We don't know what to think. Until just now, I had no idea you knew her. But based on that, it's very possible that's exactly what happened."

Claudia heaved and put her hand over her mouth, then sprinted out of the room.

Lance growled at his boss, then followed Claudia to the bathroom.

FIFTEEN

Claudia slumped against the wall and let the tears roll down her face. She had no idea. When she ran, she was protecting herself. She knew if her brother would kill one woman and get away with it, she wasn't safe. She never expected he would go after others. People he thought would help her.

Amber.

Claudia put her head against the wall and swallowed the bitter taste in her throat.

"Are you okay?" Lance asked.

Claudia hadn't heard him follow her and wondered how long he'd been there watching her quietly fall apart. "No."

"Can I come in?"

She pried her watery eyes open and looked at him. He was a blur across the room, but he was there. She'd never had anyone who was there. Who didn't abandon her the first chance they got. "You don't need to. I'll be fine."

He didn't say anything.

She wanted to cry for what could have been with Lance. If

she wasn't the sibling of a man who thought nothing of killing people. If she didn't have a mother who thought nothing of forcing herself on her own child. Claudia was never going to be a normal woman, and Lance deserved that.

"I met my last girlfriend at a fundraiser. I don't even remember what it was for, but I was there for the free food and drinks. Montgomery paid. I was seated next to Blair Mercer. She was stunning. One of the most beautiful women I'd ever seen."

Claudia was going to be sick again. She did not want to hear about Lance falling for some other woman, even if things ended.

"Blair was charming and kind. She made everyone feel special. When I admitted I was there because my boss paid, she asked what I did for a living. We talked the whole night, danced, and when the event was over, she asked if she could see me again. I was flattered, and there was no way I was turning down a chance to see her again."

"Why are you telling me this?" Claudia whispered.

"For the next few months, I tried to balance the life Blair had with the life I had. She hated my apartment and wanted me to move in with her. She thought my job was a waste of time and set up interviews for me with people she knew who had more prestigious careers. She wanted to control me and my life. I thought it was her way of making me better, so I went on the interviews, but I was never offered any of the jobs. I argued that I had a lease and didn't want to break it. I thought I was in love with her, so I kept going along with all her craziness. She wanted to go out of town all the time. All these expensive vacations. The last one she tried to talk me into was a cruise on a yacht. The cost of a week was more than I made in a month. She was angry when I said I couldn't afford it."

Claudia drew a breath. She could sense where the story was going.

"She went anyway. Told me she went with a friend, like she frequently did. I didn't realize until she got back that this particular friend was less friend and more fuck-buddy. A man who could not only easily afford the trip but could pay for them to have the nicest suite onboard, private dinners with the chef, all the excursions they wanted, and everything the ship had to offer."

"I'm sorry, Lance."

He shook his head. "I'm not. I was never going to fit into the life she wanted. I didn't want that life. I was raised by a single mother who worked her ass off to provide for me. When she died, her best friend took me in. I joined the military as soon as I turned eighteen because there was no money for me to go to college, but the military gave me a career and eventually paid for me to go to college. When I got out, I came here because Rose Protection Agency was a good fit for me. It allowed me to keep helping people. And when I was needed the most, I failed you."

"You didn't fail me," Claudia argued. "None of this is your fault."

"It's not yours either, Claudia. You had no idea Michael would go after Amber, or anyone else. You kept your distance from him, and you tried to help when you witnessed what he did. But none of it is your fault."

"How do I accept that? Amber is gone, probably dead, because she was nice to me. Because she was my friend. How is that fair?"

"It's not fair. It's not right. Just like it's not right that he killed any of the people he's killed, or who ended up dead because of drugs he sold them. He's not a good person. And I know he's your brother and you care about him—"

"He needs help."

"He does, if he's willing to get help. But first, we need to find him. If you think he's going to come back here, we need to be prepared for that. We need to know what his plan would be. It would be better if we could find him now, before he has a chance to get close to you."

"I don't know what he would do or where he would go. It's been a year since I left. He could be anywhere."

"But he never moved out of the house you grew up in. He stayed there, even when he knew the police were investigating him. Did you see other people in the house? Do you remember anyone else he spent time with before you left? Any voices or names or places?"

Claudia shook her head the whole time Lance spoke, but stopped when something slithered up and tingled her brain. "A cabin. I heard Michael and Hector mention something about a cabin. I don't know where it is, but there was definitely a cabin somewhere."

"Okay, good. We'll look into it."

Claudia was sure Lance would leave, but he didn't. He stayed at the door and watched her. "I don't remember anything else."

"I'm not standing here for that, Claudia. I hate you being so far away from me and knowing you don't want me to come any closer."

"Lance, you deserve more than me."

"Fuck that," he spat.

She jerked at the tone he used.

"I'm sorry, but you're wrong. If you don't want me, just be honest with me, but don't hide behind something like what I deserve. That's bullshit. What everyone deserves is someone who is good for them. Someone who makes them the best version of themselves. Who makes them want to be the best version of themselves. That's you, Claudia. You make me want to be a better man." He exhaled roughly and shook his head.

"But that's not how you feel about me, so I'll give you space." He backed up a step and turned.

"Lance," she blurted.

"Yeah?" He didn't turn toward her again, but he did wait.

"I don't know how to rely on anyone else."

"You have to decide that for yourself, Claudia."

"I... When I first saw you, I knew you were different. I'd never known a man like you. Someone who would help others like you did with that girl in the gym. But I manipulated things to get close to you, and I'm sorry for that."

"You have nothing to apologize for."

"I wish we'd met under different circumstances."

Lance turned back to her, his gaze sad and resolute. "Me, too."

"But..."

Lance drew a breath.

"I'm happy I met you. I... I want to be a better person. You make me want to be a better person."

"Claudia, what are you saying?"

She pushed off the floor and moved toward him. "I'm saying I've never had someone like you in my life, and I am not ready to let you go. If you're okay with that."

Lance moved toward her and wrapped his arms around her waist. He leaned down to kiss her, but she stopped him.

"Let me brush my teeth first."

He chuckled and kissed her cheek. "Deal, but as soon as you do, I'm getting another kiss."

"I think I can handle that."

Lance left her alone in the bathroom, his voice joining those of his teammates after a few seconds.

Claudia thought about Amber and all the others Montgomery showed her. They had to find Michael. They had to put him away. He needed help, but he needed to pay for what he did to all those people.

And she had to help stop him from doing the same to more people.

LANCE TOLD Montgomery about the cabin. A few minutes later, Claudia came back into the room. They went through more pictures, but it wasn't long before Montgomery left.

Griffin headed to the bedroom for a nap, and Damien sat in front of his computer.

Lance asked Claudia if she was hungry and got to work in the kitchen. Claudia sat on a barstool and watched him cook.

"You said your Aunt Jackie taught you to cook?"

"Yep. She helped me figure out how to be an adult. She taught me to cook, made sure I knew how to work hard and when to relax and enjoy life, and what it means to love another person. She's amazing."

"Is she in the area?"

"No, unfortunately. She lives in Oregon. I haven't seen her in way too long."

"That's hard."

Lance nodded and thought about Aunt Jackie. She always said how proud she was of him. She gave him the strength he had to keep going when things were not easy, and they usually weren't easy. Claudia had never had that. She never had anyone who taught her to push through adversity. No one to lean on and know they would always be there for her.

He wanted to be that person for her. To have her know she could always count on him. No matter what.

Without stopping to think about what he was doing, Lance walked around the island and cupped Claudia's face in his hands. He tilted her head back and swooped down to capture her lips.

She melted under him, her hands grabbing the hem of his tee and holding on. She sighed and parted her lips when he requested entry.

Lance's heart pounded as he kissed her. He'd never felt so much from a kiss. Like everything was right in his world. Like there was nowhere else he'd rather be than right there kissing Claudia. Not in bed, not working, not doing anything but kissing her.

Damien cleared his throat, and Lance withdrew just enough to meet Claudia's gaze. "Hi."

She smiled. "Hi."

Lance smiled and walked back around the island, unable to wipe the smile off his face as he worked on food for them.

After they ate, Claudia excused herself to take a shower. Lance wanted to join her, but he thought she might need some privacy. He didn't want her to get sick of him.

He took a seat on the chair next to where Damien worked at the table close to the balcony. The blinds were open, giving them a view of the city. "Are you finding anything?"

Damien looked up at Lance. "I'm finding out you two have a lot more going on than you let any of us believe."

"I told Montgomery I kissed her before she disappeared."

"Sure, but you didn't tell anyone you were sleeping together."

"We weren't," Lance defended.

"But you are now."

Lance knew it wasn't a question. "Why are you on this?"

Damien stared at Lance for a long moment. "Do you think she's going to be able to face her brother and know she's the one who put him away?"

"Yes," Lance said, but he knew why Damien was asking.

"No you don't," Damien said.

"Look, all I know is she reported him when she saw him

kill that woman. Then she ran when the police didn't arrest him. She isn't the bad guy here."

"I know. But she didn't have all the information before."

"What information?"

"About what her mother did."

Lance sighed. He couldn't lie and say he didn't worry about how that would mess with Claudia. It clearly had, and when she faced her brother again, there was no telling how it would impact her.

"Michael has been the only constant in her life. He's her family. I don't think she's going to be able to put him away. To testify against him and admit what he did."

Lance wanted to argue. To tell Damien he was wrong. But he didn't know if he was. Could Claudia put her brother away for the rest of his life? She'd said more than once that he needed help. Would she stand in the way of him going to jail?

Lance didn't know the answers to those questions. And when Claudia joined them again and curled up next to him on the couch and turned on the TV, he knew it would make the difference in everything. Because if Claudia said he needed to go to a mental health facility, Michael would get away with everything he'd done.

And Lance could not stand by and let that happen.

MICHAEL WALKED out of the house and closed the door behind him. He swung the keys around his finger and went to the car parked outside. It was a risk to take a car in the same town where he ditched Hector's truck, but he needed to switch vehicles. It wouldn't be long before the police were looking for the truck.

Claudia was singing like a bird, telling the police way more than she should have known. If Michael could kill Hector again, he would have. The stupid son-of-a-bitch ran his damn mouth when they were in the house, talking about the cabin. Claudia must have heard him and told the cops.

He'd gone out to get supplies when the camera he set up told him someone was there. It would take the cops a while to find the wildlife camera on the roof of the little cabin, but when they did, they would know he'd been watching them.

Getting away from there and never going back was the only option. His fucking sister was ruining everything. All he wanted was to take care of her, and she was working with the damn authorities to put him away.

For what? A few whores and addicts who died? Big fucking deal. There were more everywhere. Like the one inside the house he'd just left.

Michael checked the license plate on the car. For a day, he could get around. Within twenty-four hours, he needed to make a change. He got in and started up the vehicle, backing out of the little driveway on the edge of town where no one would notice a car missing or a dead woman inside for a little while.

Michael headed east, his blood pumping with each mile he drew closer to Claudia. He had to pull over once to jerk-off into a napkin he found in the door. Hector never should have touched her, but the look Michael got of her with her clothes torn and her breasts on display was enough for him to never forget.

Claudia was perfect. Even more perfect than Lilian had been. He knew she would be, but he hadn't thought he'd get a chance to find out. She wasn't a tease like Lilian. Claudia was modest and sweet. She never acted on the attraction between them, even though Michael knew she felt it, too.

He got back on the road and kept going, passing through one sleepy town after another as the sun crept toward the horizon in front of him. Another state down. He was getting closer. It was a long drive, but if he could stop every afternoon, find someone who wanted to trade with him, and get a new car out of the deal, he'd be in Niagara Falls within three days.

And he'd make sure Claudia never left him again.

It was time she understood she belonged to him, and only him.

SIXTEEN

Four days after Claudia looked at pictures with Lance's boss, Montgomery returned to the hotel to talk to her.

"We found the cabin you mentioned." He didn't look as happy to share the news as Claudia expected him to be. "We found a lot more than that."

"What do you mean?"

"There were multiple graves on the property."

"Graves?" Claudia breathed.

Montgomery nodded. "It appeared as though someone was disposing of bodies there, burying them in shallow graves and assuming no one would notice since it's pretty remote."

"Oh my God," Claudia whispered. "How many?"

"They've found eight so far."

"So far?"

Montgomery nodded. "They are bringing in more advanced technology to scan the entire property. There is reason to believe more are there."

"What reason?" Lance asked.

Montgomery spared him a glance before focusing on

Claudia again. "Hector's body was one of the ones they found."

Claudia closed her eyes. She didn't feel sorry for the man who assaulted her. She wouldn't mourn him or miss him, but she was to blame for his death. "It's my fault."

"None of it is your fault," Montgomery said forcefully. He grabbed her hand and waited until she looked up to speak again. "Your brother is responsible for his own actions. Not you or anyone else."

"If I'd known what he'd been through, I could have pushed him to get help."

"He's sick," Lance said.

"He's still my brother," Claudia argued. She knew Michael was damaged. He would never be normal, but he deserved a chance to get help. He should have that.

"There was a camera hidden near the cabin. A trail camera. The kind hunters use to see if there is activity in an area before they go out there to hunt. It was fairly new." Montgomery raised one eyebrow as if his news would mean something to Claudia.

It didn't. "Are you expecting me to understand what that means?"

"It means someone put it up recently. If it was Michael, he would know there are people out there right now looking at the property. They've taken it down so he no longer has access to what's happening, but it doesn't really matter now that he knows we're onto him."

"Which means he'll be even more determined to come here," Claudia whispered.

"Not necessarily," Lance told her, taking a seat next to her and holding her hand. "He could just run."

"He didn't run last time. He came after me."

"Last time he thought he got away with what he did."

"Did they find the woman I saw him kill?" Claudia asked,

feeling a tiny bit of hope that her family would have some closure.

Montgomery nodded slowly. "They did."

Claudia saw the look on his face and knew that she wasn't the only woman they found. "No. No, tell me you didn't find Amber there, too."

"I'm sorry, Claudia, but they did."

Claudia lost it. She felt like she was kicked in the chest. Pain and anger and hopelessness flooded her. If she wasn't sitting, she would have collapsed. As it was, she could barely stay on the couch.

Tears poured down her face. Voices were distant, as if they'd moved to another room. Amber was dead because of her. Because Claudia went missing, and her brother wanted to find her. It wasn't fair. It wasn't right.

"I've got you," filtered in above the noise of her cries. "I'm so damn sorry. I'm here."

Claudia focused on the voice and realized Lance was holding her. He'd pulled her onto his lap and wrapped his arms tightly around her.

Claudia couldn't stop crying. She couldn't hold back her tears or her heartbreak. Amber was a good person. Someone who wanted to help others. She was kind to Claudia. Her only fault was that she was friends with someone with a ruthless monster for a brother.

"It's not fair!" Claudia shouted.

"No, sweetheart, it's not fair. It's not right. Amber shouldn't have had to die. She should be out there living her life." Lance soothed her with his words and rocked her as though she were a child.

It was an odd thing for Claudia since her own mother had never treated her the way Lance was. She'd never been soothed when she was upset. She'd been told to get over it and move on. Claudia always did, but having Lance acknowledge her emotions and not shy away from them validated the way she was feeling. It told her she was allowed to be angry and hurt and broken and scared.

"He didn't have to go after her. He had no right."

"No, he didn't. He needs to be stopped. Eight bodies so far, with more likely. We need to stop him."

Claudia shook her head. "I wish I knew where he was going. I mean, we know he's coming here. Where would he go? What is he after?"

"You," Lance said simply. "He wants you. Whether for revenge or something else, he wants you."

Claudia shivered at Lance's words. "I can't let him hurt anyone else. I can't, Lance. I need to do something. I need to help."

"Okay. Then let's help."

"We can't stay here."

"Whoa, what? No. You can't go out there. If he finds you—"

"Montgomery said if he wanted me dead, Michael would have killed me already. He had me chained up for weeks. He could have killed me anytime. But he didn't. He doesn't want me dead."

"He also left you to starve and be assaulted. He wasn't doing you any favors."

"No, but he's my brother. He won't kill me. But he will kill others. Let me help, Lance."

Lance looked up at his boss.

Claudia followed his gaze and saw Montgomery nod. "Thank you."

"That's not a free-for-all. You might trust him, but the rest of us don't. We will still want you in some kind of protection," Montgomery said.

"I understand," Claudia agreed readily. "I just want to help."

Montgomery ran a hand down his face. He closed his eyes and looked less than happy.

"Can I leave here? Maybe go back to my apartment?" Claudia asked.

"No," all three men said at once.

Claudia flinched. "Okay."

"He knows where you lived. That's the first place he'd look for you," Lance said.

"Then maybe that's why I should be there," Claudia reasoned. "If he's coming here for me—"

"We don't know he is," Montgomery said. "All we know is the cabin you told us about is a surrounded by a graveyard."

"If he went after Amber—"

"It's likely she's been there for months. Since Lance got you out of that house, we don't know where he's been." Montgomery looked as happy with that news as Claudia felt.

"But he's not at the house, and he's not at the cabin. Where else would he go?"

Montgomery looked at her and raised an eyebrow. "You said you wanted to help. How about helping us figure that out?"

LANCE WANTED to hit his boss. The insinuation that Claudia was hiding information was more than insulting. Montgomery didn't see her chained to that bed, the conditions she was living in. If he had, he would never question her loyalty to the man who held her there.

"He never left town. I don't remember him going anywhere. But obviously he was here. He told me the cops were asking questions about my disappearance and thought he had something to do with it. That's why he came here. He wanted to make sure I proved his innocence."

"How did he know where you were?" Lance asked.

Claudia shook her head. "I've been wondering about that."

"Then let's retrace your steps. You said you ran a year ago, but you've only been in Niagara Falls for a few months. Where were you between then?" Montgomery asked.

Lance watched Claudia. He'd never thought to ask the question. And she'd never volunteered any information. Could she be hiding something?

"I didn't have much money, and I definitely don't have experience disappearing. I started out going west, into Colorado. I didn't go far, though. I was only an hour or so away from home, and I didn't think it was far enough. Then I went north and ended up in Nebraska."

"How did you pay to travel?" Montgomery asked.

"I hitchhiked for most of it. There are lots of places that don't ask questions when a woman shows up like I did. I looked for places that had older women working and knew if I talked to them, they would hire me."

"They assumed you were running from someone." Lance was impressed and angry that the situation was common enough that Claudia could hide in plain sight. No one should have to run to save their lives, and it definitely shouldn't be so damn common that people didn't blink at it.

"I was, but I never corrected anyone when they said something about a husband or boyfriend," Claudia said.

"So you worked at these places. Is there a record of your employment?" Montgomery asked.

Claudia shook her head. "I'd pick up a shift or two, especially at first. I was a server for a lot of years growing up, so I could fill in without any real worries. I worked for tips, leaving my paycheck to whoever let me work. After a few months passed with no sign of Michael, I'd stay somewhere a little longer. A couple of weeks, a month at one point."

"Until you got here," Montgomery said. "Why?"

Claudia's gaze slid to Lance. He met hers evenly, wondering if she really stuck around for him.

"I went to the gym to shower. They have day passes, so I told them I was visiting from out of town and got a pass. Gyms are good places because they look at your ID but don't usually run it or pay much attention to it. I figured if I exercised a little bit, it was good for me. But then I saw Lance..." Claudia's cheeks turned red.

Lance's grin was automatic. He didn't notice Claudia at the gym, but he was thrilled she saw him.

"He was helping a young woman with a black eye. He approached her, and I couldn't hear what he said to her, but after a minute, she relaxed and nodded. He showed her some moves, how to throw a punch. He never once touched her, though. He was very careful with her, helping her but not taking advantage of her," Claudia explained.

"So you decided to stick around because Lance is a good guy?" Montgomery asked.

Claudia shook her head. "No, not right away. I considered it, but I knew if I was going to stay, I needed to find a job. I found the diner and picked up a few shifts. Even though Mallory wasn't the manager, I met her on the first day. She waited on me, and she was so sweet. I thought maybe I could stick around for a little while. A few days later, I went back to the gym and saw Lance again. I..." She blushed when she looked at him. "I thought anyone who helped a stranger who was in danger was someone who might help me, too."

"And no one knew who you were or why you were here?" Montgomery clarified.

Claudia tore her gaze from Lance and shook her head. "No. No one."

Lance remembered her boss at the diner. "Your boss. Evan. He said he'd seen your real license."

Claudia's face paled. "Do you think he had something to do with this?"

Montgomery shook his head. "No. We already looked into him. He's clean. It sounds like it took a bit to get him to admit he knew your ID was fake. Either he's a great liar, or he didn't have anything to do with Michael showing up here."

"But this is a tourist city. Michael could be here and no one would pay attention. If he looks like a tourist, the locals will ignore him," Lance said.

"True, but we don't know that he's here. No one has seen or heard anything from him since before you got Claudia out of there," Montgomery said.

"Then let me out of here. Let me go back to my life. Let me pretend everything is normal. Either he'll find me or he's not here," Claudia said.

"We can't do that," Montgomery said. "You're a witness, and a victim of his crimes. We can't put you in danger."

Claudia jumped up and threw her arms up. "You said you'd let me help. You said you don't know if he's here. It sounds like I'm not really going to be allowed to help."

"Ms. Reynolds—" Montgomery began.

"Oh, screw the Ms. Reynolds crap. Don't act like I'm someone valuable. The only reason anyone cares about any of this is because Lance figured out I was missing. These kinds of things happen all over the country every day. Women go missing. Men get away with abuse. People are murdered and assaulted, and no one does a damn thing about it. I want to help. I want to stop my own fucking brother from hurting more people, and you want me to sit here because I saw something. No. I don't accept that. The worst thing he can do is kill me, and if he does, then you prove what he did. You don't let him get away with it again."

Claudia's chest heaved with her breath. Her face was flushed and angry. She scowled at Montgomery.

Lance was impressed with her. He didn't like the idea of her ending up dead, but most people wanted to hide. To stay out of sight and not risk getting hurt. He didn't blame them, but for Claudia to insist she was allowed to go free...

"Claudia..." Montgomery stood. "I don't think—"

Claudia spun to face Lance. "Am I required to stay here? If I leave, am I breaking a law or something that will get me arrested?"

Lance shook his head slowly.

"Then I'm leaving," Claudia declared. "I'm not going to sit here while God knows how many more people are hurt or killed because he wants me instead."

Lance didn't move as she stalked past him and to the bedroom. She slammed the door, letting him and everyone else know she didn't want company.

"She's not wrong," Damien said from the corner of the room. He'd been quiet the whole time Montgomery spoke to Claudia, but without her in the room, he spoke on her behalf.

"I know she's not wrong," Montgomery said. "But that doesn't mean I like it."

"You're not the one sleeping with her. Imagine how he feels," Damien said, jerking his head toward Lance.

Montgomery glared at Lance. "You're what?"

"Thanks," Lance growled at Damien.

"It's important for him to know. We're not going to just let her go back to her apartment and not worry about it. But if you're already sleeping with her, she could stay with you and it won't be awkward," Damien suggested.

"No. Fuck. What the hell is wrong with you guys? First Austin, now you? What is rule number one?" Montgomery snarled.

"Don't fuck the client," Lance mumbled. "But she's not a client. She's not paying us."

"No, but the fucking FBI is!" Montgomery shouted. "You can't protect her when you're thinking with your dick."

"I'm not thinking with my dick," Lance hissed.

Montgomery glared at him, taking in his posture and narrowing his eyes.

Lance knew standing up to his boss like he was could be career suicide, but he wasn't going to back down. He liked Claudia, and leaving her in the hands of one of his teammates was not in the plans.

"Fucking hell," Montgomery said. "I can't think of another option, so I guess Damien's right. Take her home with you. We need to check your security, though. Clearly the building sucks."

Lance sighed with relief as the bedroom door opened. All three men turned to see Griffin emerging from the second bedroom, rubbing his head.

"What the hell is going on?" Griffin demanded.

Claudia threw her bedroom door open and paused long enough to answer. "I'm leaving. Nice knowing you."

"Whoa, whoa. No. Wait." Lance moved toward her before she could unlock the door and leave.

"We'd like you to stay with Lance," Montgomery said from across the room.

"No," Claudia argued.

"I know you want to stop Michael. We all do. But the way to stop him is not to have him kill you. You left because he killed someone else. Even if that was an accident like he told you, he buried her. He hid her body and pretended nothing happened. It's possible she wasn't the first person he killed, and we know for sure she wasn't the last. The only way to stop him is to put him away for good."

Lance watched Claudia as Montgomery explained his reasoning to her. Lance wanted her to be okay with it, to get it.

"Okay," she finally said. "I'll stay with Lance. But I'm not going to be captive. If I am, it'll be no different from staying here. Or chained to a bed in Kansas. I want to help."

"Deal," Montgomery said, walking across the suite and offering her his hand.

Claudia shook Montgomery's hand, then looked at Lance. "I guess I should have asked if you're okay with this."

"All I want is for you to be safe. Which is why I want to ask you to give us one night."

"Why?"

"We need to make sure the apartment is safe. That we have security and can see who's coming and going. Make sure that if your brother shows up, we know it and can stop him. Can you agree to that?"

"One night? Then we can leave here?" Claudia asked.

Montgomery nodded. "Yes."

Claudia drew a breath, then nodded. "Okay."

SEVENTEEN

Michael opened the door to the diner and smiled as the bell chimed to let everyone know he was there. He looked around, his gaze landing on the pregnant woman he was there to see.

"Welcome. Sit anywhere, and I'll be right over," she said.

Michael nodded and took a seat at a booth along the side wall. He grabbed the grimy menu from the corral on the table. He forced his smile into place, knowing if he wasn't friendly, he wouldn't get anywhere.

"I'm Mallory. I'll take care of you today. How are you doing?" the pregnant server asked.

Michael widened his grin. "I'm good, Mallory. You? You've got to be dying on your feet all day."

She groaned and chuckled. "It's not easy, but you do what you have to do, right? Can I get you a coffee or a water while you check out the menu?"

"Coffee would be great. Thanks, Mallory."

"You got it."

Michael watched her walk away, letting his gaze linger on her round ass as she stepped behind the counter that ran the length of the opposite wall in front of the kitchen. She was a little bigger than he usually preferred, but he wasn't there for her. She wasn't the kind of woman he could snatch without someone noticing. He had to get information the old-fashioned way from her.

"Here you go," Mallory said, flipping the mug on the table and filling it up from the pot she carried. "Do you need another minute?"

"I do, if that's okay." Michael smiled up at her, laying on all his charm.

"Of course. Take your time." Mallory smiled and waddled away to put the coffeepot back on the hot plate.

Michael studied the menu carefully, keeping his gaze on the door in case he needed to get away in a hurry. He decided what to order, keeping the menu in front of him as he studied the other patrons.

Old couple by the door, two men at the counter, young mom with two kids in the back corner. Mallory could handle all of them without help, but if more people showed up, she would be overwhelmed. It was an easy talking point, and one that could get him the information he needed.

Michael set his menu back in the caddy and sipped his coffee. It was better than he expected, but he didn't really give a shit about the coffee.

"Have you decided?" Mallory asked.

"Club sandwich, please."

"Side?"

"What do you recommend?"

"If you like crispy fries, I definitely suggest those. If not, the coleslaw is pretty good."

"I'll do the fries. Thanks."

"You got it."

"Thanks."

Mallory waddled away to put in his order, then came back with a glass of water and the coffeepot. "Refresh?"

"Sure," he said. "You're not getting a second to relax, are you?"

She chuckled, a husky, pleasant sound. "No, but that's okay."

"You should have someone else here helping you out. Especially so far along. When are you due?"

She rubbed her oversized belly and smiled. "About a week. But we're on watch every day."

"Is it your first?"

She nodded. "Yep. A boy. We can't wait. My husband is making me a little crazy, if I'm honest. He wants me to quit working now, but I just can't yet."

"Are you the only one who works here?"

"No, no. The other servers usually work the busier shifts. There was someone else working with me for a while, but she hasn't been here in a few weeks."

"That's ominous," Michael said, chuckling to soften the inquisition.

"Unfortunately, it might be. A few cops came in here looking for her. I haven't heard from her. I just hope she's okay."

"Wow. That's scary. Did they tell you what happened?"

A bell dinged and drew her attention. "I'll be right back."

Michael sipped his water as Mallory rushed to grab food from the window. She picked up silverware wrapped in a napkin and carried both back to him.

"Here you go. Anything else I can get you?"

Michael shook his head and focused on the plate. "All good. Thank you." He grabbed a fry as she turned. "You were right. That's good."

She laughed. "Happy to hear it."

Michael chuckled with her, wishing he'd gotten an answer about Claudia and what the cops said happened to her. He'd have to work it in somehow, but until then, he focused on his food.

The sandwich was good, and he had to admit the fries were too. But he wasn't there for the food. He was there to find his sister.

Mallory gave Michael space to eat his food, but when he was almost finished, she checked in with him, asking if there was anything else he wanted.

"That pie on the counter has been tempting me since I walked in. What kind is it?"

Mallory grinned broadly. "We have apple and pumpkin."

"Ooh, the apple. Please."

"Good choice. It's delicious."

"Can I buy you a slice? Talk you into sitting down for a minute to get off your feet?"

"You don't have to do that."

"No, but I'd rather buy you a slice of pie than have you delivering that baby before you deliver my pie." Michael winked at her.

Mallory laughed. She looked around the diner at the one table left. "Okay. You talked me into it. I'll be right back."

Michael watched her go and smiled as she came back with two large slices of pie, both with a generous scoop of vanilla ice cream on top. She slid one plate in front of Michael, then wedged herself opposite him in the booth.

"Are you going to stop working after you have the baby?" Michael asked, scooping up a bite.

Mallory shrugged. "I don't know yet. My husband wants me to, but kids are expensive."

"So is daycare, I hear."

"Very true. Do you have kids?"

Michael laughed. "God, no."

"No? You seem like a nice guy."

"You're sweet. And I would want to be settled before I had kids. My life is not very calm."

"Do you live around here?"

Michael shook his head. "No. I travel a lot for work and haven't been to this area before, so I decided to stick around. I hear there's a waterfall nearby that is pretty impressive."

Mallory laughed. "Yeah, a lot of people say it's a true wonder."

Michael chuckled. "Good to know. I'll have to take a look at it."

"You should." Mallory closed her eyes and enjoyed her bite of warm pie and cold ice cream.

"This is so good. You haven't steered me wrong yet, Mallory. I think I need to check out the waterfall you suggested."

Mallory laughed fully, resting her hand on her belly and wiping her eyes. "You're funny. If my friend was here, I'd introduce you to her."

"The friend the police are looking for?"

Mallory nodded, her face dropping. "Yeah. I really hope she's okay."

"Any idea what happened to her?"

Mallory shook her head. "No. They didn't tell me much. But people are looking for her."

"She's single, you said?"

"Yeah. Well... She was, but before she disappeared, she kissed her neighbor. So, I guess I wouldn't introduce you. She was so excited about it. She really likes him. He came in here to find her. He was pretty determined."

"That's good. I hope he does. It has to be pretty terrifying to have her leave with no word, and then to find out the police are looking for her."

Mallory drew a slow breath and nodded. "Yeah. It's so

scary. But her guy was on it. I don't think he's going to rest until he finds her."

"Good. See? That's why I'm single. I probably wouldn't have even noticed if someone was gone."

Mallory laughed and picked up her last bite. "I doubt that." She maneuvered out of the booth and stood. "Let me get your check. So you can go check out that waterfall."

Michael grinned and finished his pie as Mallory walked away. He pulled out his borrowed wallet and a few bills. Hector didn't need the cash anymore, but Michael did.

Mallory came back with his check, and Michael doubled the price of his meal so she had a really good tip. She gushed and told him it was too much.

"Not nearly enough," Michael said as he stood. "You told me about the fries and the pie and the waterfall. And you kept a lonely guy company for a little while. I will never forget that, Mallory. It means a lot."

"You are too sweet," she said. "Thank you. I hope you enjoy the rest of your time in the area. And I hope you stop in again before you leave town."

"I will make sure I do that. It was so nice to meet you, Mallory." Michael grabbed her hands and squeezed them.

"You, too." She hesitated a minute, then reached out and hugged him, her giant belly stopping her from getting too close. "I'm so happy you came in today."

"Me, too." Michael extracted himself from her grip and moved toward the door. He was almost to the door when she called out to him.

"Hey, I didn't catch your name. We haven't settled on a name for our son yet."

"Michael. I'm Michael."

"Michael. Nice name. Classic. Nice meeting you, Michael."

"You, too, Mallory."

He walked out of the diner and smiled. So, Claudia had a boyfriend who came to her rescue. A boyfriend who lived near her. Maybe that was why she opened the door when he had a fake package. Claudia was screwing around with the neighbor, and he came to her rescue.

Guess his instinct was right about her going back to Niagara Falls, but he was not expecting her to be shacking up with some asshole who thought he had a claim to her.

No one had a claim to her. No one but him. And he was going to make sure they both knew that.

CLAUDIA FELT BETTER when they finally left the hotel. It was beautiful, but being stuck there was no different for her than being chained to her old bed in Michael's house. She needed to know she was free, and until she stepped outside, she didn't feel like she was.

The only day she'd been in Lance's apartment was the night he kissed her. First, when she helped his stuff balloons into the box for the gender reveal, then when he insisted on patching up the cut on her shoulder. She tried not to touch anything when she was bleeding, but living with him was a totally different story.

"Montgomery had all your stuff moved here this morning," Lance said, rubbing the back of his neck. "Damien and Griffin are going to stay in your apartment. If that's okay with you."

"Why are they in my apartment? Is that safe?"

"They will be close if anything happens, and if Michael tries to get into your place, they can hold him until the police arrive."

"Oh. I guess that makes sense." Claudia hated that her

brother caused so much trouble. How did she not see what was going on with him?

"Are you hungry?"

Claudia shook her head as her stomach rumbled.

Lance chuckled. "I guess you are." He opened his freezer and looked inside. "I haven't been to the store in a while, but I have some frozen meals if you're okay with waiting for something to heat up. Or we could go out."

"Go out," she blurted. "If that's okay."

Lance closed the freezer and walked over to where she stood in front of the couch. He reached for her hands, bringing them to his lips. "I'm sorry we kept you locked up. I never thought about how it would feel after where you were."

"It's okay," Claudia said. "I didn't think about it either. Not until I realized I couldn't leave. I enjoyed my time with you."

"I hope being here is okay. I can sleep on the couch if you want me to. You staying with me doesn't mean—"

"I know," Claudia interrupted. "I slept better with you there. And I enjoyed everything else, too."

Lance grinned and tugged her into his arms. "I did, too."

Claudia didn't move as he held her close, sinking into the feel of a loving touch. She'd never known what it was like to be around someone who didn't hesitate to touch her and hold her. Lance had been quick to do both since he rescued her from Kansas.

"What are you hungry for?" Lance asked, pulling back to kiss her lips softly.

"Do you think it's okay to go to the diner where I used to work? I'd really like to check on Mallory and apologize to Evan." Claudia held her breath while she waited for his easy no.

Lance shrugged. "I don't see why we can't. Are you okay with Griffin and Damien joining us?"

Claudia nodded. "Really? You're okay with it?"

"I don't love the idea, but you've been through enough. If you want to see your friend, I'm not going to tell you no."

"Thank you!" Claudia launched herself into his arms.

Lance caught her without hesitation, holding her close and burying his nose in her neck.

Her breath hitched when he kissed her throat.

"Let's go see if they're up for food," Lance said, pulling back before he did anything else.

Claudia felt the loss of his touch immediately and laughed at herself. She'd just said she'd never known someone like him, and she was already missing it when he wanted to feed her instead of fuck her the minute they got to his apartment.

Lance thumbed out a quick text, then smiled when he got a reply immediately. "They're in. They were just figuring out the same."

"Sounds good. The food isn't the best, but they were good to me," Claudia said, feeling embarrassed about the diner. After spending a few days with Lance, she knew his tastes were a lot more elevated than hers. He might bristle when he went there.

"I don't know anyone who doesn't enjoy a diner. I might not go to one every day, but trust me when I tell you I'm not going to judge you or anyone else there."

Claudia sucked in a breath and nodded. "Okay."

"Let's go." Lance took her hand and led her out to the hallway where Damien and Griffin were waiting for them. The men kept Claudia between them and loaded into Griffin's SUV. Claudia and Lance sat in the backseat together, her hand in his.

Griffin went to the diner without Claudia having to tell them where it was, and she remembered Lance saying he'd been there when she disappeared.

The chime above the door told everyone inside they were

there, and Claudia burst into tears when she saw Mallory behind the counter.

Mallory rushed over and wrapped Claudia in her arms. "You can't cry around a pregnant woman. It makes me cry, too!"

Claudia laughed and hugged her friend, tears running down both their faces. "I'm so happy you're okay. And that you're not mad at me for disappearing."

Mallory shook her head. "I knew you wouldn't just vanish without a word. When your hunky man showed up asking about you, I was so scared for you. I see he found you. And you found two more hunky men. Look at you, girl."

Claudia chuckled. "He found me. How are you? I thought for sure you'd have had the baby by now."

"This little man keeps cooking. He's not ready yet, I guess."

"It won't be long," Claudia said.

Mallory laughed. "I hope not. My feet are getting more swollen every day, and my back is killing me. Andrew is pushing for me to stop working, but we really need the money."

"Can I help you?" Claudia moved to go behind the counter and get the coffeepot. She hated seeing Mallory working alone. "Why isn't someone else with you?"

Mallory nodded to Lance. "When they showed up, Evan was sure you'd be back. He didn't want to give your job away." Mallory squeezed her hand. "Let me go tell him you're here."

"No, let me. If that's okay," Claudia said, looking at Lance.

Lance nodded. "I'll go with you."

Mallory smiled and looked at Damien and Griffin. "I'll get these two men seated and get coffee and water for everyone?"

"Please. Thanks, Mal."

"I'm just so happy to see you, Claudia. So happy you're okay."

Claudia hugged her friend again, then went through the kitchen to the small office in the back. She knocked and waited for Evan to answer before she opened the door. "I heard you've been saving my job."

Evan's head jerked up at the sound of her voice. He jumped to his feet and rushed around the desk to stand in front of her, gripping her shoulders. "You're okay? Thank God." His gaze slid past her to Lance. "Thank you for finding her."

Claudia spent two weeks chained to a bed, thinking no one missed her and no one cared. Finding out she was wrong was the greatest gift she'd ever received. "I'm sorry I disappeared."

"Oh, please. It sounds like you didn't do it on purpose. But you're back. Are you okay? What happened?"

Lance cleared his throat, telling Claudia she needed to keep the details to herself.

"Hopefully one day I can tell you all about it. For now, I'm back, but I can't come back to work yet."

"Why not?" Evan slid a glare to Lance.

"Because the man who took me is still out there. Until he's behind bars, I am helping the police find him."

"Shit, Claudia. Seriously? Are you safe here?"

Claudia nodded. "Lance and two of his coworkers are with me around the clock."

"Well, I'm glad they found you."

"You are the reason we did," Lance said. "Thank you for what you shared. If we hadn't known where she might be, she'd still be there."

Evan looked at Lance, and for a minute, there was silence. Then Evan nodded, a small smile lifting the edges of his lips. "Good."

"Mallory is taking care of us, but as soon as I can, I want to come back. If you'll have me."

Evan grabbed her hands. "There will be a place here as long as you want one."

"Thanks, Evan."

Evan moved to go behind his desk again, then paused. "Mallory finally came up with a name for the baby, by the way. She met a customer yesterday who she gushed over all day. Said she's going to name the baby after the man."

"Oh, yeah? What's his name?"

"Michael."

EIGHTEEN

"Wʜᴀᴛ ᴅɪᴅ ʏᴏᴜ sᴀʏ?" Lᴀɴᴄᴇ ɢʀᴏᴡʟᴇᴅ. Iᴛ ʜᴀᴅ ᴛᴏ be a fucking joke. There was no way.

Evan gave him a confused look. "Michael. He was a customer. Mallory said he was really nice. Why do you two look like that?"

Lance met Claudia's petrified gaze. She shook her head, but they both knew it was exactly what they were thinking.

Michael was in town. And he'd been there a day before.

"He knows who she is," Claudia whispered. "She needs to be protected."

"Who knows what? What are you talking about?" Evan asked.

"The man who abducted Claudia was named Michael," Lance explained.

"What? How do you know who took her? Why is he not in jail?" Evan barked, coming around his desk again.

"He's my half-brother," Claudia said.

Evan stopped. "He's... Your half-brother is the one who took you?"

Claudia swallowed roughly and nodded. "It's a long story,

and not one I can get into right now, but if he was here, he knows I used to work here. He knows I was friends with Mallory. She's not safe."

"Are any of us safe?" Evan asked.

Lance looked at the older man. He was nice enough before and helpful, but he wasn't someone who was equipped for danger. He was more skin and bones than muscle. He looked like he'd be more likely to kill someone with the greasy food served at the diner than out of self-defense. Lance understood Evan's anxiety.

Claudia went to the door, but Lance stopped her.

"Hold on. We need to make sure we're not overreacting. What did this man look like?"

Evan ran a hand over his balding head. "I didn't see him. I was back here. Mallory talked to him for a while, though. She can tell you."

"Let's go ask her," Lance said, resting his hand on Claudia's back as the three of them filed out of the office.

Mallory was talking to Damien and Griffin, smiling at something one of them said. She looked up with the same smile when she noticed Claudia and the two men approaching, but it faded quickly. "What's wrong?"

"I told her about the man you met yesterday," Evan said.

"Oh, I wanted to tell her. Don't you love the name Michael?" Mallory asked.

Griffin and Damien stiffened the same way Lance and Claudia had, something Mallory noticed.

"Or not?"

"Mallory, what did this man look like? Can you describe him?" Lance asked.

"Why are you asking about him? What does it matter?"

"Because the man who kidnapped me was named Michael, and we think he might be who you spoke to yesterday," Claudia said with little emotion.

"What?" Mallory gasped, her face and knees sinking.

Damien and Lance were able to catch Mallory before she fell and guided her to a chair. Claudia took a seat next to Mallory, with Evan on the other side.

"How... He was so nice. Why...?" Mallory breathed the broken questions and looked at the floor.

"What color was his hair?" Lance asked.

"Brown. Shorter on the sides, but he was wearing a hat," Mallory said.

"Skin?"

"He was white, kind of pale. Stubbled jaw that looked like he hadn't shaved in a few days. Brown eyes."

"Piercings?" Claudia asked.

Mallory looked at her and nodded. "Both ears."

Claudia closed her eyes.

"What else? Thin, heavy, muscled, skinny, what was he wearing? Anything?" Lance prodded.

"He wore a leather jacket. Black. Zippers on the wrists. I noticed his fingers were stained. I figured he was a smoker, but I didn't smell it on him. He had a scar on his cheek. Below his left eye."

"He fell out of a tree when I was little," Claudia said. "Caught a branch. I don't remember it, but he's had that scar forever."

Mallory's hands shook. "Oh my God, it was him. And I was going to name my son after him."

"What did he say to you? What did he want to know?" Griffin asked.

Damien moved away, his phone to his ear. Lance nodded his thanks to Damien for getting in touch with the team.

"He was friendly. We just talked. He said he was here for work and decided to see the sights a little. There was nothing about him that made me think he was lying or playing me. God, I'm so stupid," Mallory cried.

"You aren't. He's manipulative, but he's also dangerous," Lance told her. "Did he ask anything about Claudia?"

Mallory shook her head, then looked at Claudia. "No, but I told him about you."

Claudia sucked in a breath.

"What did you say?" Griffin asked.

Mallory's eyes filled with tears. "I'm so sorry. I didn't think. He was saying something about how I should have help, how I shouldn't be working alone, especially pregnant. I said Evan was holding your job and that the police were looking for you. And..." She trailed off and looked at Lance.

"And?" he encouraged.

"And that her neighbor boyfriend was looking for her and I knew she'd be back," Mallory finished.

Lance met Damien's gaze just before the other man's eyes slid closed. Damien turned and walked farther away, the muscles in his back tense with the new information Michael had.

"I'm sorry. I shouldn't have said anything. I'm so sorry." Mallory burst into tears.

Claudia gathered Mallory into her arms and soothed her friend. Claudia's face was a mask of pain.

Lance wanted to pull Claudia into his arms and take away her pain. She was worried about her friend, but she needed to be worried about herself. Michael knew a lot more than any of them realized, which meant he either spent more time in Niagara Falls when he first grabbed Claudia or he had a way to get information now. Either way, it wasn't good.

"Montgomery is on the way," Damien said quietly.

"Who's that?" Mallory asked.

"That's our boss. He's going to want to put you in protective custody until this is over."

"I can't do that. I'm... Oh!" Mallory stopped, then peed herself.

"What the hell?" Griffin hissed, backing up to avoid the gush.

"My water just broke," Mallory whispered.

CLAUDIA HELD the baby boy close to her chest and smiled at the peacefulness on his face as he slept. Mallory and Andrew did not name him Michael, but the whirlwind of a day that brought him into the world made it impossible for them to discuss other names, so he was still just Baby Boy.

Claudia had never been around someone when they went into labor. Mallory was prepared for it and possibly the calmest one of them. She told Evan to take care of the customers, but he refused to let her go to the hospital without Andrew and packed up the food for the customers to go. Evan told the cooks to clean up and take the rest of the day off with pay, then he ushered everyone out the door.

Griffin and Damien brought the SUV to the door and got Mallory inside, handing over her keys to Lance to drive him and Claudia to the hospital. Evan followed behind in his own vehicle.

When they all arrived, Mallory was whisked away, and the rest of them were told to sit in the waiting room. Andrew arrived and thanked them all for taking care of her, then said they didn't have to wait. None of them moved.

Griffin went to the cafeteria to get food for all of them since they missed lunch. Montgomery came back with Griffin and added to their vigil. When dinner rolled around and they were still there, Damien talked to the nursing staff about getting something delivered and ordered enough pizza for the staff in the maternity wing.

It was nearly midnight when Andrew came out and told

them the baby was born and both he and Mallory were doing well. He tried again to get them all to go home, but none of them were willing to.

Andrew came out again an hour later and asked if Claudia wanted to meet the baby. Andrew said Lance could come with her, only because the hospital knew there were extenuating circumstances. Mallory handed the baby to Claudia as soon as she walked into the room, then apologized for putting her in danger.

"You did nothing wrong," Claudia assured her friend. "I'm sorry he came to you."

"Is he dangerous?" Andrew asked.

"Yes," Lance answered. "Which is why none of us are leaving. My boss wants to make sure you are all safe."

Andrew let out a shaky breath. "Thank you. I... Having a baby is enough of a worry, but then this... We would appreciate the help."

"Can we speak for a minute?" Lance asked Andrew, nodding to the other side of the room.

Andrew nodded, and the two men stepped away, their voices too soft for Claudia to hear.

"He's very protective," Mallory said.

"He's already a great father," Claudia told her.

Mallory snorted. "I meant Lance, silly."

Claudia shook her head. "He's just doing his job."

"No, he's not. He likes you. When he came into the diner, I knew exactly who he was. He had a look in his eyes. He was scared he'd never see you again."

Claudia looked at Lance, her cheeks warming when he looked up and met her gaze.

"That man has it bad."

"Oh, it's not like that."

"Are you going to stand there holding my newborn baby

son and tell me I'm wrong and you're not sleeping with that sexy man over there?"

"I didn't say that," Claudia said, burying her face in the sweet smelling little boy.

"I knew it," Mallory hissed. "Good for you. It's about time you enjoyed things a little."

Claudia sighed. "I just… It's a weird situation."

"Of course it is. Your brother kidnapped you, your boyfriend stole you back, and your brother is here to get you again? That's made for TV weirdness. If you told me it was an ex, I'd almost get it, but your brother?"

"I saw something he didn't want me to see," Claudia whispered.

"Oh." Mallory was quiet for a minute. "I'm so sorry I said anything to him."

Claudia shook her head. "Stop. You did nothing wrong. How many times have we told customers things? You had no way of knowing it would be an issue."

"Still, I feel bad."

"Look at this beautiful boy and stop feeling bad," Claudia said, ducking to transfer the boy back to his mother.

Mallory accepted him into her arms and smiled. "He's pretty perfect, isn't he?"

"Yes, he is. You just need to name him."

Mallory groaned. "Ugh. I know. Maybe we should name him Lance?"

Claudia snorted.

Mallory chuckled. "We'll figure out something."

"What about Evan?"

"Damien?"

"Griffin?"

The two of them giggled as the men came back to them.

"What are you two laughing about?" Andrew asked.

"We're trying to find a new name for your son," Claudia told him.

"I was thinking Callahan," Andrew said.

Mallory gasped. "What?"

Andrew shrugged. "We don't have to, but..."

Mallory's eyes filled with tears. "It's perfect. And maybe Elliott for his middle name?"

Andrew nodded, a shaky smile lifting his lips. "Yeah."

Andrew leaned over and kissed her. He pulled back and kissed the top of the baby's head. "Callahan Elliott."

They shared a sweet smile and another kiss before Mallory looked up at Claudia and Lance. "Callahan is my maiden name, and Elliott is Andrew's middle name."

"Oh, that's so sweet," Claudia said.

Lance slid an arm around her waist. "Better than Lance."

Claudia and Mallory chuckled.

Mallory yawned, and Andrew took the baby from her arms. "You need to sleep."

"We'll head out. I'll be back in a minute," Lance said to Andrew.

Andrew nodded. "Thank you."

"Congratulations," Lance said.

Claudia hugged Mallory and offered her congratulations, then followed Lance out of the hospital room. "Why are you going to be back?"

"Montgomery wants to introduce himself to them both. He's going to stay here tonight. He's already spoken to hospital security and has shared Michael's picture, but he wants someone outside their door." Lance held her hand as he led the way back to the waiting room.

"I hate that they're dealing with this," Claudia said.

Lance nodded. "Yeah. The good news is it's unlikely he's going to go after them. He got what he needed. He found out about me. If he was going to hurt her, he would have when he met her."

"I hope you're right," Claudia said. Lance signaled to Montgomery, then left Claudia to wait with Griffin and Damien.

When Lance returned, the four of them went back to the apartment. It was almost three in the morning, and they were dragging, but the men insisted on checking both apartments for anything out of place before they settled in for the night.

Claudia felt awkward using Lance's bathroom and climbing into his bed. He assured her he wanted her there, but they still didn't know each other well.

Lance slid under the comforter next to her and pulled her into his arms, kissing the top of her head. "You looked really sexy holding that baby."

"What?" she asked with a laugh.

Lance shrugged. "I don't know what it is about seeing a beautiful woman holding a baby, but it was all I could do to not drag you into a storage room."

"You have to be joking."

Lance shook his head. "Not even a little."

"So, I take it that means you want kids."

Lance exhaled slowly. "I never really thought much about it. I've spent so much time working, and I never met anyone I wanted to spend the rest of my life with. Having kids wasn't a priority for me."

"Then why did you... Why did you like seeing me?"

"I don't know. But when you picked Callahan up and smiled at him, you just looked like nothing in the world could get to you, and if anything ever tried to get to him, you'd burn the world to the ground to protect him."

"I would," she said without hesitation.

"That's hot," Lance said, leaning over her to kiss her.

She inhaled sharply, her body tingling as his fingers found the bare skin between her shorts and tank top. He came to bed in shorts and a tee, but the night before, he slept naked. So did she.

Claudia hitched her heel over Lance's calf, encouraging him to get closer. He moaned and rolled on top of her, his erection notching between her thighs and lighting her up. He didn't make a move to hurry things along, sliding his hands up to support himself on his elbows as he kissed her slowly.

Claudia rocked against him, wrapping her legs around his and trembling at the feel of him on top of her. She lifted his shirt and dragged her nails over his skin.

He moaned at the scrape and lifted to yank his shirt off. "I've dreamed of having you in my bed for months."

"Months?"

He nodded, barely visible in the dark. "I can't tell you how many times I've woken up wishing you were here with me."

"What would you have done if I was?"

He groaned and jumped up. "First, I would have made sure you were naked."

She smiled as he slid off the bed. He pressed her shirt up and followed the path with his lips, kissing her skin as he exposed it. When he reached her breasts, he sucked her nipples into his mouth, then removed her shirt. He did the same with her shorts and panties, then dropped his clothes to the floor.

"That's it?" she teased him.

"Oh, Claudia, that's nowhere near it." He opened his nightstand drawer and grabbed a condom from the neat pile contained in the organizer.

"You have more than one here."

He bent over her and nodded. "I'll buy more tomorrow."

She laughed. "There have to be a dozen in there."

"Later today," he said, sharing her laughter against her lips.

Claudia didn't think there would be anything to laugh about when they found out Michael was in town, but Lance helped her to forget why she was in his apartment instead of her own. He helped her to feel like she was a normal woman and they could be a normal couple.

Lance kissed her as she laid back onto the mattress, bringing him down on top of her. He supported himself over her and slowly pulled away from her lips to trail his lips down her throat. He paused to appreciate her nipples again, then kept going, settling between her thighs and pressing them wide.

"Second, I'd make sure you were too tired to leave my bed anytime soon."

Before she could remember what he was talking about, his tongue was inside her. "Oh, yes."

He hummed in agreement and licked his way through her folds to circle around her clit, returning to her entrance and plunging his tongue into her.

Claudia writhed on the bed, eager for more as she fought to reach her first orgasm. It continued to stay just out of reach. The penetration inside didn't reach far enough, and the attention on her clit didn't last long enough.

She groaned and huffed, making Lance laugh at her antics.

"Are you getting frustrated?" he whispered against her thigh.

"Yes," she mumbled.

"What was that?"

"Yes! Oh, fuck, yes," she moaned as he sucked her clit into his mouth. "Holy. Fuck. Yes. Oh, fuck."

He didn't reply with his mouth otherwise occupied, making her scream nonsense. Lance pushed two fingers inside her while he tortured her clit, thrusting her up and over the edge in seconds.

Claudia came with a shout and some begging for him to do it again.

Lance didn't give her a chance to come down before he was sending her right back up, adding a third finger inside her and flicking her clit with the tip of his tongue until she whimpered. He curled his fingers and nipped at her tender flesh, and she soared once more.

"Oh God, oh God, oh God. Yes. Fuck, yes!" Claudia shouted, riding out her orgasm and feeling the edges of her consciousness fading.

"Damn, you taste good," Lance said, kissing the inside of her thigh before dragging his lips up her body. He tore open the condom and rolled it on before Claudia was fully aware of what was going on.

She looked at him as he poised at her entrance.

His gaze strayed to his cock, then back to her face.

"Don't hold back on me," she whispered.

He plunged inside her, not stopping until he was fully seated. They both moaned as their bodies connected. Lance stilled inside her, reaching for her hands before he pulled back.

Claudia held his hands, pushing back on them when he leaned forward and pulling him closer when he drifted too far away. With her legs hanging over the edge of the bed, she had no leverage, but she wrapped her thighs around his hips and held on as he pounded into her, his body taking what it needed from hers.

"Fuck. Claudia."

She felt him swelling just before he slammed into her and stopped, his cock pulsing with his release.

"Oh, fuck. Yes." He grunted, his body twitching slightly before he stilled. "Jesus."

She smiled up at him. Breathless. Boneless. Fully sated.

"Wow."

She chuckled, pulling him toward her to let him rest for a

minute on top of her. "Yeah." She held him in her arms and wondered when she'd started to fall for the man who didn't want kids until her, took care of everyone around him, and made her feel like the sexiest woman alive.

Because she was no longer falling. She was there. And she was in big trouble.

NINETEEN

Lance laid in bed long after Claudia fell asleep, thinking about what they knew so far. When he met her, he never thought they'd be where they were. In his bed, for one, but also protecting her from a threat.

He loved one, not the other.

If Michael was in Niagara Falls, he was definitely there for Claudia. And now he knew about Claudia and Lance. Was going to the diner because he knew they would find out, or did he think he could be there unnoticed?

And did it matter? All that really mattered was that Michael was in town, and he was there for Claudia. To silence her for good, most likely.

Lance hugged her sleeping form closer, squeezing her until she pushed him away in her sleep. He released his hold just enough for her to settle again, then pressed his nose into her hair and inhaled to draw her scent into him.

He laid like that, breathing her in, until he drifted to sleep.

He woke with a start hours later when he heard footsteps. He bolted upright to peer around the room.

"Sorry," Claudia whispered from the bathroom door. "I needed to use the bathroom, and I was going to make coffee."

Lance looked at the window, seeing the first glow of sunlight around the edges of the blackout curtains. "I'll start the coffee."

Claudia closed the bathroom door as Lance swung his feet over the side of the bed. He scrubbed a hand down his face and padded to the kitchen. He scooped grounds into the basket and added water, pressing start before Claudia walked up behind him and pressed her naked body to his.

"That's better than coffee to wake me up," Lance said, his voice rough with sleep and desire.

Claudia chuckled and kissed his back. "I agree."

Lance turned in her arms, kissing her quickly and realizing her breath was minty fresh. "Did you brush your teeth?"

She nodded. "I didn't want to horrify you with my morning breath."

"I could never be horrified by you, but now I have to do the same thing since I know it bothers you."

Lance kissed the top of her head, then hurried to the bathroom to brush his teeth. He used the bathroom and washed his hands, returning to the kitchen as the coffeepot sputtered its last puffs.

He opened the fridge to get creamer, and Claudia poured two mugs of coffee. They fixed their mugs and carried them to the couch, curling up together in front of the dark screen.

Lance was used to noise. He always had the TV on, and at the office, it was always busy. Sitting in the quiet with Claudia, without feeling the need to fill the silence, gave him a peace he didn't know was missing from his world.

Claudia finished her coffee and leaned against his side. He wrapped an arm around her without hesitation, enjoying the feel of her body against his. He stroked up and down her arm, occasionally copping a feel of her breast. When she sucked in a sharp breath, he set his mug on the coffee table.

She sat up when he moved. Lance grabbed her hand before she could go too far and pulled her onto his lap. He slid one hand into her hair and tilted her head to the side so he could kiss her.

She returned his kiss, her tongue peeking out to touch his lips. His cock surged against her hip, wondering if it was time for him to get in on the action.

Lance wasn't in a rush to get to an endgame with Claudia. Holding her, kissing her, felt like enough at the moment. His mind raced with the events of the last few days, and having her close and knowing she was there with him was all he needed.

A gentle knock on the door sifted through the haze of their kisses, dragging his lips from hers and reminding him they were both naked. "Go to the bedroom."

"What are you going to do?" she whispered.

"Find out who's at the door." Lance watched as she hurried to his room and closed the door before he went toward the front. He looked through the peephole and groaned when he saw Damien on the other side.

"Are you going to let me in?" Damien asked.

"Not unless you want an eyeful. Give me a minute."

"Copy," Damien said.

Lance knocked on the bedroom door and opened it slowly. "It's Damien."

Claudia visibly relaxed. She was already dressed in sweats and a tee, but her heavy breasts swung free beneath the fabric. "What does he want?"

Lance shrugged. "I told him to give us a minute." Lance grabbed a pair of shorts from his drawer and tugged a tee on, then led Claudia back to the living room. He opened the door, letting Damien and Griffin in. "What's going on?"

Damien and Griffin nodded at Claudia before focusing on Lance.

"Montgomery checked in. He had a quiet night at the hospital. Zeke's been running Michael through facial rec in the area, and he's hit a few times." Griffin glanced at Claudia as he spoke.

"Where?" Lance demanded.

"Mostly around here. We know he was in the apartment, and since he now knows about you, it makes sense he would be in this area."

"The plan doesn't change," Lance said.

Damien and Griffin exchanged a look.

"What?"

"We need to find him before he hurts anyone else."

"Agreed. And?"

"Are we just going to sit here and wait for him to show up?"

"What did you have in mind?"

"We've been analyzing his movements. Looking at where he's been and how he's getting around. We think he's staying close by, and we've narrowed it down to a few places."

"Okay? Let's go check them out," Lance said, ready to put Michael behind bars.

"Something about it doesn't feel right," Damien said.

"What?" Lance asked.

"It's too easy. Too basic."

"What the hell does that mean?"

"It means I think he's playing with us. He's fucking around. He knows we're watching him, and he's trying to get us to do what he wants us to do." Damien was frustrated. His body language showed his agitation.

"What does he want us to do?" Lance asked.

Damien shook his head. "I don't know. That's what I'm struggling to figure out. But this is a guy who went unnoticed for years. No one knew he existed or cared. Claudia ran, and he was still unknown, even to the cops in his own town. He managed to get here, swipe her out from under your nose, and hide her for weeks in his own damn house, and now he's back and he's just walking around like he's an innocent man? It doesn't make sense."

"Then what does?"

"He's setting us up," Damien reiterated.

"Again, to do what?"

"We don't know," Griffin said. "But I think Damien's right. Reynolds is not changing his actions. He's walking the same roads, he's sticking to the same places. He's even gone to the same bar every night for the past few days."

"So we go fucking get him," Lance barked. "Why the hell are we sitting here and talking about this?"

"It's too easy," Claudia said.

Lance wanted to argue, to tell them it didn't always have to be difficult, but Claudia's comment made him stop. "Not everything has to be hard."

"No, but Michael is smart. He didn't do all of this to get caught. He is doing all this because he wants me. He's not going to be careless. Not after all of this." Claudia's tone was resigned.

"So what do you think? You know him. What is he trying to do?" Lance asked.

"I think they're right." She gestured to Damien and Griffin. "He wants the FBI to tip their hand. To show up where they think he's going to be so he can be somewhere else."

"We can't just let him walk around and not try to stop him," Lance argued.

Claudia shook her head. "No, but if we fall into his trap, we're not going to stop him."

"Where would he go?" Griffin asked, directing his question to Claudia.

Claudia shook her head. "I don't know."

Lance closed his eyes and shook his head. "Where have you seen him? Where has he been going?"

Griffin and Damien looked at each other like he was crazy.

"Maybe if Claudia knows where he's been, it'll help her figure out where he could be hanging around," Lance said.

"Oh, good thought," Griffin said.

Griffin handed his phone to Claudia and sat next to her on the couch, sharing the information they had.

Lance hung back, grabbing their forgotten mugs and retreating to the kitchen with Damien following him.

"Took you a minute to let us in," Damien said.

Lance slid a glare his way. "And?"

Damien shrugged. "Just commenting. She looks like she just rolled out of bed."

"We were drinking coffee."

"And?"

"And nothing. What do you want from me?"

Damien examined him closely, not missing anything. None of them did. It was their job to see things others wouldn't see, and until Lance was being studied by his teammate, he saw it as a good thing.

Not anymore.

"Are you sure about this?"

"About what?"

Damien jerked his head toward Claudia.

"About her? What the hell do you mean?"

"Listen, I agree with what she said. I said it, too, but I don't love how easily she agreed to holding off on going after him."

"So now you think we should?"

"I didn't say that."

"Then what are you saying?" Lance growled.

Damien held Lance's gaze for a long moment. Long

enough that Lance knew he wasn't going to like what Damien said. "Is she protecting him?"

"You think she'd protect the man who kidnapped her and chained her to a bed?" Lance hissed. He slid a look toward Claudia, who wasn't paying attention to him. "Why in the fuck would she do that?"

"He's her brother. I think anything is possible."

"Not that. She wants to stop him. If she didn't, she wouldn't have gone to the police a year ago."

"Things have changed."

"Yeah, he's proven he's an even bigger psycho than she thought he was. We found his burial ground. Why would she want to protect him?"

Damien shrugged. "I just wanted to put it out there."

"You don't trust her."

"I don't trust many people without a damn good reason. I trust my gut, and I trust myself. But no, I don't trust her. Not fully. She's not proven to me she can be trusted."

"She's the one who needs protection. She's not the one we're protecting someone from."

"Maybe, but something isn't adding up."

"And you think it's her?"

Damien stared at Claudia, studying her carefully. After a minute, he shook his head. "I don't know. All I know is Michael Reynolds is here, and he's after her, and he's not hiding that he's around. It's all too easy, and all I can think of is there's no way it's this easy unless there's something else that we're missing."

Lance wanted to argue, but if he was honest with himself, he agreed. Michael showing up at the diner could have been a mistake where he didn't think he'd be found out, but him wandering the city and not bothering to hide his routines was not the same thing.

He was playing with them.

"Claudia has an idea," Griffin said. "Want to check it out?"

"All of us?" Damien asked, sliding a look toward Lance.

"We can get something to eat while we're out," Griffin said.

The four of them shrugged and nodded. "Let's get ready to go."

CLAUDIA FOLLOWED Lance into his bedroom. He closed the door behind them, keeping Griffin and Damien on the other side of the door. She grabbed a bra and tossed her shirt aside.

"Do you think he'll be there?" Lance asked, his gaze stalling on her naked breasts. He wanted to forget all about Michael and tackle Claudia into bed, ignore his responsibilities and focus only on her.

Claudia shrugged, slipping her bra into place and dislodging his plans. "I don't know. But I don't have a lot of guesses. He wouldn't stay somewhere expensive because he doesn't have money for that."

"And you think this would be where he would go?"

"I don't know," she said with a sigh. "I don't know. He didn't call me up and say, 'hey sis, I'm coming to town to kidnap you again, and while I'm waiting to get you alone, I'll be staying at the fleabag motel five minutes from your place. Come say hi.'"

Lance looked at her like she was unhinged, and she felt a little like she was. She wanted Michael caught, but she was worried about him. She hadn't been able to stop thinking about what he told her since he confessed the details of his relationship with their mother.

"I don't want him to end up dead," Claudia whispered.

"Michael?" Lance spat.

Claudia nodded. "Yeah. He needs help. He needs someone to talk to. He suffered something horrible, something no kid should have ever gone through. He deserves a chance to heal."

"And what about the people he killed? What do they deserve?"

"That's what I'm talking about," Claudia cried, spinning on Lance. "That attitude. Michael was damaged. Our mother, the person who was supposed to protect him, caused this. She assaulted him and forced him to be someone he's not."

"You can't blame someone else for his actions. You can't say he isn't responsible for what he did. For the lives he took."

"I'm not saying that. All I'm saying is he needs help."

"It's too late for that, Claudia. He had you chained to a bed. Unable to move. He broke your nose, then broke it again when he straightened it. He murdered a man who touched you, and a woman who was your friend, and many, many others. He would have killed you eventually. And you want him to go talk to someone about how bad his mother was?"

"How can you judge him? You don't even know him!"

"I know enough. I know he's a psychopath who doesn't value life. He takes what he wants from others without regard for their lives. How can you protect him?"

"Because he's still my brother," she whispered.

"And Amber was your friend. But he ended her life when he thought she might have helped you to get away from him. How can you let him get away with that?"

Thinking about Amber brought tears to Claudia's eyes. Lance was right. Amber was dead and gone because of her.

"We have to stop him. We won't go in there with the intention of hurting him, but if that's how it ends up, we're not going to hold back because he had a fucked up childhood."

Claudia glared at him.

"Do I feel bad for the guy? Yes. That's the truth. No one should have had to go through what he went through, but do I think that gives him the right to go around killing and kidnapping people? Fuck no."

Claudia swallowed the lump in her throat. She didn't have an argument, but she knew if she was there, she could try to protect her brother. She could make sure he was safe. He would listen to her.

A knock on the bedroom door had her hurrying to finish getting dressed. She turned her back to Lance as she pulled her shirt over her head, then took a minute in the bathroom to gather herself.

She was going out with three protectors to face a man she'd been alone with most of her life.

And she was going to do everything in her power to make sure all of them came out of the situation alive.

TWENTY

Michael leaned against the fence and watched his puppets dance. He pulled the string, and they did exactly what he wanted. What he expected.

He shook his head. It was almost too easy.

He watched from his hidden spot as three men stalked toward the motel room he'd rented. Claudia was in the middle of them, her gaze swinging around the parking lot as they drew closer to the room.

Michael's fingers itched to go to her. To touch her. To pull her into his arms and keep her away from these other men.

It was easy for him to pick out the one she was fucking. The white guy kept looking at her, as if he worried the most that something would happen to her. He stayed in front of Claudia, with the Black guy in the back, and the Asian one leading the way. None of them had any clue what they were about to walk into.

Michael took a deep drag of his cigarette, then dropped it to the ground, rubbing it out with the toe of his shoe before slowly letting out the breath he was holding.

The Asian man knelt in front of the door, the others

flanking him to watch for threats. Like he'd fucking rush them when they were doing exactly what he expected them to do.

"Dance, puppets, dance," Michael mumbled.

The door opened, and the neighbor and the Black guy disappeared inside while the Asian man stood and spun to keep Claudia safe.

Michael stared at her, his breath frozen in his lungs as he watched her chest rise and fall with her rapid breathing. In, out, in, out. His dick hardened as he stared, his gaze focused on Claudia and only Claudia, his mind blocking out everything and everyone else until she was all he could see.

She didn't understand how much he loved her. That they were meant to be together. She'd never understood it. He thought she would eventually, but she started making plans to leave him. Talking about moving out and getting her own place.

Everything that happened in the last few years was her fault. He snapped when she said she was moving out. Like any man when the woman he loved said she was leaving him. How could she expect him to act any differently? To not fight for her?

All those other whores he fucked were replacements until Claudia saw the truth and came to him. Admitted she belonged with him.

Her choosing to stay was step one. And she finally agreed. Once he told her he needed money. Once she knew he was counting on her. He thought things could go back to normal, but then she ran.

Straight into the arms of the fucker who dared to touch her as Michael watched.

The neighbor pulled Claudia into his arms, and she clutched his shirt. She buried her face in his chest. He kissed the top of her head, then cupped her jaw and brought her lips to his.

Lips that belonged to Michael. Lips he was meant to kiss for the rest of their lives. Lips that were tainted by the asshole who thought he had a right to touch the woman Michael loved and swore to protect forever.

He would pay for that. He would die for that. Because no one touched what belonged to him.

And if Claudia was dumb enough to let him, Michael would show her the error of that behavior. Because she belonged to him. She was always meant to be his. And if he couldn't have her, if this protector was going to stand in the way, no one would get to have her.

LANCE COULDN'T LET GO of Claudia. Not after he saw the inside of the motel room. With pictures of her everywhere. Pictures of her when she was chained up, going to class when she was younger, pictures of her since she'd been back in Niagara Falls with him.

Some had Claudia alone, some with Amber, some with Lance. Michael had been stalking them, following them, close enough that he was taking pictures, and Lance didn't know it.

He felt violated. He knew she would feel the same when she saw the pictures. He wanted to show her and wanted to protect her from it at the same time.

"How bad is it?" Claudia asked against his chest.

"Bad," Lance said.

"Can I see?"

Lance sucked in a breath. "I don't want you to."

Claudia responded with a nod.

"Montgomery is on his way with Agents Sloane and John-son. They're all a little pissed we didn't wait for them," Griffin said.

"We didn't know what we were walking into," Damien replied. "It was a hunch, no proof of anything."

"That's what I told them. They still wanted to be kept in the loop," Griffin said.

"Next time," Damien said, rolling his eyes.

Lance steered Claudia away from the door. He pulled back enough to meet her gaze. "Are you okay?"

She laughed mirthlessly. "Do you really think there's an answer to that question?"

His lips lifted slightly in a smile. "I fucking hate this."

"Me, too." Her words were sadder, more broken.

Lance pulled her back into his arms as a car with lights blazed into the lot. The police car screeched to a stop right in front of them, and two cops jumped out with guns pointed at the four of them.

"Freeze!" one cop shouted. "Hands where we can see them!"

"Whoa, what?" Lance snapped back.

The cop closer to him swung his gun to Lance, putting Claudia directly in the line of fire. "Let me see your hands!"

Lance moved swiftly, tucking Claudia behind him.

Both cops shouted, both guns pointed at Lance and Claudia. Griffin and Damien tried to be heard over the cops, but no one was standing down or pausing to hear what was going on.

Another car with lights pulled into the lot, slower. The siren whooped as they drew closer, then Agent Sloane and Agent Johnson got out of the vehicle.

"What the hell is going on here?" Adam demanded.

"We got a call about three men and a woman breaking and entering at this motel," one of the cops said.

"Put your guns down," Lorelei snarled at the cops.

"Excuse me, ma'am, but who are you?"

"We're special agents with the FBI, and these four people are working with us on an active case. Kidnapping, homicide, and narcotics. So unless you'd like us to bring you in for impeding that investigation, put your damn guns down," Lorelei growled at the cops.

The two cops exchanged a glance before one turned his focus toward the agents. "Can we please see some identification?"

Lorelei and Adam already had their badges out and on display for the cops.

"Thank you," the one said. "All good." He lowered his gun, prompting his partner to do the same. "We apologize. The call came in a few minutes ago, and we were close. There was nothing in our system to tell us that this was part of an active case."

"It was kept quiet so we didn't tip off the man we're looking for," Adam said with a sidelong glance at Lance and the others. "We have reason to believe he was staying in this room, and we didn't want him to run. It looks like we weren't so lucky."

"Who called it in?" Lance asked. There was no way it was just a coincidence.

The cops shook their heads. "Anonymous tip."

Lance shared a look with Adam and Lorelei. "He's watching us."

Claudia tensed behind Lance, her grip on the back of his shirt tightening. "What?"

"Check the room," Lance told the agents instead of answering Claudia.

Adam and Lorelei shared a look before moving toward the open door. They disappeared inside with Damien, with the cops looking at each other.

Griffin stepped forward. "Can we get some information from you?"

The officers let Griffin lead them away. He spoke quietly to them and nodded toward the room.

"Michael is here right now?" Claudia asked, her voice shaking and quiet.

Lance turned to face her, protecting her with his body in case there was a threat lurking. "We didn't do anything to draw attention to ourselves. We had a key from the attendant. Griffin checked that there wasn't a trigger on the door before he swiped it open. None of the other people staying here would have any reason to think we weren't supposed to be here. But if Michael is watching us, he could have called the police to try to get us arrested."

Claudia shuddered, her gaze sliding past Lance and searching the area. "Then we can bring him in."

"We will set up a search, but he's probably already gone. He might have been here when we arrived."

"Why would he stick around?"

Lance paused. "That's... The room." Lance ran toward the room. "Get out! Get the hell out of there! Go now!"

"What?" Adam came out of the room with Lorelei and Damien right behind him.

"Go!" Damien shouted, pushing the agents forward.

All of them started to run but only got a few steps away before the door ignited.

Lance moved back as the rest of the room went up in flames.

"What the hell?" Lorelei breathed.

"He had it all rigged to ignite. It would have trapped anyone inside," Damien breathed.

Griffin shouted at them to move back and ran toward the room with a fire extinguisher. He stopped, pulled the pin, and squeezed the trigger.

The foam spurted from the end of the short hose, dousing the flames on the doorframe. Griffin moved closer to the room, working to put out the fire at the door so he could go inside, but before the doorframe was clear, the extinguisher was empty.

"Find another one!" Adam shouted to the two cops who were gawking at the scene.

Lance stood and watched as the entire room lit up. Curtains flickered and went up quickly. The bedding on both beds in the room ignited, burning all the pictures Michael had laid out on one of the beds. Clothes, furniture, every piece of evidence in the room went up in flames in a matter of minutes.

The cops rushed back with fire extinguishers as Montgomery pulled into the parking lot, followed by two fire trucks.

The next few minutes were a mad rush of moving vehicles to give the firefighters access to the room. The captain refused to send anyone into the room when he heard there was no one inside.

Lance and the others stood and waited for the fire to be put out, knowing with complete certainty that everything that would help them was gone.

TEARS RAN down Claudia's face. It was late, and they were finally back at Lance's apartment, and she felt like she'd been crying for hours.

Lance didn't want her to see the pictures Michael had of her, but she knew about them. She knew he'd been following her in Niagara Falls, had been trailing her at home before she ran, and had a camera in her bedroom at home.

She couldn't help but wonder if there were more pictures of her. The ones of her chained to the bed were recent, but when did he put in a camera? Judging by the pictures, it was somewhere near the door to her bedroom. But did he have older pictures? Of her in there alone? Of her before she ran? Naked. Touching herself.

She shuddered at the thought. If he had those, he didn't lay them out. What did that mean?

Claudia didn't know how she was supposed to feel. There was no guidebook for *my brother is a psycho and seems to be in love with me*.

"What can I do?" Lance asked.

Claudia shook her head.

"I'm sorry you had to hear about all of that."

Claudia drew a breath and let it out slowly. "Was there any sign of him?"

"No," Lance said, sounding as angry as she was.

"But he was there."

Lance nodded. "There was a small pile of cigarettes near the fence at the edge of the property. It looked like he'd been waiting for us, ready to set the fire."

"He knew we were going to show up there." Claudia squeezed her eyes shut. "He knew I would think that was where he'd be. How does he know me so well?"

"The same way you know him. You're siblings. You're family. You've lived with him your entire life. You know things without really knowing how you know them."

"But he's still a step ahead of us. What if he did the same thing to your apartment? Set up charges to go off when he decided it was time." Panic was flooding in, making her voice climb with her adrenaline.

"He didn't do that," Lance said, sounding far too sure for a man who'd spent most of the day with her answering questions.

"How do you know? What if he was here when we were out there looking for him?"

"Hey, hey. He wasn't. I know he wasn't because I have security cameras. I always had one that could see the door, but when you came to stay here, we added more. There are cameras in the hallway leading to our floor, pointing at both ends of the hallway, and on the other side of the hall covering our doors."

"What?"

"It's why we took a day before we came here from the hotel. I didn't want to freak you out by telling you everything we'd done, but we have eyes on this place. Damien and Griffin are watching all the time."

"Like Michael was. I'm sure he didn't want to freak me out by telling me he'd put a camera in my bedroom," she snapped.

"I'm not like him," Lance said sadly.

Claudia closed her eyes and drew a breath. "I know. I'm sorry. I'm just..."

"I know. We should get some sleep."

Claudia nodded and followed him to the bedroom. "I'm going to take a shower."

"Okay," Lance said.

Claudia wanted to fix things with Lance. She didn't blame him for what was going on. She knew he was helping her, protecting her. And him putting up cameras to watch anyone coming toward their apartments was not the same as Michael installing a camera in her bedroom.

She hurried through her shower, wishing she could scrub off the feeling she got whenever she thought about Michael having pictures of her. When she got out of the shower, she dried off and wrapped her hair up in the towel, then brushed her teeth and got ready for bed. She walked out of the bathroom with the towel wrapped around her body.

Lance was sitting on the edge of the bed, and when she came out of the bathroom, he slid past her and mumbled something about taking a shower.

Claudia stood in his room and listened to him go through

his routine. She dried her hair with the towel and pulled on one of his shirts, then slid between the sheets. She curled on her side and waited for him to emerge.

Lance turned off all the lights in the bathroom before he opened the door, wearing shorts but no shirt. He glanced at her as he walked out. He grabbed her towel off the edge of the bed and hung it up, then turned off the lights in the bedroom. He hesitated by the door before taking a step toward the living room.

"Don't go," she whispered.

"I didn't think you'd want me near you."

"I overreacted. I'm sorry. Please."

Lance nodded, barely visible in the dark room, and approached the bed. He climbed into bed on his side, lying on his back and not reaching for her.

Claudia turned to face him, sliding over to put her head on his chest. "Is this okay?"

"Yes." He cleared his throat when his voice cracked. "Yeah."

"I'm not mad at you."

"Okay."

"I wouldn't have been able to handle any of this without you. I know what you did was to make sure I was safe. What he did..."

Lance tensed at the mention of Michael. "I hate that he's doing this to you."

"You will stop him. I know you will."

"I don't." Lance vibrated with tension. "I want to kill him. I want to hurt him. I want him to understand the pain he caused. The pain he inflicted. Not just on all the people he killed, but on you. He's put a look on your face that is..." He drew a breath that lifted her head. "He needs to pay for what he's done."

"I agree."

Lance seemed to relax at her words. "You should get some sleep."

"Are you going to sleep?"

"I will when you do."

"I don't know if I can sleep."

"It's been a long day, Claudia. You're safe with me. I'm not going to let anything happen to you."

She drew a breath and nodded. "I know. I've always known that."

"Good. Then try to sleep, sweetheart. It's been a long day."

Claudia wanted to argue, but his soft voice was already lulling her to sleep. "Keep talking to me."

"Okay," he whispered, then told her stories about his childhood until she drifted to sleep.

TWENTY-ONE

Lance crept into the room quietly, wondering how he got there. Everything was fuzzy, like it wasn't real. He didn't recognize where he was or know why he was there, but something was pushing his feet to keep moving forward.

He heard voices, one male and one female. As he drew closer, he recognized Claudia's voice. He called out to her, wondering where she was. He didn't see her, but he heard her.

"Lance," she cried out, drawing his attention to the other side of the room.

Lance saw her, chained to a bed like when he'd rescued her from her brother's house. The bed wasn't there before. What was going on?

He rushed toward her, dropping to his knees next to the bed. "What happened?"

"You have to get out of here. He'll kill you."

"Who will? I'm not leaving you."

"Lance, go. Michael is home."

Laughter rang out from the darkness surrounding them. A haunting sound of a man who was unhinged, separated from reality.

Lance turned to see the man they'd been chasing, but instead of a man, all he saw was smoke. Smoke that had glowing red eyes and grew in size, then streaked toward him as if flying.

Lance woke up choking, struggling for breath as if the smoke had actually choked him.

"Lance! Lance! Are you okay?" Claudia shouted at him.

Lance let the dream fade and reached for her, tugging her close to his side as his lungs filled with clean air.

Claudia snuggled against his side, her arm across his body and holding him tight.

They were silent for several long moments before Claudia spoke. "Are you okay?"

Lance nodded. "Just a bad dream."

"You were calling for me," Claudia said.

"I'm sorry I woke you."

"It's okay."

Lance laid there for another five minutes, unable to slow his racing heart or the twitchy feeling the dream left inside him. He kissed the top of her head, then slid out of bed.

Lance padded to the kitchen and opened the fridge. He grabbed the carton of orange juice and poured himself a glass, leaning against the counter to drink it. He closed his eyes and tried not to remember the dream.

He saw the red eyes as if they were real, as if they were right there. Lance had fought against some of the worst humans in existence, but he'd never been so personally invested in winning the battle. In the military, he followed orders. He did what he was told to do. He didn't question it, and he had no intention of doing so.

Even after joining Rose Protection Agency, he was doing a job. Protecting people who needed their help. He liked the work, liked feeling useful. But this job was different.

Protecting Claudia was not like anything he'd ever done.

Because if he failed, Claudia would be gone. She wasn't just his neighbor, his client. She was… more.

"Are you okay?" Claudia whispered.

Lance jumped. She was leaning against the bedroom doorframe, wearing his tee. His cock jumped at the sight. She was his. Maybe not forever, but for now, she was his. She was in his shirt, sleeping in his bed, and loving him with her body.

The dream made him ache for her. He didn't want to be away from her. He couldn't stand the thought of something happening to her. Not without her knowing how much she meant to him.

He set his glass in the sink and walked toward her. She straightened when he got closer, her gaze tentative when he stopped in front of her. "I don't want to lose you."

"Me, too."

Lance leaned down slowly, drawing out the seconds until his lips met hers. He sucked in a breath at the feel of her softness. Finally, finally, everything was okay. Everything was right. She was there. She was safe.

His hand went to her hip, the soft cotton of his shirt protecting her skin from his. He squeezed her hip, loving the way she trembled at his touch.

He needed her. Like a man possessed, he needed her. He couldn't think or breathe or function without knowing she was his, even if it wasn't forever. Even if she only wanted him because he could protect her, he had to have her. To claim her. To know she was his for a time.

Lance backed her up into his room, not stopping his progress until her legs hit the mattress and she lost her balance. He followed her down, not letting their fall break their kiss. He covered her body with his, bunching his tee to expose her flesh to his greedy hands.

He groaned when he found nothing beneath his tee. "You don't have panties on," he whispered against her lips.

She shook her head, wrapping her arms around his neck and holding him to her.

He thrust his tongue between her lips, filling his hand with her supple body. He needed to know what every inch of her felt like and tasted like. He couldn't walk away from her until he did.

Probably not even then, but he wouldn't have a choice when the threat against her was over and she could live her life. She would leave him.

But she was there now. In his bed. Writhing against him. Begging him with her body for what he could do to her.

Lance slid off the bed, dropping to his knees. He looked up at her, catching her gaze as her breath hitched. He pressed her knees wide, getting a peek at the sweetness waiting for him. He skimmed his hands from her knees upward, rubbing his thumbs over her muscles until he reached her center.

Her breath faltered again, and he looked up to find her watching him, propped up on her elbows.

He kissed her right knee, then let his tongue follow the path his thumbs had taken, sliding all the way up her thigh until he reached her center. He skipped over her sensitive flesh, nipping her left thigh when she groaned at him.

She gasped, her hips shifting to find him.

He kissed his way down her left thigh to her knee, then lifted her leg up onto his shoulder.

"Lance."

"You're so damn beautiful, Claudia."

"Lance."

He looked up at her, seeing the question in her gaze. "I need you."

She sucked in a breath but didn't say anything.

He could feel her unease. He knew that claiming her the way he needed to was more than what he'd done. It was pushing the boundaries. It was crossing over into more than just sex. More than just two people who were forced into the same place.

But he was already there. He wasn't just sleeping with her because she was around. She wasn't convenient for him. She was the only woman he wanted. The only one he couldn't wait to touch and kiss and make laugh.

Not that he could say any of that. She wasn't in a place to start anything. But when she was, he wanted her to remember what she deserved.

Lance grabbed her right ankle and lifted that leg over his shoulder, zeroing in on where he wanted to be. He used his thumbs to spread her wet flesh, to expose her clit to his view and his tongue. He licked the tender nub.

Claudia gasped, her hips surging off the bed. "Lance."

He wanted to tease her, to drag out her pleasure and make her beg him for more, but one taste of her and he was gone. He was like a man possessed, needing to hear her cry his name and feel her come over and over again until she didn't want to leave his bed ever again.

She pressed her hips closer, meeting his tongue on its way to another taste of her. She gasped, and he groaned.

Lance grabbed her knees and pulled them down, giving himself more room to work between her legs. He flicked her clit with his tongue and growled at her mewl. He wanted her to scream, to beg, to coat his tongue and never forget the way he made her feel.

He brought his hands to her soft skin and teased her inner thighs. She lifted one leg from his shoulder and dug her heel into the mattress, shifting away from him. He looked up at her as she did the same with the other heel before dropping her knees to the bed, exposing herself completely to him.

Lance cupped her ass and brought her body to his mouth. He pressed his tongue into her channel and tasted the burst of her flavor on his tongue.

"Oh, God, Lance," she whispered.

He pulsed his tongue inside her, licking his way to her clit once more and tugging her open with his thumbs on either side of her entrance.

"Please," she cried.

He didn't know what she was asking for, but he pushed his thumbs into her, licking her clit at the same time. She whimpered and wiggled against him, her breath rushing from her in pants and gasps as he worked her body toward orgasm.

She went still, like she'd fallen asleep, but the ripples inside her said she was close.

Lance closed his lips around her clit and sucked hard, coaxing the nub out with the tug. He replaced his thumbs with two fingers, thrusting them deep into her and curling them to tip her over the edge.

"Oh, fuck. Yes." She moaned, her body trembling with her orgasm as she made noises that had his cock surging.

He released the suction on her clit and fought back against the pulsing in his cock. He wasn't done with her yet. He added a third finger to her core, pumping faster in and out of her body.

"Lance. Yes. Oh. Oh!" Her channel rippled around his fingers, pulling him in.

He reached up with his free hand to cup her breast and found his tee blocking his progress. He retreated, finding the edge of his shirt, then slid his hand beneath the fabric until he brushed the underside of her breast.

She moved, her body rocking from side-to-side. The shirt tugged over his hand until it disappeared.

Lance looked up from his position, finding her gaze on him.

"I wanted to see your hand on me," she said.

His dick jumped. Fuck. One hand inside her body, his

tongue on her clit, his other hand fondling her breast. All while she watched him.

He couldn't tear his eyes from her, staring at the hungry look on her face. Her gaze slid to his fingers on her nipple, then back to his face, mostly hidden by her curves. When she looked down at him, he nipped at her clit.

Her core flooded when he did.

"You like that," he whispered against her body.

"Yeah," she whispered, as if ashamed by her reaction.

"Don't hide from me, Claudia. I want you to feel good." He licked her clit and brought it to his teeth.

She shook against him, her belly rippling with her movement. "Lance. So good. Please."

Lance didn't make her ask. He knew what she needed, what they both needed. He tugged on her clit gently, then sucked hard, pinching her nipple at the same time and pounding his fingers into her.

"Oh, fuck. Yes. Fuck. Lance!" She cried and came, her body gushing all over his hand. One hand landed on his head and gripped his hair, holding him in place as she rolled from one orgasm into another, aftershocks and orgasms becoming one while he wrung every bead of pleasure he could get from her before tipping over the edge with her.

Her hold on his hair finally eased, and he yanked the nightstand drawer open. He tore open a condom and rolled it on, holding himself still as he positioned himself at her entrance.

"Please," she whispered, prying her eyes open.

Lance watched himself disappear into her, every inch of his cock welcomed in by her warm and willing body.

"Lance."

He looked up at her, meeting her gaze and seeing all the things reflected back at him that he'd been feeling.

He wanted to look away, to hide from how he felt. He

wanted to protect himself and save a piece of himself for when she was gone, back to her whatever life she wanted to have.

But he couldn't.

He stared into her eyes, wishing he could watch the colors change as he loved her. Next time, he needed the lights on. To watch the flush on her body and the pleasure on her face as he made love to her.

His body moved, his base instincts taking over as he poured all of himself into her. He wanted to tell her how he felt about her, to beg her never to leave him, to say the words on the tip of his tongue. But he didn't. He slammed into her, letting his body say all the things his mouth couldn't. He shifted until she gasped, then doubled his efforts to send her flying again.

She reached for him, her hands finding his in the dark. She held onto him, her muscles fluttering.

He pulled one hand from hers and leaned over her, knowing the angle would help her.

She opened her mouth in a silent O. She brought her hand to his cheek, and he leaned into her touch.

Lance couldn't hold back. Her touch, her body, her sounds. He grunted. "Claudia. Fuck, Claudia."

"Yes," she moaned softly, her body rippling around him and giving him that last nudge over the edge.

Lance surged into her, stilling inside her as her body drew him in until his energy was depleted. He collapsed onto her, devoid of everything except love for her.

Claudia held him, her breath as labored as his was, and her body shaking with the same tingly energy.

Lance found his strength and kissed her neck before retreating to the bathroom. He took care of the condom, then washed his hands and went back to the bedroom.

Claudia was on her way to the bathroom but stopped in front of him. She lifted her chin and smiled at him.

Lance leaned down to kiss her, giving her time to back away.

She wrapped her arms around his neck and held onto him, not letting him pull away after a quick kiss. "Thank you," she whispered against his lips.

"Thank you," he said, smiling.

They traded places, and Lance waited for her to join him in bed. She curled against his side, holding onto him the way she did when he woke from his dream.

He shook off the dream and held her tighter. She was there. She was safe. He wasn't going to let Michael hurt her. And when Michael was gone, Lance would tell Claudia he loved her.

CLAUDIA LOOKED up from the TV and smiled as Lance walked into the room. Spending days with him continued to amaze her. She thought he would get bored with her, or maybe she'd get bored with him, but every day brought something new to discover.

She couldn't wait to... If she was honest, she couldn't wait to spend the rest of her life learning everything there was to know about him. The two weeks they'd been living together, even knowing Michael was out there looking for her, were the best of her life. She didn't want it to end, even after she was safe, and she felt like he could be thinking the same. It felt presumptuous, but she wanted to spend the rest of her days with him. To learn all the things that made him tick. Find out what made him laugh and cry and—

Scream?

"What was that?" Lance asked, his smile morphing instantly to a scowl.

Claudia was on her feet, following him to the door, where the scream came from. "Do you think..." Claudia didn't voice her concerns.

Lance checked the peephole, then opened the door. "Did you hear that?"

"Yeah, I—"

"It sounded like someone fell," Griffin said at the same time Claudia spoke.

Lance moved into the hallway, looking both ways. He turned back to Claudia and said, "Stay here," then pulled the door closed behind him.

Claudia watched through the peephole as Griffin and Damien rushed past the door. All three men moved to the stairs and disappeared from her view.

She wanted to know what happened. If someone was hurt. But she didn't dare leave the apartment. She was fine inside. She was safe.

Claudia forced herself away from the door and went to the kitchen to get a glass of water. She didn't like feeling like she couldn't do anything.

The door opened, and she set her glass down. "Hey, what happened? Is everyone okay?"

Lance didn't answer her, so Claudia moved out of the kitchen to see him.

"Lance, what..." She gasped. "Michael."

"Hey, sis. Nice to see you. I thought we could have a chat while the boys are... otherwise occupied." Michael flipped the lock, the sound of the deadbolt like a gunshot.

Straight through her heart.

TWENTY-TWO

Claudia gasped, freezing in place. She always thought that if she was in a truly life-threatening situation, she would be able to react. To fight. To do the right thing.

But standing face-to-face with her brother, a knife in one hand and a gun in the other, all she could do was stare at him.

"Aren't you going to offer me a drink? Or maybe we should just get right to it."

"What…" her voice was soft, almost inaudible to her own ears.

Michael moved closer. "What am I doing here? Well, I'm glad you asked. I'm here for you, sis."

"What do you want?" Claudia managed to ask.

"I want you. And before your boyfriend comes back, we should get out of here."

"I'm not going anywhere with you."

Michael chuckled and rolled his eyes. "You will, but it's so much easier if you go willingly. Don't you think?" He rubbed his thumb across his nose, reminding her of what he did to get her to leave with him last time.

"Lance is right outside the door. I could scream, and he'll be in here in seconds."

Michael waved the gun at her. "And he'll be dead in seconds. As soon as he steps in the door, I'll shoot him. Do you really want to be responsible for another death, Claudia? Amber and Rachel and Adrian helped you get away from me a year ago. Then there's Hector. He touched you. I had to put him down for it. Did your new boyfriend touch you? Because if he did, I'll happily put a bullet in his head, too."

"No. Leave Lance alone. He didn't do anything."

"No? He didn't touch you? He didn't fuck you, sis? He didn't make you fall in love with him and promise you a future where he'd never let anything bad happen to you?" Michael moved closer with each word until he was right in front of her.

Tears flowed down her cheeks as Michael spoke. She backed up, putting herself in the corner, trapped and scared.

Michael caressed her hair, tucking the loose strands behind her ear and letting his fingers linger on her neck, the gun brushing her skin as he did. "He doesn't deserve you, sis. He's not good enough for you. But if you say he didn't touch you, I'll let him live. As long as you come with me. Did he touch you, sis?"

Claudia shook her head, hoping Michael didn't see the lie in her eyes.

"No? Do you promise me? Because I want you to be pure. To be innocent for me. Are you, Claudia?"

She swallowed the bile rising up in her throat. Tears ran faster down her cheeks. She wanted to scream. To run. To get the hell away from Michael. But she couldn't have him kill Lance.

Michael's hand tightened around her neck. "Answer me, Claudia. Did you let him touch you? Did he fuck you?"

Claudia shook her head. "No. No. He didn't do anything."

Michael's hand stayed tight on her neck, cutting off her air. He stared at her, his dark eyes studying her carefully.

Claudia's eyes burned with the loss of air. She reached up to grab his hand, and he released her. She collapsed, sucking in a breath as Michael took a step away.

"We need to go."

Claudia watched him move around the apartment, stalking toward the sliding door off the dining room. Lance didn't have a table in the dining room, just a bar and stools for entertaining.

Michael moved around the bar and pushed the vertical blinds aside to see out the back door. "Let's go."

Claudia glanced at the front door of the apartment, wondering why Lance wasn't back yet. She took a step toward the door, but heard a growl coming from behind her.

"I wouldn't do that, sis."

She turned and saw the gun pointed at her head.

"I'll kill you first, then him. Or maybe I'll just hurt you, so you can watch him die. And I'll make sure it's not easy for him. He will feel every single heartbeat as he gets closer to death. Every gasp for air. Every last bit of hope that he might survive this to live up to those promises you claimed he didn't make you to protect you and keep you safe."

"Michael."

"Your call, Claudia. Life with me, or death with him?"

LANCE EXHALED as the ambulance drove away with Mrs. Mitchell in the back. She was still unconscious, but the paramedics said it was expected with the fall she had.

Lance had no idea what happened to the older woman. She woke up a few times, but she wasn't able to tell them anything about how she fell.

It didn't sit right with Lance. Mrs. Mitchell wasn't a young woman, but she never seemed to have trouble with the stairs or any mobility issues. How did she fall? Was she pushed?

But who would do that? Someone could have been in a hurry and it could have been an accident, but then why leave her there?

It bothered Lance the entire time he was with Mrs. Mitchell. Judging by the looks on Damien and Griffin's faces, they were thinking the same thing.

"That was weird, right?" Griffin asked.

Lance nodded. "Yeah. Very weird."

"Is she normally unsteady?" Damien asked.

Lance shook his head. "Not that I've ever known."

"Do you think she was pushed? Someone bumped into her?" Damien asked.

Lance shrugged. "I wondered that, too, but why would someone knock her down and not stay to help?"

Damien, Griffin, and Lance all came to the same conclusion. They turned and took off up the stairs. Lance got to the door first and found it locked. He knocked on the door.

"Claudia. Sweetheart. Open up. It's safe now. Let me in." Lance pressed his ear to the door as Griffin clenched his fists beside him. "Claudia!" Lance pounded on the door.

"Move," Damien barked, coming out of Claudia's apartment. He held up a key.

Lance moved to the side to let Damien unlock the door. Damien opened the door, stepping inside first.

Griffin tugged Lance's arm, holding him back.

Lance jerked his arm free. "What the hell are you doing?"

"Just wait a minute," Griffin said.

Lance flinched when he realized what Griffin was worried about, then pushed past his partner to go into the apartment.

"It's empty," Damien said, walking out of the bedroom. "Balcony door is unlocked."

"That's not possible," Lance barked, crossing the room to the balcony. "I never use it. It's always locked."

"I'm guessing they went out that way."

"They?"

Griffin and Damien shared a look.

"Go check the footage," Lance demanded.

Griffin left the apartment, going to Claudia's to pull up the footage of the hallway. It should show them any activity from the hall, including if anyone went into the apartment when the three of them were checking on Mrs. Mitchell.

"How the hell did he get in here? And why would she leave?" Lance hated that Claudia was vulnerable again. With her monster of a brother.

"He knocked Mrs. Mitchell down the stairs. Hit her first, then shoved her down. He waited around the corner, and walked in here when we were all checking on Mrs. Mitchell," Griffin said, bringing a computer over for the three of them to look at.

Lance watched the footage, his stomach turning when he saw Michael hit Mrs. Mitchell and push her backward. The asshole hid just out of sight, tucked in a little corner Lance didn't pay attention to when he went to check on Mrs. Mitchell.

When Michael let himself into Lance's apartment, Lance wanted to reach through the screen and kill the fucker right then and there.

"Where did they go?"

Lance stared at the screen and waited for them to walk out. To go down the hall to the other stairwell. To see her again and know she was alive when she left the apartment. That she didn't leave on her own.

"There's another camera," Damien said.

"What? Where?" Lance snapped, glaring at the two of them.

Griffin tapped the keyboard, and another view appeared on the screen.

Lance ground his teeth as Claudia's feet hit the ground. "Go back."

Griffin clicked the screen to go back, the video skipping to where the balcony was empty. Griffin hit play, and the three of them stared as Claudia and Michael appeared on the balcony. Michael had a gun trained on her. He tucked a knife into his waistband.

Lance wanted to vomit.

Claudia said something to Michael.

"Is there audio?" Lance asked.

Griffin clicked something else and the sounds of outside burst from the computer. Griffin paused the video and did something, then hit play again.

"Where are we going?" Claudia asked, stalling on the balcony.

"Away from your protector," Michael growled. "Where he won't find you."

"Are you taking me back home?"

Michael looked back at the apartment, then pointed the gun at her head. "Move, sis. Now."

Claudia flinched, then moved to the edge of the balcony. She swung one leg over the railing, then the other. She held on to the metal handrail, then reached for the support structure at the corner.

Lance watched as she climbed down the corner rail. Michael was right on top of her, jumping the last few feet when Claudia was on the ground by herself.

"Let's go, sis." Michael slung his arm around her shoulders and pulled her to him.

Claudia slid her arm around his waist.

"Why is she touching him?" Lance whispered.

"What did they say?" Damien asked.

Griffin tapped the volume and backed up the video, then hit play again.

"I love you, Claudia."

"Me, too."

Lance took a step back. "No. No. She didn't... No. Fuck!"

Griffin slapped the laptop closed, ending the video as Lance stalked to the other side of the room.

"Lance..." Damien tried.

"No. Just. I need... She didn't mean it."

"She said it, though," Griffin said.

"Shut up! Just... stop."

Lance paced his apartment. There was no way. No way Claudia meant it. No way she loved him.

"She was lying. She doesn't love him. Not like that. Not at all. Not after everything he did to her."

"He's her brother, man. I mean, can you ever really not love a sibling?" Griffin asked.

"She knows he needs help."

"So she's on his side now?" Griffin asked.

"No. No. She's just pretending. You saw the gun. And the knife. She's not on his side," Lance said, wishing he felt as confident as he sounded.

"I agree," Damien said.

"What?" Lance asked. After the way Damien questioned him the week before, his insistence that he didn't trust Claudia, hearing Damien defend her was the last thing Lance expected.

Damien looked at Griffin, then slid his gaze to Lance. "My gut tells me there's more to it. We have no idea what he said to her during the time they were in here. I don't think she would have left with him unless there was a damn good reason."

"Like he had a gun. And a knife?" Griffin suggested.

Damien shook his head as Lance nodded.

"No. She's tough. She's not going to let something like that bother her. I think it was more than that," Damien said.

"Like what?" Griffin asked.

"I don't know, but I feel like there's more to it." Damien stared for a second, then shook his head.

"All that really matters is that I find her. Whatever the reason is that she left, I need to find her." Lance went to his room, needing to gather everything he would need to track her down and save her.

"What the hell? What are you doing?" Griffin asked, on Lance's heels.

"I'm going to find her."

"Alone? Again? You're going to pull this shit again?" Griffin snapped.

Lance turned and looked at his partner. Griffin was right. And Lance knew it. "I need to find her. I know she didn't go with him because she wanted to. I can't leave her with him."

"Then let's do this the right way. Let's do this together."

Lance met Griffin's gaze and nodded. "Okay."

CLAUDIA SAT on the bed and watched Michael pace the motel room. He hadn't said much to her since they arrived at the seedy motel on the outskirts of the city. She'd never been to it, and she would have been happy to have never been. A mouse ran past the door when they arrived, and a spider spun a web in the corner of the room.

She was going to die in that room. She knew it as well as

she knew Michael had completely detached from reality. He was mumbling to himself, ignoring her almost entirely.

She never thought she'd wish she'd died back in her bedroom in Kansas, but as she sat there and wondered what in the hell Michael was doing, she wished he'd gotten it over with before. She wished she'd never known what life could have been like with Lance. Never loved him, and felt his love for her.

Maybe it was resolution or fear or just acceptance, but Claudia convinced herself that what she and Lance shared was love. She was afraid of those feelings, big feelings, when she was with him, but sitting on the dirty bed, in the disgusting room, she wished she could have told Lance she loved him. That she could have thanked him for saving her from Michael, and could have made him realize how much that meant to her.

She'd never see him again, but maybe he'd know. Maybe he'd look back at the time they shared and know she loved him in the only way she could.

"No. No!" Michael shouted, punching himself on the side of the head.

Claudia wanted to ask who he was talking to, but she was fairly sure she knew the answer, and she wasn't going to like it.

Michael started pacing again, and Claudia just sat and watched him. She'd ignored all the signs, all the things that seemed so obvious as she stared at the man she thought she knew.

Michael was always eccentric, marching to his own beat. Claudia thought it was charming at times and irritating other times, but she never saw the depths of her brother's torment. She never understood that he was truly fucked up.

Their mother did that to him, but Lance was right when he said Michael could have made other choices. He could have chosen to be a better person. The difference between two people who experienced the same thing could be paramount.

Michael could have turned around the hell in his life, he could have gotten help.

It took a strength her brother didn't have to ask for help. To admit that there were things in his past that weren't okay. Claudia had worked with children who'd been victims of abuse, and she knew the trauma they faced, even as preschoolers, would likely stay with them forever. But Michael...

Michael made it sound like what their mother did to him was okay. That he was happy he'd been in a relationship with a woman who should have been protecting him, not sleeping with him.

"You're mine," Michael said, stopping in front of Claudia.

He seemed to look through her, not at her, and she kept quiet.

"I'm the man of the house. It's my responsibility to take care of you. To love you. To never let anything bad happen to you. I was always there for you. Why didn't you just stay with me?"

Claudia wasn't sure if he was talking to her or not, but then his gaze slid to hers.

Anger. Lust. Heartbreak.

All of it was in her brother's eyes. Focused on her for the first time since they walked into the motel room.

"Why didn't you love me back, Claudia? I've loved you since the day you came home from the hospital. I've always known we were meant to be together. Lilian told me to take care of you, she made me promise. I told her I would love you the way I loved her." He broke off with a twist of his lips.

Claudia swallowed hard. She wanted to scream. To run. To get away from her brother. But she couldn't move.

Michael went to the dresser on the other side of the room. He opened the top drawer and removed something, then closed the drawer again. He was still for a minute, then turned to face Claudia again, holding up the watch she'd taken from him when she first left.

"I think Lilian would have wanted you to have this. I was angry before because it was all I had left of her. She was gone too soon, but I forgot that you miss her, too. I want you to wear the watch. I want to see it on you."

Putting the watch on was the last thing Claudia wanted to do. The way Michael was looking at her wavered between the way Hector looked at her to even more disturbing.

If that were possible.

"Will you wear it for me, Claudia? Will you let me remember what it was like when we were all together? You, me, and Lilian?"

He was deranged. And she was definitely going to die.

TWENTY-THREE

Michael held the watch out to Claudia. It had been a long time since he had seen it on the wrist of the woman he loved. She was just as stunning as Lilian. In a different way, of course. A man never forgot his first love.

Claudia finally took the watch from Michael and slid it onto her wrist. He grabbed her hand and flipped it over so he could secure the watch to her wrist. He flicked the clasp and smiled.

He didn't release her hand, turning it in his grasp. His thumb brushed over the cold metal of the watch. "Did you know I got this for her?"

"What?" Claudia breathed.

Michael nodded. "It was right after you were born. She was having a hard time because you cried a lot. It stressed her out, and she would scream or cry herself. The only time you would be quiet was when she gave you a sip of her drink."

Claudia gasped.

Michael smiled, remembering the day he presented Lilian with the gift. "I came home from school one day, and she'd put you in the bedroom. She was on the couch, sleeping. You were screaming your head off. I checked on her, and she woke up, smiling at me. That was the first time she kissed me. She held me and loved me and told me how much I meant to her. I knew I loved her in that moment."

"You were a child."

"I was old enough," Michael snarled. "I loved her. I took care of her. You didn't do anything to help."

Claudia sniffed and nodded. "You're right."

"After that day, I knew I needed to get something for her. She loved when she got things, and so did all the other women I knew. We were out one day when I saw the watch." Michael lifted Claudia's hand to look at the delicate silver watch that had graced Lilian's wrist for years.

Claudia tried to pull her hand away, but Michael held firm.

"It was in a fancy store, but the owners were not very smart. I walked in there one day when they had a bunch of customers. It wasn't the first time I'd taken something, and it was even easier to grab that watch than any of the other things I'd taken. Lilian was so happy when I gave it to her. She loved me even more after that. Moved me into her room so she could tell me all the time how important I was to her."

Claudia swallowed roughly, tears running down her cheeks.

"She said she loved me most. I hated when she fucked other men, but she always told me I was her favorite. I was the one she always came back to." Michael slid a glare at Claudia. "You never said the same thing."

"I... I didn't know you needed to hear it."

"But you did love me?"

Claudia drew a shaky breath and nodded. "Of course."

Michael stared at her, watching the way her eyes dilated and slid around the room warily. "You're lying."

"No. I'm not. Why would I lie to you?"

"You wanted to leave me. Then you did leave me. Everything I ever did was for you. To make sure you were safe. No one would dare touch you. Any man who did paid for it."

"What?" Claudia breathed.

"You are mine, Claudia. You always have been. Even if you needed extra time to accept it, we belong together. I've always known it."

"What are you saying?"

"Why do you look confused? You said you love me. When you love someone, you don't make a fool of them. You've been making a fool of me for too long. I made sure every man who touched you knew the mistake they made. You're mine."

"What did you do?" Claudia whispered.

Michael shrugged. "What needed to be done."

"Are you telling me you killed every man I've ever been with?"

"Been with? You told me you were pure for me!"

"I am. I... I meant dated."

"Dated. Sure. And no, I killed every man who dared to touch you. Whether it was a kiss, a touch, or having the audacity to fuck you, they got what they deserved. Because I know you lied to me. You aren't pure. You haven't been for years. I know, Claudia. I know you were running around on me like Lilian. But you never let me love you like I was meant to."

Claudia gasped. "No."

"You belong to me. All those other men didn't have the right to touch you. You're making it seem like killing them was the wrong thing to do. They needed to know you are mine."

"I'm not yours!" she shouted. "I'll never be yours. You're sick, Michael. You're my brother, not my lover. You're never going to be my lover. I don't feel that way about you. We're siblings. What Mom did to you was wrong, and your misguided affection for me is no less wrong."

"Don't you dare say what I had with Lilian was wrong. You weren't there. You don't know."

"I know she raped you."

"She did not," Michael growled.

"Yes, she did. Even if you thought you chose that, you were a child. You weren't old enough to make that kind of decision. She was supposed to protect you. Both of us. Instead, she made you into a monster."

"I'm not a monster!" Michael shouted.

"You are. You're a murderer. You killed people for no reason."

"I had a reason. They weren't allowed to touch you. You're mine."

"No. I'm not. And I never will be." Claudia scampered off the bed and raced toward the door.

Michael was faster, and he got to her before she could open the door. He pressed his body against her back, letting her feel how much he wanted her. He grabbed her wrist, Lilian's watch still in place, and pinned it to the door.

She inhaled deeply, her breath shuddering out of her.

Michael smiled against her ear. He licked the shell. His cock nestled against her body, finally getting to feel her.

She'd whored herself out for too long. Too many years of making him wait for what was his.

But he was done. She would understand what she had done wrong. She would know she was finally where she was meant to be. And after he had her, he would make sure no one ever touched her again. They would be together for all eternity.

"Michael, please."

"You don't have to beg me, Claudia. I'm going to give you exactly what you want. We belong together. Just the two of us. No one else will ever touch you again. We're finally going to be together. Forever."

LANCE SAT in the front seat as Griffin raced across town. The motel they believed Michael took Claudia to was fifteen minutes from the apartment, nine if Griffin would fucking step on it.

"Almost there," Damien said from the backseat.

Once they watched the video of Claudia leaving with Michael, Damien called Montgomery. Montgomery had access to more video cameras, including a few Captain Marcus Patrick had given Montgomery access to for emergency purposes, and Montgomery was able to track Michael through the city to a motel.

Lance checked his watch. It had been two hours since Michael forced Claudia out of the apartment. He had a few minutes of doubt, but he knew Claudia didn't go willingly. There was more to it. More going on than they knew. She wouldn't have left with Michael unless she felt she had no option.

Even death.

Lance's gut churned the entire drive, and when they pulled into the parking lot for the motel, they saw they were not alone.

"Room one-six-three," Adam said. "The clerk said he checked in three days ago, paid cash, and hasn't been seen since."

"He has her. We saw the video," Lance growled. He didn't care if the FBI agent was the one calling the shots, Lance was going into that fucking motel room and getting Claudia out. No matter who tried to stop him.

"We know, but we need to be smart about this."

"He has her!" Lance shouted.

"And crashing into the room is not a guaranteed way to get her back alive," Adam said.

The words sent Lance stumbling backward. He hit the brick wall of the building and leaned against it for support.

He couldn't imagine the possibility of Claudia being dead. He had to get her back. She had to be okay. Losing her when he'd just found her…

No. He couldn't go there.

"What's the plan?" Griffin asked.

"We have to find out if they're in there. Both of them or just one of them. We don't know. No one saw them go into the room."

"You just said—" Lance barked.

"Michael Reynolds checked into that room, but the clerk hasn't seen him since then. He could be in that room, or he could have broken into another one. We don't know," Lorelei said, her voice calm.

"Then we need to find out," Lance said.

"Exactly." Adam raised an eyebrow at Lance.

"What?"

"Are you going to let us do our job?"

"We all want the same thing here," Damien answered for Lance.

The agents didn't take Damien's word. They waited until Lance nodded before they turned to walk toward the room.

"We have a small camera that we're going to try to use to see inside the room. The clerk said the room next door is vacant. We're setting up in there," Lorelei explained.

Lance followed the agents into the silent room. He looked around as they worked. One person was against the wall with a listening device. Another had a tiny drill positioned at another spot on the wall. Lorelei and Adam went to a woman on the opposite side of the room staring at a computer screen. Lorelei tapped the woman on the shoulder, and she removed her headset, passing it to Lorelei.

Lance wanted to know what was going on. To hear inside the room, see inside. But all he could do was wait until the FBI agents gave him permission to do something.

A shout from the other room came through the wall, and Lorelei took the headphones off. "Let's go."

"What happened? What's going on?" Lance demanded.

"We need to get in there. Stay here."

"No, I need to—"

"You need to listen," Adam said, blocking Lance's path. He raised his brows at Lance, arms crossed until Lance nodded. "We will let you know as soon as you can see her. I understand how you feel, and I promise you we will get you to her. But first, we need to do this the right way."

"Save her," Lance said.

"We will do our best."

Lance knew that was the best he was going to get.

FEAR WAS A COMPLICATED EMOTION. Claudia had experienced all the normal reactions to fear. She froze when Michael walked into Lance's apartment. She fled when she saw him kill that woman a year ago. And as the true meaning behind his words dawned on her, she became still. Acceptance filled her and seemed to displace her from her body.

Claudia was no longer in control of herself. As soon as she felt Michael's erection against her backside, she knew he was going to rape her. He was going to claim her body. He was going to do whatever he wanted to her.

Because there was no one there to help her. No one to save her.

Claudia walked out of Lance's apartment to save him, and she was going to take his place. She would die before the night was through. But only after Michael had his way with her.

Michael brushed the hair back from her neck and kissed her shoulder. "I've always wanted to be allowed to touch you like this. I can feel you shivering. I know you want this, too."

"It's wrong," Claudia said, her voice coming from far away. Someone else's voice.

"No, it's not. The people who say that just don't understand us. They don't matter, though. None of them matter. All that matters is you and me right now. Tonight, we become one. And for the rest of our lives, for the rest of today, we are united."

Claudia wanted to scream, to cry, to punch him or kick him. To fight back and get away from him. But fear had taken over. She'd always toed the line, refusing to rock the boat. Her mother was an emotional mess, and quick to anger. Michael marched to his own beat. Claudia craved acceptance from her mother, but she never knew how to get it. How to be someone her mother looked at the way she looked at Michael.

Now... Now Claudia knew there was nothing she could have done to gain her mother's love and acceptance. Her mother was a sick woman who preyed on a child. A child who grew up to be a man who was now twisting the same affection onto Claudia.

"Why... Why does it have to be now? I... We should be somewhere special. Somewhere romantic."

That got his attention. "Is that what you like?"

Claudia sucked in a shaky breath. She nodded. "Yeah, yes. This place isn't right for us. We're... We should be somewhere with candles and champagne. Make it a celebration."

"Is that what your neighbor did?" Michael's voice was harsh against her ear. He punched the door. "You told me he didn't touch you, but how would you know what you like if you were waiting for me?"

"I—"

Michael grabbed her hair and yanked, cracking her neck as he pulled her head to the side. He lowered his mouth onto her exposed skin and bit down hard.

"Ow!" she screamed, trying to get away from him but unable to move. He'd pinned her to the door, his body tight against her back.

His free hand went to her hip and tried to move to her front. He eased up on the pressure of his hips so his hand could slide to her stomach, but Claudia didn't move.

He bit her harder, and she bucked against him. He was ready for her, grabbing her crotch as soon as she moved her hips. He avoided her move, turning his hips to the side and pressing his fingers hard against her core.

"You belong to me, Claudia. You're mine. I'm done waiting for you to accept that truth. You're going to be screaming my name, and you're never going to feel another man's touch on your skin. I'm going to erase all of them, mark every inch of you as mine so no man ever dares to come near you again. Not that neighbor, not anyone."

"Housekeeping!" someone shouted from the other side of the door.

Michael spun her away from the door, his hand in her hair. He held his other finger to his lips. "One word and I kill her."

Claudia whimpered.

"We don't need anything," Michael called back through the door.

"I have fresh towels, sir. And I can turn down the beds for you."

"We don't need that," Michael growled. "Go away."

"No need to be so rude, sir. I'm just trying to do my job."

"Thank you, but we're good."

"Fine. Have a good night," the housekeeper said.

Claudia strained to hear the woman's steps retreating, to hear her knocking on another door. But all she heard was Michael's breathing, heavy from the brief interaction.

Michael stepped up to the door slowly, his hand in Claudia's hair, pulling her with him. He looked through the peephole so quickly she wasn't sure how he saw anything, then moved to the door more slowly. He looked again, pausing and staying at the door for a few seconds.

Then the phone rang.

"What the fuck?" Michael barked. He stalked to the phone, dragging Claudia with him. He released her, shoving her onto the mattress as he stood in front of her, between her and the door. "What?"

Claudia could hear a voice, but she couldn't understand what they were saying.

Michael sighed heavily. "I don't need any housekeeping. I told the lady at the door that. Why the fuck are you bothering me?"

Claudia held her breath. Was it possible? Could she hope the interruptions were Lance's team? Was he there? Outside right now waiting to rescue her. Again.

She stared at Michael. He was angry, shaking his head as whoever was on the phone continued to speak.

He pulled the phone away from his head, but the man kept talking. Claudia heard *service* and *help*. She didn't know what either word was in reference to.

"I said we're good. I shouldn't have to put that stupid sign on the door for you to leave me the hell alone. Please stop calling me and knocking on the door. I don't need anything."

The person was still talking when Michael hung up the phone.

"Where were we?"

Claudia knew she had one chance. Only one. If she was wrong, she was dead. If not, maybe she would survive and get away from Michael. "I need something to eat. I'm starving. And I don't want to pass out and have you disappointed in me."

Michael smiled. He slid one finger down her cheek. "I'd never be disappointed in you."

She snorted. "Well, I wish I could say the same."

"What?" he snarled.

Claudia shrugged. "Just saying I wish I was so confident I wouldn't be disappointed. I mean, especially after feeling you against me. You're not even half the man Lance is." She held two fingers close together, examining them closely. She spread her fingers wide and smirked. "Not even half."

"You bitch!"

He shoved her onto the mattress, but she was ready for it. He wouldn't put up with her questioning his manhood.

He climbed over her, but before he dropped his weight onto her, she brought her knee up and connected with his crotch.

Hard.

Michael screamed and rolled off her, aided by her shove.

Claudia scrambled off the bed, racing to the door. She was almost there when the door swung open in front of her.

Claudia screamed and jumped back, but someone grabbed her and yanked her outside.

A gunshot split the doorframe, inches from her face.

Then the door slammed shut.

TWENTY-FOUR

Claudia screamed. She swung. She did everything to get away.

Lance tugged her farther from the door, trying to pull her into his arms.

She kept fighting him. "Let go of me! No!"

"It's me. Claudia, it's Lance," he said, his hands going to her face to force her to look at him.

"Lance? Lance! He said he was going to kill you. He had a gun. He came in when you were in the hall, and he said if I called for you, he would shoot you before you could even get into the apartment. I couldn't let that happen. I couldn't watch him kill you." Claudia crumpled as she rushed to explain what happened.

"I know, sweetheart. I figured that was what happened."

She shook her head and let him pull her against his chest. "I thought I was dead. He was going to kill me."

"I was not going to let that happen," Lance said.

"Michael. He has a gun. He…" Claudia looked around and seemed to realize they weren't alone. "Who are all these people?"

An FBI agent was standing a few feet from them, watching their every move. Lorelei and Adam thought Lance needed to be at the front of the line when they got Claudia out of the room, but they wanted the two of them protected as soon as Claudia was free. They had an agent with them, and more surrounded the room.

"The FBI is in charge. They want Michael alive."

"He's not himself," Claudia said, her voice sad and resigned. "Or maybe he is, and I never knew him."

"Can you tell them anything that might help?" Lance asked, hopeful Michael wouldn't slip through their grasp again.

Claudia nodded, and Lance met the gaze of the agent standing guard. The man turned and signaled to Lorelei, who immediately joined them.

"Claudia, you remember Lorelei," Lance said.

Claudia nodded. "Thank you for being here."

"We're happy you're safe. Do you have any ideas for getting Michael out of the room?"

Claudia swallowed roughly. "He's a victim, but he admitted he killed more people. He has a twisted sense of love for me."

Lorelei's brows shot up, but the agent didn't make a comment.

"He was going to..."

"Did he touch you?" Lance breathed, rage coursing through him.

Claudia stilled. "He crossed a line, but I'm okay. The housekeeper and the phone call... That was you guys?"

Lorelei nodded. "It was. We heard you scream and knew we were running out of time."

"Michael is angry and trapped. I don't know what he'll do, but if I can help, I want to," Claudia said.

Lance wanted to wrap her up and drag her away from the

whole thing. He wanted to protect her and keep her as far from her brother and his obsession with her as possible.

But he couldn't. Michael was her brother, and Claudia would never forgive herself if she didn't do everything she could to help him.

"Maybe you can talk to him. We can call the room again." Lorelei nodded to someone who brought over a phone. "If you're willing."

Claudia took the phone, and Lorelei tapped the screen. It rang, the sound echoing inside the motel room.

"I told you to leave me alone."

"Michael, it's me. It's Claudia."

"Claudia. Why did you leave me? You abandoned me. How could you?"

"Michael, you need to come out. You need help. What you're doing, what you've done, it's not okay."

"Everything I've done has been for you, Claudia. I've been taking care of you, protecting you from the ugliness in the world. I've been waiting for us to be together. I love you."

"Killing people is not protecting me, Michael."

"I did it for you! I told you, those men who touched you had no right. You are mine. And I'm going to kill that neighbor who keeps stealing you from me. Is he with you right now? Is he listening to me?"

Claudia lifted her gaze, and it collided with Lance's. Lance wasn't afraid of Michael. He wasn't afraid of anything now that Claudia was by his side.

"Lance Kilgore. I'm coming for you. I'm going to kill you slowly. You touched what belongs to me. You will never touch her again."

Claudia dropped the phone. She trembled at Michael's words.

Lance wrapped her up in his arms, holding her close. "It's okay, Claudia. He's not going to touch me."

"He'll kill you. He said he was going to kill us both and make me watch you die."

"I promise you, I'm okay. He's not getting away this time."

"You don't know him."

"No, but I know the FBI."

Lorelei picked up the discarded phone. "Mr. Reynolds. This is FBI Agent Lorelei Sloane. We have your room surrounded. Surrender now and come out with your hands up."

"Bitch! Claudia, how could you? How could you go to the fucking cops? You turned me in. You said you loved me. You said we could be together. This is because of him. Because of that neighbor. He twisted your mind. Is this what you want to happen? You want me in jail? I'll never do it. Never! I love you, Claudia, but I'm not going to let them corrupt what we have."

The phone went silent.

"He hung up," Lorelei said. "Are you okay?"

Lance didn't let go of Claudia and felt her suck in a breath.

"No. How can I be okay?"

"We will get him. We will bring him in, and he will stand trial for all the things he did. I pro—"

A gunshot rang out, interrupting Lorelei's words.

"Shots fired. It came from the room," someone behind Lorelei said.

"Michael!" Claudia cried.

Lorelei slid a look to Lance, and he held Claudia tighter. Lorelei drew her gun and moved into place with Adam and the other agents.

Lance kept Claudia from following them as they broke down the door to the motel room. All the agents disappeared, a dozen of them vanishing in seconds as they all poured into the room.

Claudia held her breath as they waited for someone to tell them what was going on.

Lorelei stepped out of the room first. She met Lance's gaze, and he saw it in her eyes.

Claudia cried out, her knees giving way as she saw the same thing Lance did.

Michael was dead.

Lance picked Claudia up and brought her into the room where the agents had set up. He sat on the bed with her in his arms and held her as she cried for the brother who would have killed them both if he'd had the chance.

But he was still her brother.

CLAUDIA ANSWERED QUESTIONS FOR HOURS. Her eyes were gritty, and her limbs felt like lead. She wanted to sleep for days.

She told the FBI agents everything Michael told her. About their mother, and the watch Michael stole for her. She handed it over, happy to be rid of the item that made her sick to feel on her wrist. She told the agents about the men Claudia had been with and Michael killing all of them. About him selling drugs to support them. Everything he confessed to.

Claudia didn't know why it mattered since he was dead, but she hoped the news could bring closure to some of his victims' families.

Lance never left her side. Even when the agents asked him to, he refused. He held her as she cried, then gripped her hand tightly as she answered questions. And when the medical examiner arrived and took Michael's body away, zipped up inside a black bag, Lance caught her when she fell and held her again.

When the police finally let them go, Claudia followed Lance to a dark SUV. She leaned against the window as he drove, the events of the day and the motion of the vehicle lulling her into a restless sleep that she came out of all at once when Lance parked the vehicle.

Claudia looked up, confused when she didn't recognize where they were. Panic gripped her for a second.

"I figured you wouldn't want to go back to my apartment. Or yours. We can stay here for the night and figure everything else out tomorrow," Lance explained.

Claudia finally recognized the place. They were back at The Davidson Hotel. The classy place where they'd stayed when he first brought her back from Kansas. She nodded, touched that he thought ahead to bring her somewhere she would feel safe.

Lance checked into the room and led her upstairs. He unlocked a room and pushed open the door for her to go in first.

It wasn't a suite like they'd been in before, but it was still a very nice room. The bathroom was large and lavish. Fluffy white bathrobes hung on the back of the door. Sheets were tucked tight into the bed.

"How about a bath?" Lance asked, moving into the bathroom where a large tub was in the corner.

Claudia nodded, drawing a breath as the water ran.

Lance helped her into the tub, then moved to the door.

"Where are you going?"

"I was going to let you relax."

"Will you join me?" Claudia asked, not wanting him out of reach.

Lance nodded, his throat working as he swallowed. He dropped his clothes to the floor and climbed into the tub behind her, his thick erection making his presence known against her back. "Ignore it."

Claudia giggled and leaned back against Lance. "Thank you for saving me."

"I think you pretty much saved yourself. I just opened the door and caught you as you ran out."

Claudia exhaled and long breath. "Is it bad that I'm sad he's dead?"

Lance's arms tightened around her. "He was your brother. It would be strange if you didn't feel sad. I'm guessing you're also angry and hurt and confused and maybe a little scared."

Tears streamed down her cheeks as she nodded. She'd never known someone who understood her the way Lance did. Who could make her craziness feel normal. "He took care of me when I was little. Our mom never cared much about me. I was always jealous of how close they were, but now I know it wasn't a healthy relationship. He was never allowed to be a kid."

"It's not right."

"No, it's not. And I know what she did doesn't explain his behavior. But how many other kids have been through something like that? How many others have had no one to turn to?"

"Probably too many."

"I think I might want to help them. To be the person Michael never had."

"I think that's a great idea."

"You do?" Claudia asked, turning in the tub to meet his gaze for the first time since she shared the thoughts that had been running around in her mind all night. "You don't think I'm crazy for wishing I could have helped him?"

Lance shook his head and leaned closer, placing a gentle kiss on her lips. "I think you're amazing. I think Michael was never given a chance to be his own person. He was a victim, and he was a criminal, but he was also your brother. There were parts of him that were good."

Claudia nodded. "Yeah, there were."

Lance pulled Claudia against him again. She rested her head on his chest and let his steady breathing relax her. The warm water, the hot man, and the end of her hell had her eyes closing, and her body relaxing in a way she hadn't for over a year.

Water splashed and woke Claudia up. She sat up quickly, sending water rolling through the tub.

"I was trying to figure out how to wake you up. Sorry," Lance said.

"It's okay," Claudia said sleepily.

Lance climbed out first, then offered Claudia his hand. He wrapped her in a towel before tying one around his waist. He rubbed the towel down her arms and over her curves before squeezing the moisture from her hair. He held one of the robes for her, and she snuggled into it.

Lance dried himself quickly, then put the other robe on and led her to the bed. He turned on a movie and curled up on the bed, holding her close as Claudia let his presence soothe her back to sleep.

CLAUDIA WOKE UP EARLY. She felt rested, but she was hit with a soul-deep knowledge that her life would never be the same.

She eased out of Lance's arms and moved across the room to a chair by the window. They'd forgotten to close the curtains the night before, and Claudia curled up in the chair and watched the world outside wake up as she thought about her life.

She meant what she said the night before about wanting to help others who were like Michael. She knew he made his own choices, especially at the end, and she wished things could have been different, but Michael chose his path to violence.

By the time the sun was shining over the horizon and Lance stirred, Claudia had made a few decisions about her future. And when Lance sat up and immediately looked for her, she knew the biggest one was the best one.

"I love you," Claudia whispered as Lance's gaze landed on her.

"What?" he asked.

Claudia drew a breath and cleared her throat. A small smile lifted her lips. "I love you. I don't expect you to say it back, and I don't expect anything from you, but I spent too many years not saying things. Not wading into the middle of what was going on with the people around me. I've always tried to keep to myself and make sure everyone around me was okay, was taken care of. I pushed my own needs to the back, and I... I'm not saying this to force something. I just wanted to share how I feel. I wanted you to know that you're important to me. I have never felt this way about anyone in my life, and even if you don't feel the same, I wanted you to know I love you. I love you for coming after me, for keeping me safe, for never giving up on me, for giving me what I needed last night, for every word and touch and moment since we met. Thank you for showing me what love could truly be."

"This sounds like a goodbye," Lance said, swinging his feet over the edge of the bed. He faced her, not moving from the mattress. He leaned forward, his elbows on his knees. His robe gaped in the middle, giving her a peek of the solid muscles that held her all night.

Claudia shook her head and tried not to be disappointed he didn't say the words back to her. "It's not goodbye. But Michael is dead. He was working alone. There's no threat to me anymore. You have a life to get back to. Others to protect."

"I do. It's my job. But... Are you going back to Kansas?"

Claudia snorted. "No. It's not home. It hasn't been for a long time. I have too many bad memories from there. Even more now."

"What are you going to do?"

She drew a breath and let it out slowly. "I'm staying here. But again, I don't expect anything from you. Niagara Falls has felt more like home than Kansas ever did for me. But I don't want you to feel pressured."

"You have no idea how I feel about you, do you?"

"Um, no. I don't."

Lance stood, his body straightening as he unfolded himself from the bed. He took two steps to stand in front of her and reached for her hand. He urged her to her feet. One hand slid across her cheek.

Claudia nuzzled against his hand, still warm from sleep. Her eyes slid closed as she inhaled his sleepy morning scent.

"I love you, Claudia."

Her eyes flipped open. "You don't have to say that."

He exhaled a laugh. "I know. But it's the truth. Finding out you were missing made me realize how much I enjoyed seeing you every day. Seeing you chained to that bed..." He broke off his words, turning his head away.

She cupped his jaw and brought his gaze back to hers. "You saved me."

"I was so scared I'd never find you. And yesterday, when I saw the video of you climbing down the balcony... I thought you were gone forever."

"I never asked how you found me."

"Traffic cameras, mostly. The city is full of them, and since the case was already open, it was easy to get access to them."

"That was convenient."

"It was the longest two hours of my life. When we arrived and I heard you scream—"

"I'm safe now."

Lance pulled her close and kissed the top of her head. "I'm never letting you go. I love you. I want a life with you. We can find a new place to live, something that's ours. Something where we can make new memories."

"Good memories," Claudia said.

Lance pulled back and met her gaze. "All good memories."

Claudia lifted onto her toes and kissed the man she loved. "I love you."

His lips quirked. "Damn, I like hearing that."

"I like saying it."

"I love you," he said against her lips.

She vibrated with joy. "I like hearing that, too."

His hand slid between the sides of her robe. "How much do you like hearing it?"

She moaned softly. "I'll like it even more when you're inside me."

"I was hoping you'd feel that way," Lance said, leading her back to the bed. He spent the rest of the morning showing her how much he meant those three little words.

TWENTY-FIVE

Claudia let out a breath, hands on her hips, feeling flustered and overwhelmed and terrified.

She'd never met a man's family before. Ever.

"It's going to be fine. They're going to love you," Lance said, as if reading her mind.

It was scary how he'd been able to do that even more over the last month since they moved in together. Either she wore her feelings on her face or he was incredibly perceptive.

"I love you, and they're going to love you. Stop worrying." Lance slid one hand low on her back and brought the other up to cup her jaw. He brought her lips to his and teased his way inside, his tongue stoking a blaze in her that was wholly inappropriate when his family was literally on the way to their new apartment.

A knock on the door had Claudia jumping back.

Lance tugged at the tie on her dress, nearly pulling it loose.

"Lance!"

He chuckled as she reached for the fabric that kept her wrap dress in place. "You are beautiful. Take a breath."

Claudia did just that, the air shaking on the way out of her lungs as Lance went to the door.

"Hi, Aunt Jackie," Lance said, ducking to hug a woman Claudia couldn't see.

Claudia checked that her dress was secure, then double-knotted it before her playful boyfriend threatened to leave her naked in a room full of people. She looked up, and her gaze connected with a beautiful Black woman with gray-streaked braids and the kindest smile Claudia had ever seen.

"Claudia?" the woman asked.

Claudia nodded and approached as Jackie released Lance and handed him off to a tall man with light brown skin and a sleek dark ponytail. "It's so nice to meet you, Jackie." Claudia offered her hand to the woman approaching.

Jackie looked at Claudia's hand and shook her head. "We hug in this family, sweetheart. And I've been wanting to hug you since Lance first called and told me about you."

Claudia shook with her inhale and let herself be pulled into a hug with a woman she'd never met.

Jackie held her tight, her smaller height not stopping her from enveloping Claudia in a motherly embrace unlike anything Claudia had ever experienced.

She felt loved, safe, warm. It was like Lance hugging her, without the sexual energy. Claudia sank into the feeling.

"Don't scare the girl, Jackie. We want her to stick around," Rico said.

Claudia chuckled, not letting go right away. Jackie loosened her hold, and Claudia smiled as she let go, too.

Jackie cupped Claudia's cheeks and smiled. "She's not going anywhere. She knows she's a truly loved part of this family."

Claudia trembled with love for the woman who'd raised the man she loved. "Thank you."

Jackie smiled as though she knew all the things Claudia

was thanking her for. "No thanks necessary, my love. I'm so pleased to meet you."

"You, too."

Jackie stepped back to allow Rico to hug Claudia. His hug was less enthusiastic but no less welcoming. "It's nice to meet you, Claudia."

"It's nice to meet you, too."

Lance grabbed their suitcases and carried everything to the spare bedroom. After everything that happened, the apartment complex didn't hesitate to allow them to move out of their previous building and into a two-bedroom unit in another building. Claudia and Lance were happy to be away from the bad memories, but they didn't want to go far from the place where they met and fell in love, yet.

"What can I do to help? I'm so sorry our flight was delayed. I'd hoped to be here hours ago to cook with you," Jackie said.

Claudia waved her worries off. "It's fine. Lance is a wonderful cook. I like to bake, but he took care of dinner."

"Her brownies are epic," Lance said, winking at Claudia.

Her cheeks warmed with memories of what they did the last time she made brownies for him. She made bug-eyes at him, and Lance chuckled.

"You can hang out with me," Rico said, wrapping an arm around Claudia's shoulders and steering her away before anything else was said. "The two of them are masterful in the kitchen. It makes my head spin."

Claudia chuckled. "That's how I feel. Baking is easy because I can follow directions, but I don't have a lot of experience creating new things in the kitchen."

"We all have our strengths," Lance said, returning to the living room as someone else knocked on the door. He went to let Damien and Griffin in, then introduced them to Jackie and Rico. The last knock on the door was Mrs. Mitchell, who'd been their first visitor after she was released from the hospital.

"Ooh, you two have made this place a home," Mrs. Mitchell said, leaning on her cane to move through the space. She'd suffered a severe concussion and a broken femur when Michael hit her and pushed her down the stairs. Michael blamed her for Lance finding Claudia, and that was why he attacked Mrs. Mitchell.

Claudia hated Mrs. Mitchell was another person hurt by her brother for trying to help her, but she was incredibly kind and did not blame Claudia at all. When Lance invited her to their apartment for Thanksgiving, Mrs. Mitchell readily agreed and asked what she could bring.

"They did well, didn't they?" Jackie asked, moving over to introduce herself to Mrs. Mitchell. The two women were immediate friends and crowded into the kitchen with Lance while Claudia and the other men found drinks and settled in the living room.

"I think I need some cooking lessons before you go back west," Griffin said. "Everything smells amazing."

Rico laughed. "Lance did most of it, but he learned from Jackie. She keeps me fat and happy." He rubbed his belly, which was not fat, but the man was definitely happy.

"No shit?" Griffin said.

Rico nodded. "I've always been pretty helpless in the kitchen. I just don't have the talent for knowing what works well together. Those two talk about food, and I think they're speaking another language."

Claudia chuckled, agreeing with every word.

"I like the grill, but it's pretty basic. Cooking something like all this is way outside what I could do," Damien said. "But I'm happy to enjoy the fruits of their labor."

"Agreed."

It wasn't long before Lance, Jackie, and Mrs. Mitchell

declared dinner was ready and everyone filled plates. Lance took a seat next to Claudia and asked if she was okay.

Claudia looked around the room and nodded. She had everything she never knew she was missing. A family, friends, and a man who loved her and would never let anything happen to her.

"I'm great," she told him.

Lance winked at her and joined the conversation.

JACKIE TOOK a pie out of the oven and set it on the trivet Lance had out. "Your friends are pretty great."

Lance nodded. "They are. I'm lucky to have so many people in my life."

"Yes, you are." Jackie patted his cheeks. "And Claudia?"

Lance's blood buzzed at her name. Everything about her made him want more. "I love her."

"Oh, honey, I knew the night you called me. I'm happy to see things have worked out. Finally. I know it wasn't easy getting here."

Lance shook his head. "No, it wasn't. But it's worth it for the right one, isn't it?"

"Every time," Jackie said, sharing a grin with him.

Another knock on the door had them all calling for whoever it was to come in. Austin peeked his head around the door, smiling when he saw he was in the right place and pulling Lacey inside behind him. She waddled as she walked, but she glowed. A look Lance hoped to see on Claudia one day.

Austin and Lacey hugged Damien, Griffin, and Claudia. Claudia introduced them to Mrs. Mitchell and Rico, then pointed to Jackie and Lance.

Austin had his arm around his wife, the two of them back from their babymoon turned honeymoon a few days earlier.

"Welcome back," Lance said.

"Thanks, man. Good to see you." Austin hugged Lance, clapping him hard on the back.

"You, too. Hi, Lacey." Lance leaned down to kiss her cheek. "How are you feeling?"

"Like I'm ready to pop," Lacey said. She smiled and slid her gaze to Aunt Jackie. "Are you the one making it smell so amazing in here?"

"I can't take all the credit. I'm Jackie. We're happy you could join us. Lance said you were with your mom today? She could have come, too," Jackie said.

Lacey hugged Aunt Jackie. "Thank you, but she had other company."

"Kirk and Stephanie were with her," Austin told Lance.

"Other teammates," Lance explained to Aunt Jackie. "Close friends of Valerie and Samuel."

"Oh, you're Samuel's daughter. I'm so sorry. I didn't realize." Aunt Jackie smacked Lance's shoulder. "Why didn't you tell me?"

"I thought I did!" Lance defended himself.

"I apologize, sweetheart. How is your mom doing? The first events are the hardest," Jackie said.

Lacey nodded. "Yeah. This is the first major holiday. I think having Kirk and Stephanie with her is good. Montgomery, Zeke, and Nina were there for dinner, too. They left when we did. I think the baby is a good distraction for my mom."

"I imagine so. And Lance said you two just got married? Come sit. You don't need to be on your feet." Aunt Jackie guided Lacey to the couch.

Damien gave up his seat, then joined Lance and Austin in the kitchen. "Your aunt is amazing," Damien said.

"Yeah, she is," Austin agreed.

"I know. She's checking up on me but doesn't want me to know it," Lance told them.

"You're lucky to have her. Not everyone has someone like that in their lives," Damien said.

"Too true," Lance said, sharing a look with Austin.

"I do now," Austin said, smiling when he looked at Lacey. Austin left them to go check on his new wife.

"You following them down the aisle?" Damien asked.

Lance shrugged. "Hopefully eventually. It hasn't been that long, though. I think she might want to get used to being free. I don't want her to look around in a year or two and wonder how she got stuck with me and think it's too late because we rushed into a marriage she didn't really want."

Damien snorted. "That woman is head over heels for you, man. You could ask her right now, and she'd be dragging you to the courthouse to say I do before the end of the weekend."

"What makes you say that?"

Damien glanced at Claudia, then back at Lance. He shrugged. "I trust my gut. And my gut says Claudia will never look at another person the way she looks at you. The only one who will ever come close is if you have kids."

Lance looked at Claudia and found her staring at Lacey's baby bump. Her gaze lifted to Lance's, and he sucked in a breath at the intensity staring back at him.

Claudia pregnant. With his child. Rocking a baby, chasing a toddler, sharing her love with them. Lance could see it all.

And he couldn't fucking wait for it.

THANK **you** so much for reading Lance and Claudia's story! This story went places I wasn't expecting, but these two were the guiding lights through every page. I loved watching them find love together and overcome all the shit from their past. They are the kind of couple that prove love conquers all.

The series continues with Damien and Harmony. She was just looking for a cup of coffee, not to witness a heist. Too bad what she thought she saw wasn't the full truth. And the man behind it all wasn't looking to be saved. Preorder Rescuing His Curvy Girl today!

STACEY THOUGHT Wray was her forever. He picked her, but he lied and he stole and he broke her. There would never be anyone else for her, but without trust, what did they have? Wray won't give up on them so easily, especially when he learns someone is threatening their family. *FURY* is available now!

ABOUT THE AUTHOR

USA TODAY Bestselling Author Mary E Thompson spent most of her childhood wishing she had a few less curves. She hid in the pages of books because her favorite characters never cared what size her clothes were. Now, neither does Mary, and she writes stories that celebrate women like her. Real women who have curves, chase dreams, and find love, because we should all be happy, no matter our dress size.

Mary spends her non-writing time with her husband and two kids, watching too much TV, cheering for her hometown football team (Go Bills!), and hiding chocolate from her family.

Visit https://MaryEThompson.com/ to sign up for Mary's newsletter, **Romancing the Curves**. Subscribers get free ebooks and other fun stuff, like exclusive, members only content and giveaways, plus are the first to know about new releases and sales!